SECRETS

OF THE LILIES

...words worth reading

SECRETS

OF THE LILIES

By

Deana McGill

Secrets of the Lilies

Editor: Earl Tillinghast and Regina Cornell

Cover Design: 3SIXTY Marketing Studio - 3SIXTYprinting.com

Interior Design: 3SIXTY Marketing Studio - 3SIXTYprinting.com

Indigo River Publishing

3 West Garden Street, Ste. 352
Pensacola, FL 32502

www.indigoriverpublishing.com

Ordering Information:

Quantity sales: Special discounts are available on quantity purchases by corporations, associations, and others. For details, contact the publisher at the address above.

Orders by U.S. trade bookstores and wholesalers: Please contact the publisher at the address above.

Printed in the United States of America

Library of Congress Control Number: 2018944944

ISBN: 978-1-948080-30-9

First Edition

With Indigo River Publishing, you can always expect great books, strong voices, and meaningful messages. Most importantly, you'll always find...words worth reading.

Chapter 1

Troubled Heart

The glow of taillights shimmered in the evening rain as they backed in behind a house. A shaggy, overweight man got out of the truck and began looking around in the rain. Just as he bent down to pick up something, the back door to the house quickly opened and a small-framed woman leaped out and yelled, "Hey! What does your stupid ass think you're doing?"

Prunella was standing fifteen feet away from her husband, Barlow Brown, as he stood there in shock that she was home. She was furious at the sight of him holding her yellow mop bucket. She yelled at him again, "Hey! Just what are you doing with my mop bucket?" Barlow stood there dumbfounded, mumbling something as he placed the bucket on the back of his truck with some recognizable items from her father's shed.

She adamantly asked him to repeat himself, to which he replied, "Your daddy gave it to me."

Appalled at his lie, she placed her hands on her hips and said, "I highly doubt that, Barlow! I know Daddy didn't give that to you. Besides, you haven't mopped a damn thing in your life." She dropped one hand to her side, leaving the other on her hip, cocked her head, and added with a touch of sarcasm, "Barlow, you know it would take instructions for you to use it, and guess what? That particular model does not have any!" She then snapped her finger and pointed at the ground. "Now take it off the truck!"

He grabbed the bucket from the pile of stuff and slung it at her feet. She jumped aside just before it hit her. Barlow cursed at her as he jumped in his truck, spun out in the grass and down the driveway. He revved the engine down the blacktop road as if he were in a mad race. Prunella picked up the mop bucket and took it inside. She'd had enough of people sneaking around and stealing things!

***

The next morning, in April of 2012, rains were saturating the southern lands of Mississippi, where a large red-brick home sat being drenched in silence. The yard was a mess; bushes were overgrown and covering some of the windows. A small gray dilapidated house trailer sat decaying about twenty-five yards away from the home. Many Mississippian critters now inhabited this place, crowding around the far-gone memories. The flower beds in the front yards were lifeless, with sticks and twigs replacing their beauty. The only color in the entire yard was behind the house, where an assortment of lilies grew under a tall, twisted mulberry tree. A huge oak tree stood tall and strong just at the edge of the brick home. Its long limbs grew over the roof, covering one end. The winds blew, causing the branches to scrape and scratch on the rooftop. Rolls of thunder rumbled over the house as a soft breeze tossed leaves under the carport to join the ones already harbored there. Spiderwebs clung to all of the angles of the windows and doors; some were even spun sporadically around the ceiling with crispy corpses of dead flies clinging to them unwillingly.

Through its overgrown walkway, this once-beautiful home now looked abandoned. What had been wonderful memories were now drowned in painful pictures everywhere. All of the rooms felt cold. The warmth had grown weak and faint, then vanished with a dying breath. The rain clouds concealed the dawn's soft glow, and only the security light broke the morning's darkness. Droplets of water rolled from the roof and fell onto a faded Coke can, lying at the edge of the concrete front porch.

Plagued by memories of her father and the constant tapping against her window, Prunella had a hard time sleeping. Her long blonde hair tangled as she tossed and turned. Her blue eyes opened, and she grunted at the sight of the alarm clock alerting her in bright green that it was only 5:00 a.m. She flipped back what covers were on her body and threw her legs over the side of the bed in disgust. She stood up quickly and slipped on her soft, sparkly slippers and shuffled into the kitchen. She turned on the light, illuminating the outdated kitchen. She walked over to the coffee pot and made a pot. As the water seeped through the coffee grounds and released their aroma into the room, Prunella walked around the small bar that was littered with old mail. She opened the carport door and stood there gazing out at the dark morning for what the yard's nightlight might reveal. She unlatched the metal screen door and pushed it open to feel the morning's damp breeze. She then quickly closed it, as her pajamas didn't provide a warm barrier. Still gazing at the morning from the door, she watched the drizzling mist gently fall to the ground.

Sleeping through the rain wouldn't be possible because her mind was spinning out of control. The doctors had prescribed medication to help with this, but she soon found out the pills didn't help. They just caused her to make dumb decisions. "Oh, come on, happy thoughts," Prunella spoke out loud.

The final sound of steam from the coffee pot indicated its completion. She shut the door and made her way back to the coffee pot. Just as she was reaching for a cup from the cabinet, the unexpected ringing of the phone caused her to shriek. She reached for the phone above the bar and placed it to her ear. "Who the hell is calling me so early?"

"Hey, Prunella. It's me, Jerry. Your sister is in the hospital." Jerry paused, waiting for questions from her, but all he got was silence. So he continued, "Well, it happened last night about 11 p.m."

Prunella stood there for a moment continuing to be silent. Then, placing her hand on her hip and rolling her eyes, she said, "Well, hmm, OK." Then she added smugly, "Well, Jerry, I don't know what to tell you, other than good luck with that."

Hanging up the phone before Jerry could say another word, she ran her fingers through her hair in frustration. She stepped over to the coffee pot and fixed a cup, then sat down at the kitchen table where her father used to sit. It had been the perfect spot for her father to watch television if dinner was at five. This had also been her mother's favorite seat, while preparing her concoctions of comfort. Prunella sat there staring off into the living room as her mind pondered the phone call. She had been so frustrated with her sister for so long and no longer cared.

Sitting and listening to the sounds of the rain as it began to beat on the roof like a drum, Prunella knew she had to do something with the house. It looked like someone had shaken it up and poured out the contents, reminding her of a garage sale. The hoard of stuff from her parents only collected dust, and she wanted to rid herself from seeing it all anymore. Prunella had tried to do something with the house and its contents, but it was just too overwhelming. Her sister and her boyfriend had been entrusted to help, but she had quickly found out that someone was helping themselves. No longer able to find anything, not even the important papers that her father had left, Prunella placed her head down on her arm stretched across the table and covered her face with her other hand in aggravation. She muffled the words "Why was I so trusting?" Feeling more alone than ever, Prunella wanted to give up, but knew she couldn't. Looking slowly around the house, everything was a mess, just as her sister and her boyfriend had left it when she ran them off.

Thinking back, she realized that as her father's health had begun to fade, so had the house. It seemed as if everything had started to fall apart. Trying to keep it up alone was too much for thin, pale Prunella. Her only help had been her once-attractive husband, Barlow Brown. Despite her father's warning, they had married at a young age. "Do you realize your name will be Charlie Brown if you marry that fella?" he had said. The marriage was soon in shambles, and she had sworn off trying to fix what was completely broken. Now, not only did she regret the legal name she carried, but Barlow's constant cheating and lying left nothing to fix. So when the opportunity came along, she had moved in with her father. Prunella sat there staring mindlessly at an old newspaper, as she bowed her head feeling ashamed for marrying him to begin with.

The clatter of the phone disturbed her thoughts yet again. She looked up at the clock; it hadn't been long since the last call. *Damn! I'll bet that's Jerry*, she thought. *What now?* She answered with an unhappy hello.

A young, perky male voice rambled, "Hey, Prunella, I know it's early, but I been eyeballing that Corvette you got under the shed there on the side of your house. It doesn't look like you are going to do anything with it. I was wondering if you'd sell it to me?" Thankful it wasn't Jerry, but appalled at the question, she couldn't care less who it was on the line. She took no time in answering him. "Nope! Not gonna happen, buddy. I'll never part with that car!"

10

She angrily slammed the phone back on the wall, where it had hung for years, causing a picture frame hanging next to the phone to come crashing down and smash on the floor. Prunella sighed as she slid her head down her arm and began to cry. She walked around to pick it up. When she bent down, soft tears gently rolled down her cheeks and fell onto the gold-leaf frame that contained a picture trimmed with dark-green matting, a picture of three lilies that seemed to hug one another. They were perfectly angled and aligned with one another as if they were identical triplets spun from God's fingers. The beautiful yellow lilies complemented the nature around them. They had been planted by her father and grew in abundance, multiplying with the turning of the days, under the mulberry tree. A large crack now ran across the glass, breaking it in two pieces. Prunella ran her hand along the gold frame, carried it to the table, and looked at the damage. The brown paper backing was ripped enough to see the back of the photo, so she pulled it off and tossed it aside. Written in black ink down the left-hand side on the back of the picture was 'NO OOM.' *What is 'NO OOM'?* she thought.

After studying the strange lettering for a bit, she tossed it aside and found herself mindlessly looking around at the house. Daylight was now peeking through the kitchen window. Her eyes moved past the back door. Adjoining the kitchen was the openness of the living room. Next to the back door was the brick fireplace that had once released warm, glowing heat as the flames danced around the fake logs. The fireplace no longer worked thanks to her redneck husband's fixing what was not broken. Usually, once Barlow started messing with things, they never worked right again.

Prunella looked at the large window facing the backyard. Normally, it let in the morning sunshine, but today it only revealed a rainy and dreary day. Many fond Christmas wonders had been enjoyed

11

next to that window. Her mother would decorate the Christmas tree with her favorite red silk balls and slather it with icicle strings as the colored blinking lights flickered. This view could only be seen by the trespassing rednecks that tramped behind the house to shoot the deer that crossed her family's land. Now it was even worse since her father, Charles Richards Jr., had passed away in February of 2011. She turned her attention to the five-shelf bookcase built into the wall next to the window. It housed a few pictures of the family and trinkets along with the full set of 1969 special-edition encyclopedias, collecting dust as they sat undisturbed for years. Next to the shelves, hung on the wall, was a painted portrait of her older sister at age twelve. It was an eerie sight. It wasn't a bad painting of her, but the expression she held on her oil-based face was as if she knew something you didn't.

Chapter 2

Prunella's Name

Feeling frustrated, Prunella allowed her eyes to follow along the once light-colored paneling walls now dark from years of tobacco stains. She stood up and walked over to the door across from the bar. The room behind that wooden door had once been a formal dining room. Through the years of her growing up, it had become a storage room for her mother's sewing machine and materials. Her father had also turned it into his office. As her hand held the knob, she hesitated at the door; something was bothering her. Turning her head to the left, she saw a picture of her other sister hanging there. Prunella snatched it from the wall and slammed it upside down on the end table, saying out loud, "Now that feels better!"

She went on into the room and turned on the desk lamp and looked around at what needed to be moved and gone through. Her father had kept everything, including old bills from his business and stacks upon stacks of papers, in dark-brown milk crates. On the desk was an outdated 2010 calendar, which she tossed in the trash. After moving the calendar, she saw a drawing of her name that she had made in the sixth grade tucked under a thick piece of glass covering the desk. Prunella's mind drifted back to a year ago on the last day she spoke with her father.

***

Prunella remembered him lying afflicted with illness in his bed, clinching his covers, and pulling them tightly under his chin. She could still hear the haunting coughs echoing from his room along the long, dark hallway down to where she had been sitting that day at the kitchen table drinking her coffee. "Prunella!" he had bellowed between coughs, alerting her. She'd made her way to his dim, gloomy room and turned on the bedside lamp, and as she reached over to touch his dank skin, he began to complain of the room's chill and asked her to turn up the heater.

"Dad, the heater is already supplying an extreme degree of heat throughout the house. I've all but resorted to putting on my swimsuit to stay cool in here," she said, grinning. "I'll get you another blanket."

Just as she turned away, he grabbed her hand. "You know, your name is important to me. Your mama wouldn't let me legally name you Prunella. She said it sounded like an old, dried-up prune," he chuckled, "so I told your mama, 'You might not let me give it to her legally, but I'm gonna call her Prunella anyway.'"

She then gave him a smile. "I know. That had me so confused that when I started school, I kept getting mad because they were calling me Charley. I wanted to know why they were calling me a boy's name. I was like, 'Who is Charley?'"

As they chuckled about that, she looked over at the bedside clock. It was 8 a.m. and time for his medication. Once she left the room, his eyes grew heavy, and he drifted off into a dream state.

***

His mind began flipping through pages and scenes of his life. Charles Richards Jr.'s dream took him to his hometown in Mississippi in 1946 when he was eleven. He was floating above the home he grew up in that rested quietly in a small southern community. He could see his family's black mailbox at the end of the driveway with "C. Richards" painted in gold letters. He could feel the humid heat of the summer.

Beads of sweat rolled down the face of an African-American woman. The sweat dropped onto her breast next to a small gold nugget dangling from a thin gold chain. As she sang her favorite hymn, her singing echoed ever so gently among the creeks and hollows. Her singing felt to Charles as if invisible butterflies fluttered about giving a delightful sensation to the day. She was interrupted by the cool feeling of a long shadow as it blocked the warmth of the sun from her back. She turned to see a tall, slender white woman standing there, tapping her foot, with both hands on her hips.

The slender woman spoke, saying, "Now, Prunella, I'm gonna need you to remember, there is not enough time for wasting on a song. Come on now; let's get those greens on to the house, for there are other things you need to be doing." The two ladies gathered the greens and walked back toward the house. As they passed a wood-planked shed, both women looked at it. Vertical slits of light showed through the woodshed and highlighted a cobalt-blue eye, which belonged to Charles.

His eyes were opened wide, straining in the direction of sounds made by small critters jumping and leaping about in the shed. Those sounds scared him. The slits of light somewhat lit up the garden tools that hung on the walls. He was too scared to move, but wished he had one of those tools in his hand to clobber the critters if they were to attack. Suddenly, there was a click from the latch and squeaks from the rusty hinges, and the door swung open to reveal a full-figured, pear-shaped silhouette standing in the dusky light with something in one hand. Prunella, the lovely woman who had been with the family since 1902, was holding a cloth from the kitchen containing a buttermilk biscuit, while steadily balancing a glass of milk fresh from the family's cows.

"Child, you okay?" she spoke softly.

Her familiar voice calling his name caused him to jump to his feet, rush over and wrap his arms around the comfort of her. Squeezing her tightly and burying his face into her waist, he asked, "Did you come to get me out?"

"No, child. I brought this here out to you. You have got to be hungry." With gratitude, he smiled and gave her another loving hug. Her voice trembled with the thought of getting caught by his mother, Stella, who was not your average woman, because she stood intimidatingly confident and proud at five feet eleven. She was a well-respected woman in the community, and she always wanted things promptly. That meant *urgently*, for a better word. Stella didn't believe in senselessness or foolishness of any kind. She despised absurd behavior, although her son would keep her in check with this from time to time. Prunella felt that his being confined to the woodshed was no way to treat a child, no matter what he had done. Every time he was sent in there, she was sure to bring him something from the kitchen. He swallowed the biscuit and gulped down the milk, then handed her the empty glass and the cloth. With one swoop from his arm, he wiped the milk from his lips.

"Have some grace about yourself, child," she scolded him. "Here, use this," and she handed back the cloth. He wiped his mouth, then handed it back to her. She bent down and gave him a big hug and said, "I had better go before your mama catches me. I love you, boy. You know your family has taken care of me all these years, and I've taken care of them, so, child, I'm sure gonna take care of you." She kissed him on his soft, pale cheek, then backed out of the doorway.

Just as she placed the latch down, she jumped at the sound of the female voice behind her.

"Prunella! What are you doing? You know I don't like it when I'm undermined." It was Stella scolding her.

"With all due respect, Mrs. Stella, that child in there needs to eat."

Prunella had never spoken to her like that; however, when it came to Charles, she was no-holds-barred. Stella was very angry at her. She stood there stiff and tall as she angrily demanded that Prunella get out of her sight. After Prunella hung her head and scampered back to the house, she stood there for a minute with her arms folded tightly to her body as she fumed over the defiance of the two of them.

Charles could not contain himself anymore. His mother didn't take up for Prunella when the neighbor Mrs. Creel called her a dumb Negro, and at this point, it didn't matter to him if he got into trouble, because he was already locked in the woodshed. While listening to his mother rant, he let it out and scolded her for it.

She put her hands on her hips and said, "That is grown folk's business, and that's no place for children's noses." She then turned and walked back to the house, muttering her complaint: "I'm tired of people undermining me."

Her stomping steps on the wooden floor grew closer and louder as Prunella stood at the kitchen sink washing up the milk glass. Her chocolate face turned as white as a clean linen sheet hanging on the line as Mrs. Richards walked over to her and stood there towering over her five-feet-four frame. She felt like a cockroach under a high-heeled shoe. Stella put one hand on her hip and with the other, slapped the counter. This caused Prunella to jump, batting her eyes in fear and pleading with Stella not to be upset with her. She only feared her for one reason: if Stella wanted her gone, that would tear Charles Jr. and her apart.

***

The sounds of Charles's daughter brought him from his dream and back to her. "Daddy, I've got your medication." She handed him a handful of pills and a glass of water. She then expressed her dislike of the amount of pills he had to take, but in the same breath, she thanked the doctors for treating his sickness and relieving his pain. He looked at her with his pale-blue, yellowing eyes as she placed another blanket on him. "Come here and let me tell you about the woman you are named after," he spoke softly. She sat on the edge of the bed, turning her body to him so as to give him her full attention. Charles told her the following story.

***

Prunella Jackson was born in 1887, twenty-five years after slavery ended, to a couple that was from Tupelo, Mississippi. Her father, Edgar Jackson, and mother, Riva Jackson, were enslaved until October 20, 1886. A man named Arbor Harold was returning from a chicken trade in Alabama. As he was entering Mississippi, he happened upon a black couple being beaten with a whip by a scraggly man on a horse. As Arbor saw what was happening, he stopped his wagon and stepped down from it, walked over to the black couple, and looked at their faces. As they held one another, he turned to the man on the horse and asked, "Might I ask you why you are lashing these nice colored folks?"

The man only replied with a wad of tobacco spit on Arbor's boot. Arbor was a large, wiry, unkempt, gray-haired man and could take care of himself. He looked at his boot and then at the man on the horse still holding the whip. He could tell by the look in the man's eyes that at any second the whip would be singing in the air directing its vocals at him. He pulsed, calculating the distance from the man to him. Just as he said, "You two get in my wagon," the man snapped the whip as quick as a mountain lion attacks.

Arbor reached up with lightning precision and caught the whip with his large calloused hand, wrapping it around and jerking the man to the ground. Meanwhile, the couple climbed into the back of his wagon. He took the whip and tossed it into the woods. Spotting a rope on the man's saddle, he took it and tied it around the man's feet, then back to the horse's saddle. With one good slap on the horse's rear, the scraggly man was dragged away. Arbor handed them a canteen full of cool water.

Riva was pregnant with Prunella when this happened, and she kept it secret until giving birth to her between rows of knee-high corn. No one knew she was in the cornfield, and they found her too late. Riva had bled to death, leaving her sweet baby still attached by the cord.

At age fifteen, Prunella was sent to live with Charles Jr.'s grandpa, and he treated her like family. She was dressed in fine clothing and jewelry. They made sure she learned how to read, write, and use basic mathematics. Cooking and sewing were learned at her leisure; as she grew up, she found a passion for them and was very good at both. When Charles Sr. came along in 1904, she took care of him like he was her baby brother, and once he married Stella,

Prunella lived with them. Stella had her verbal moments with her, but there was never any physical harm.

***

Charles stopped the story and began to cough haggling breaths. His daughter asked if he was all right. He reassured her that he was, but he needed to rest. She tucked the covers around him, kissed him on his cheek, and turned off the lamp. Once she left the room, he began to think about his family. His eyes grew heavy, and he began to drift off to rejoin his previous dream.

***

Charles saw Prunella and Stella in the kitchen. "Why would you do such a thing as going out to the shed?" Stella inquired. "You know that was the second time I was made a fool of today! The house was destroyed, and Mrs. Creel had to go to the hospital with chest pains. He needed to be punished for all of that today."

Speaking out of turn, Prunella responded, "He meant no harm."

The immediate response was: "I am appalled at your actions today. There is no excuse for it. That frog should not have been brought into the house. Period! So now I want him to stay in there for one more hour. That is for your actions and his mouth."

"Oh, Stella, please don't punish him for what I did. I promise I won't do it again," she pleaded.

"Well, never you mind it today. Maybe both of you will get it together and remember this the next time."

Stella turned and walked out of the kitchen. As she left the room, Prunella muttered, "I don't care for that old, prodigious Mrs. Creel anyway. No more than she care for me." She raised her hands to the heavens and said, "Lord, I praise you! So do as you see fit with her."

Chapter **3**

The Frog Tale

The soft sway of country music's twang sounded slightly through the home as Charles's father took a nap. With his eyes closed and a newspaper across his chest, he lay stretched along the sofa, completely relaxed after the long workday and the fine supper Prunella had laid out for him. Soft snores escaped seemingly in time with the music. He was up at 4 a.m. preparing to work for the Mississippi Department of Transportation, day in and day out, six days a week. Sundays were the only time the family all got together.

Charles Sr. was an important man. He was a well-respected supervisor over a crew of several men. Most of his coworkers knew his wife, Stella, and they all thought she was a handful. She was beautiful and very memorable. As she sat in her chair working on a crossword puzzle while listening to the snoring rhythm from her loving husband, Prunella approached her, leaned down, and whispered so as not to disturb Charles's napping.

"Shall I get Charles Jr. ready for his bath? It's been an hour."

Without even looking at or speaking to her, Stella just tightened her lips and nodded her head yes.

Complete darkness had fallen on the shed. Prunella grabbed a light from the kitchen and made her way out to where he sat quietly. Unlatching the door, she told him to come out and reached into the darkness for his hand. Charles latched on, and they slowly walked toward the house. Unconcerned of her own steps, Prunella kept the light in front so he could safely tread the shaggy grass.

"Child, you done gone and done it this time," she said. "You know they had to take old Mrs. Creel to the emergency room. Child, I told you! Your pranks were gonna get you in trouble, if not get someone seriously hurt. You like to have scared that woman to death."

He stopped walking, looked up at her, and squeezed her hand with a smile, then cackled, saying, "Did you see her eyes? They were as big as teacup saucers. That woman is just a mean, old, fat, messy woman. She gossips about everybody and hates colored people. I overheard her say you should not be free. That's why I don't like her, because everybody should be free. What's your skin color got to do with it? That woman just gossips too much anyway. She thinks she knows everything that goes on around this town!"

Charles paused his rant, looked down at the grass, then back at her. "You know, if anybody wants to know about somebody, they can just sit next to Mrs. Creel 'cause I'll bet she'll dang sure know!"

They started walking to the house again. She knew it was true, and it made her feel loved to see that protective gleam in his eye. "I thought you learned your lesson last time you did something like this."

He laughed with fond remembrance, acknowledging, "Oh yeah... the pastor when I put that little green snake under his podium. You know I traded a pack of gum for that snake. Well, I sure thought it was funny."

Prunella tried but just couldn't scold him. She just said, "Child, that man could have broken his leg when he fell off that platform." With a slight chuckle, she added, "Good thing he's got connection to the Lord."

Just as they were about to enter the house, Charles stopped her again by pulling back on her hand. Looking up at her, he said with

25

a serious face, "I understand I must be punished for some things, and I will take the woodshed over that belt I know Daddy has. You know my friend Shorty? Well, I know his daddy whips him real good with his dang belt. I've seen him come to school with a sore butt." He shook his head, then smiled at her, adding, "You know the only regret I have about the pastor and the snake?" He placed one hand on his hip, tilted his head to the side, and said, "I sure wished I still had that pack of gum when I got put in the shed for that."

She laughed at him, then lovingly smacked him on his backside and said, "Go on! Get in there to your bath. You something else, boy!"

The early-morning roosters crowed, alerting everyone that the sun was on the rise. One old rooster, Roger, had been Charles's alarm clock for the past few years. He was a morning person, and Roger was first to be fed. He would run out and feed the farm animals every morning. His eyes slowly opened to invite the light to his day, but his first thoughts caused him to jump out of bed quickly. It was a school day, and he couldn't wait to share the adventures of his weekend with his close pals. He quickly tended to his chores and ate the breakfast Prunella had made for him. After he brushed his teeth and washed his face, he quickly got dressed.

Tucking in his shirt was the one thing no one had to get onto him about. Charles was a very sharp dresser. He was never wrinkled and always neat and clean. His shoes never lost a shine, either. His short, stubbly blond hair didn't need much tending. He said his goodbyes, grabbed his books from the table, and swung open the screen door, running out onto the porch. Right before the bam of the door, he cringed with his whole body and face. He had been told numerous times not to let the screen door slam, so he turned slowly with an apology: "Sorry. I forgot."

He began skipping down the steps as his little feet followed a path, faster and faster until they were running, to the little school just a mile from his home. The sounds of children laughing and playing filled the morning silence as he grew closer to the school. He could see his pals, Dan, Shorty, and Gordon, in the distance. Charles and the others considered Gordon the "good one" of all the boys because he always seemed to escape trouble. He struggled to keep his friends out of trouble, but it didn't always work out. Gordon was like their conscience, but they rarely listened to him. Shorty was the smallest of the boys, but he walked around like he was ten feet tall, looking to fight anyone who picked on him. Dan was the tallest and the smartest. He seemed to always have the answer to any question and could solve most problems. However, he would let Charles talk him into things from time to time. When these boys got together, it was never dull in those Mississippi woods.

The boys saw him and ran to meet him halfway. They were eager to hear what had really taken place after overhearing their mothers' gossip on the phone. They were talking about what had happened over the weekend. With their excitement, they were falling over each other to get to Charles and ask him questions. He had to slow them down by telling them, "Hey, hey! One at a time."

Shorty spoke up first: "I overheard Mom talking to Rob Hewbertson's mom, saying you put a frog in Mrs. Creel's blouse and put cake on her butt."

All the boys laughed, then agreed they'd heard about the same thing.

"No, no, no!" Charles grumbled. "Let me tell y'all the whole story. This is what really happened."

The boys leaned close, and he began. He drew in a deep breath, exhaled and said, "Saturday, Mrs. Creel came over with a dress she wanted hemmed. Prunella tried to tell her that it was gonna have to be re-pinned where the hem was going to be, but was told she didn't know what she was talking about. 'I pinned the garment myself, and I've pinned more garments than you have in your lifetime.' So once more she tried to explain that the pins were slanted and it would shift, then twist the fabric, resulting in an ugly, uneven hem. After dismissing her opinion, Prunella got tired of the disagreement and sewed the garment anyway. When done, the old bag said that it was messed up on purpose and she was just a dumb Negro. Prunella left the house and ran out to her favorite mulberry tree. Mama was standing there the whole time and didn't say anything to her. The whole thing upset me, so the next day I got payback for my pal. Mama was having one of her punch-bowl parties where they play cards, and I was sitting on the front porch with my dog, Black-Eye. Mrs. Creel came over with Mrs. Jones and Mrs. Broom."

Charles interjected to entertain his friends that Mrs. Broom's hair looked like a straw broom. They all laughed hysterically; then he went back to his story.

"I was on the steps when Mrs. Creel started walking up. I moved over by pulling Black-Eye with me to give her room, but she told me to move myself and my mangy mutt. Then the dog barked at her. I think he understood what she said. Well, she screamed for Mama to help her because they couldn't come up the steps and the dog was frightening them. Y'all know my dog wouldn't hurt a flea. Mama came outside and told me to get, and it made me mad. So I walked down to the pond. I was sitting there thinking about that hateful woman and how I wished I could scare the crap out of her one day—just to show her what being frightened was all about.

28

So as I continued to sit there, I heard a frog croaking nearby. Y'all know how she is terrified of frogs. Well, it took some wrestling around, but I caught that frog."

The boys stood there so intent, hanging on every word, knowing it was all true. Charles might have been a prankster, but he owned up to it all. If he said it, he did it. If he made a mistake, he didn't deny it. He then told of going into the house and sneaking under the cake table, telling them, "Man, that cake looked good, too. I wanted a piece, but Mama wouldn't let me have it. Anyway, when no one was looking, I put the frog under her napkin. Then I darted back under the table. Just as I got back into position, she came in and sat down. I couldn't have planned it any better. Mrs. Creel lifted her napkin, and the frog jumped into the punch bowl, splashing it everywhere! With one giant leap, the frog jumped from the punch bowl onto her old, wrinkled boobs!"

The boys grabbed their sides, laughing and rolling around, as he continued, "She jumped up screaming, knocked over her chair, and then tripped, knocking the cake off the table and onto the floor. The old bag slipped in it and fell down, and when she fell, I was face to face with her. I smiled, grabbed a piece of cake, took a bite, and ran out the door. I found out later that she had sat on a fork, and it stuck in her butt." They all continued to laugh even harder at her misfortunes. Just then, the school's bell sounded, alerting the boys to make their way to the classroom.

As they parted, Gordon put his hand on Charles's shoulder and asked a one-word question: "Woodshed?"

He replied with a one-word answer: "Yep."

Charles tried to walk through the large school doors with Gordon, but his body froze in place as Gordon walked on. Silence fell over his ears; then a soft voice called him by his full name. He turned around expecting to see someone, but there wasn't anyone there. He found himself completely alone outside the school doors. He turned back to the doors and pulled on them, and again he heard the voice. He became frantic as he tried to open the door again. Finally they opened, and he stepped through them only to find himself falling down a black hole. Just as he was about to panic, he woke up in his bed of old age and sickness. Charles wanted to cry, but he was strong. He knew it was his bad habit that had landed him in that bed.

**

Prunella tapped on his door and walked in, asking, "Are you awake?" Seeing that he was, she gave him a smile and added, "Hey, I've got a couple of turkey pot pies I'm going to fix later. Do you think your stomach can handle that?"

He quickly answered her with a stern chuckle, "Naw, I don't eat turkey." Laughing out loud, he patted the bed, wanting her to sit next to him. He adjusted himself, then laid his head back to rest on his pillow. He looked at the ceiling in search of his detailed memory bank, saying, "Now, let me tell you why I don't do turkey," then took her back in time.

**

Chapter **4**

The Turkey Hunt

It was spring break 1950, and Charles was fifteen, about to turn sixteen in August of that year. He and his cousin Oliver had planned to go hunting and camping alone after he turned sixteen. The boys' plans were going to be disrupted because Oliver's father had landed a new job in Alabama and their family would be moving next month. This was upsetting to them, for they had been looking forward to this since age ten. The two were close in age by one year. Oliver had six siblings, but Charles was his "brother." He looked up to him like no one else. Knowing that they would be moving before his birthday pained him. Charles Sr. understood his pain and, before discussing it with Stella, had told him it would be okay if they went hunting and camping together along with some other pals before he moved. The boys were responsible even though they both had spent many hours in the woodshed after having too much fun. When these two were around one another, they would entertain themselves in ways that usually resulted in a trip in there.

The Richards family had eighty acres of land that consisted of open fields and forest. That was plenty of land for the boys to have fun on. Charles Sr. was a wealthy man due to his father's dealings in the oil business, and he had taught his son everything he knew—beginning with hard work. Charles Jr. was an only child and would one day inherit everything his father owned.

While Prunella was baking a pie for Stella, Charles, Oliver, Dan, and Shorty were gathered in the kitchen, sitting at the table, anxiously waiting for Charles Sr. to come home. His father worked until noon on Saturdays, and the clock was sitting on 12:55 p.m.

Prunella pulled one of the pies from the oven and placed it on the table, giving the boys a look that told them not to touch it, telling them Stella was over at Mrs. Creel's house and was coming back to get it when it had cooled. No sooner had she gotten it out of her mouth when Stella walked in.

"Miss, you got perfect timing."

All of the boys said hello to her, but she ignored them as she walked over to the table where they sat. Giving them a look of "get out of my kitchen," she said, "What are you all doing here in Prunella's way?" Setting her purse down next to Charles and sliding the pie close to her, she expressed delightfully, "Oh! This smells wonderful, but I sure hope you strained the berries real good this time. You know how I hate those little seeds in my teeth."

"Why, yes, ma'am! I sure did. I remembered you didn't like them things. And you need not worry. These children is no bother to me."

Charles loved to aggravate Stella, and while the women's backs were turned as they looked at the second pie on the counter, he picked up a can of corned beef hash sitting on the shelf next to him and quickly dropped it into her purse. When she picked up the purse, it would throw her off as to why it was heavier. Only the three other boys had witnessed what he'd done. Charles raised his finger to his lips as if to tell his friends to stay quiet, but they began to giggle. Mr. Richards walked in about that time and asked them what they were laughing at. Charles did not want to give details, so he quickly changed the subject. "Can we go camping and hunting today?"

Mr. Richards walked over to Stella to give her a kiss and asked the other boys, "What do your parents say about this?"

He leaned in to kiss Stella on the cheek, but she pulled away, saying, "Tomorrow is Sunday, and we have church." She then looked down at her husband, who only stood five feet eight, and told him with that one look to tell them no.

Charles Sr. knew her look, but this time he spoke up for the boys. "I promised him once he turned sixteen, they could go out there and camp and hunt on their own. Now you know they won't be around each other as much. It ain't that much longer before he is sixteen, so I say let them go."

She pushed past her shorter husband and grabbed the pie and her purse. Just as she picked them up, the weight balance expected from her purse caused her to misjudge the pie. Everyone gasped as they watched her fumbled it around in her hand. Luckily, as it slid from her hand, she tossed it gently back to the table's edge. Giving Charles a stern look, she pulled out the can of corned beef hash and slung her purse onto her shoulder, then grabbed the pie with both hands. Reaching the door, she said, "Whatever, Charles Richards Sr. Have it your way." Then she walked out, slamming the door behind her.

He knew she was upset, so he looked at his son and said, "Always remember: no matter how much trouble, a promise is a promise. No matter what, you keep it." He then hung his head down after giving Prunella a quick look. "I really should have discussed this with her first, but it's too late." Then he quickly looked at Oliver and shook his finger at him. "Now you look here. I'm telling you not to be carrying a gun, period!"

Oliver shook his head with complete understanding and agreement. The boys were sitting on the edge of their seats, anxiously waiting to be excused. Their gear was sitting by the back steps, ready for their adventure. Charles Sr. could feel their tension as he looked at the back door, ready to give them the green light. He finally said, "Go on. Get out of here."

Scuffling feet and chairs scraping across the floor were followed by a flash of light from the opening of the back door, and they were gone. In a moment, Charles Jr. opened the door and stuck his head in, grinning broadly. "Prunella, I'm gonna bring back the biggest, juiciest turkey you've ever had."

She gave him a wink and a smile. "Go get 'em, boy."

The boys headed out to the back side of the eighty acres of the Richards family land where a creek ran through. On one side was an opening with a little brush, while the other side was covered with trees. It was perfect for hunting turkey. Once they got to the shallow creek, they set up camp on the tree side, giving cover to their hunt, hoping the turkeys would take pleasure in that area.

A slight breeze blew the leaves, dancing them along the forest floor. After the boys gathered wood for their campfire, Dan struck a match, giving it life. With their camp ready, all of the boys were relaxing and dreaming of the big game they intended to kill. Shorty pulled a few cans of beer from his bag and tossed each of them a can. He bragged about swiping it from his brother's truck. Oliver opened his first and lifted it to his nose. He made a horrible face at the putrid smell. "No way, man! I can't drink this." He poured the beer out and tossed the can aside and reached into his pocket, pulling out a knife; then he picked up a small piece of wood and began whittling. Dan opened his beer and took a big swallow. A woof came from him as he pulled the can from his lips. Charles chuckled at them as he sat there looking at the red label with gold lettering advertising Schlitz beer. "The beer that made Milwaukee famous, huh?"

He had heard of this brand, but had never been tempted to ever really drink the stuff. Today was different. He was a man now, so he flipped back the tab, exposing the liquid. He turned it up, taking a big swallow, and then wiped the beer from his chin. Lying to Shorty, he said, "Not bad."

"See, Oliver, it ain't bad," Shorty smugly replied. "You're just a kid anyway. Keep playing with your stick."

Charles disliked the comment and, in a protective manner, decided to get back at him. He jumped up, moved closer, and then poured his beer over Shorty's head. As he rubbed it into his hair, in a preacher's tone he said, "I anoint you with oil and dub you a dummy for thinking we wanted this stuff anyway." He fell backward on the forest floor, laughing. Dan and Oliver joined in the laughter with him. Shorty, on the other hand, was not amused. Upset with his friends, he walked away and stood at the edge of the fire-lit trees.

When he complained about catching a cold because his head was wet, Charles got up and went over to apologize. "Come on. It was all fun. Come on over and sit back down with us. I'll leave you alone."

They both returned to the campfire, and Oliver held up the piece of wood he had been whittling. Charles took it and looked it over, surprised at how well he had done. He had whittled on that stick and carved a ball free to move within a cage. He expressed his enthusiasm and rubbed his stubby dark hair. Soon their fun and games subsided, and the boys stretched out to rest for the night.

As dawn's early light began to glow, softly illuminating the forest, birds began chirping in the tall trees. The relaxing sound of the creek and the fresh smell of pine welcomed the boys awake. Stretching and yawning, Charles was the first to sit up. The early-morning light reflecting in his blue eyes was enough to make the sky jealous. He woke the others up by pushing on them and said, "Come on, girls! Let's get some turkeys." He picked up his bedding and tossed it onto Shorty. "Never mind, I got a turkey right here!" Jumping on him, they wrestled around until Shorty cried out in aggravation, "Stop! Let me go!" He might have been a fighter with other boys, but he was afraid he didn't have a chance against the quick Charles. Figuring his fist might be just as fast as his mouth, he just complained and pleaded for him to stop.

He was now in a headlock and muttered, "Why are you always picking on me?"

"Picking on you? Well, that was yesterday's promise. Today is a whole new day."

All of the boys were awake now and watching the calamity. Oliver spoke up: "Come on, Charles. Let him be."

Charles immediately released him, stood up, and extended his hand. "OK...come on, Shorty. I promise that I'll leave you alone."

Across the creek in the brush, the boys hunkered down to watch and wait for their prey. Hours passed and their bellies began to growl. Dan bumped Charles and whispered, "Hey, give me some of that cornbread I saw you tuck in your coat pocket."

Charles gave him a big smile as he pushed lightly on Dan's shoulder. "What cornbread? I ain't got no cornbread."

Dan could see the mischievous look in his eyes and could just taste it, knowing it was in his pocket. His lips began to smack as he waited for him to pull it out. Charles kept his eyes forward, trying not to look at Dan, but everyone was now looking at him as if to say "What gives?" Feeling their hungry faces looking at him, he broke and couldn't hold back the cornbread any longer. He pulled out the large piece and divided it among everyone. They were all so hungry, they took care not to drop even one of those small yellow crumbs.

"Gobble, gobble," the sounds of a turkey echoed through the field.

Shorty spoke with cornbread-spewed words, "Holy shit," for he was the first to see several turkeys creeping along without a care in the world. Turkeys were coming into the opening, pecking and scratching around like common yard chickens. "Look! Look!" Shorty yelled as he pointed in the direction of the turkeys. Oliver slapped his hand over his mouth to hush him up.

Charles picked up his rifle to aim at the birds, but Dan reached over and whispered as he pushed the barrel down, "Wait. Let's see how many there are before you scatter them."

They all began counting. Their eyes started bulging as six turkeys soon became twelve. Charles could not contain himself any longer. He raised his rifle, pulled the trigger, and made a kill shot. There went one. Charles cocked his head to the side in confusion because the other turkeys did not move. *Hmmm*, he thought, *any other time the loud sound of a gun would cause the turkeys to scatter.* He disregarded the thought and yelled, "I got one!"

The other two boys took aim, and their guns went off, leaving several turkeys on the ground. Shorty shouted, "Put your guns down. I know I got two!"

He jumped up and ran over to the mess of birds. Two were still flapping. Dan tapped Shorty on the back of the head. "Yep, there's your two. I did it for you," he said, remembering Charles's promise not to pick on him. The boys laughed, but Shorty found no humor in it.

Eight dead turkeys lay at their feet. The boys were full of excitement knowing they were each taking two of them home to their families. No one noticed as the other four birds calmly walked back into the brush. Charles, Oliver, and Dan each picked up their two birds, leaving Shorty the two still flapping.

"Shorty, go on now and get your two birds," Dan said.

Oliver burst out laughing at this. Shorty propped his gun up in his arms, poked out his bottom lip, looked at Oliver, and mocked him in a high-pitched, girly voice, "Well, little boy, at least I can carry a gun."

Charles motioned for him to stop. "Give it a rest, girls. Come on. Get your birds."

He looked at the birds, then at the other three boys, and grunted. Bending down, he grabbed the turkeys by their necks, and with one quick circular motion, he had his game. The boys rushed back to the campsite, snuffed their fire, and packed their gear. Shorty tied his turkeys to his belt, one on each hip. Charles, Oliver, and Dan threw their birds and knapsacks over their shoulders. With the feathers draping down their backs, they looked like camouflaged angels.

**

Prunella was enjoying the story her father was telling her, but she had to ask, "Well, Daddy, that really didn't tell me why you don't eat turkey."

He laughed as he added, "Those birds belonged to old man Newman. You know that fella's property that joins us in the back of our property?"

"Yes. I heard he wasn't right in the head."

"Oh! It made me and Oliver so sick when we found out that we had killed and ate that man's pet birds, and that was the worst birds I've ever tried to eat. So that's why I won't eat turkey ever again." He paused, then said, "Well, that isn't the only thing I won't eat. Apples...apples—nope, not them either.

Chapter 5

Apple Bombs

It was a beautiful Friday morning in 1953. Charles anxiously awaited Oliver's arrival. He wrung his hands and paced the floor. "Any minute now, Prunella, and he will be here. Oh, I can't wait! We are going to slip over and get some apples from Mrs. Creel's apple tree. I heard she won't be home."

Prunella instantly dropped the small bowl that she was washing and spun around to him. "Oh, child! Don't you dare go over there. I heard she was gonna sell them to Mr. Holloway by the pound, and he's gonna be picking them tomorrow. Rumor has it she's got every apple counted." She shook her finger at him and warned, "You stay as far away as you can, child."

He stopped dead in his tracks and exclaimed, shrugging his shoulders and flapping his arms wildly, "Every one of them counted? Aw, come on! You can't believe that."

She gave him the stink eye, then shook her finger at him again. "Child, stay away from that tree!"

He turned away from her because he could not give her that promise. Outside, there was the sound of rocks crunching up the driveway. He jumped from the kitchen chair and flew to the door. As he looked out, she asked, "Well, is it him?"

With a sigh, he replied, "No. It's just Gordon. Looks like he is with his grandma." Charles stepped out to meet them.

Gordon opened the passenger door of his grandma's car and said, "Hey! We came by to see if you wanted to join us at church. There is gonna be..."

Before he could complete his sentence, the car Charles had been waiting on pulled up. Unaware of his rudeness, Charles left him and ran around the car. He ducked down to peer into the station wagon's windows to search through the sea of children.

Just then, Oliver climbed over his sister and sprang from the back seat, saying, "Man! I can't believe you are going to be eighteen this year."

Oliver's father, Russell, overheard them talking as he opened the passenger-side door for his wife, Sylvia. As she gathered up the other children, Russell walked over and put his arm around Charles. "Eighteen, huh? Any plans, son?"

"Yep, I sure do." He pointed at the house and indicated that everyone was inside.

Oliver stopped his dad and asked, "Can we go see Dan?" Russell gave him a nod.

Gordon and his grandma were still there waiting for an answer. Gordon then proceeded to tell them there would be a picnic lunch on the church grounds. The boys declined the offer because their minds were on more "important" things. Oliver grabbed his bag from the station wagon.

The boys ran as fast as they could, but suddenly Oliver stopped running and sat down on the ground. He dug around in his bag, pulled out a wooden pipe, and began to pack it with tobacco. Charles was ahead of him, weaving his body through a barbed-wire fence, and realized he was alone. He looked back to see Oliver relaxing on the ground and yelled, "Come on!" Oliver wasn't getting up, so he weaved his body back through the fence and headed back. As he got closer, he could see smoke curling around Oliver's head and suddenly realized he was puffing on a pipe.

Laughter echoed at the sight of his young, little, skinny cousin smoking a pipe. "Dang, Ollie, when did you start smoking a pipe? Them thangs are for old men."

A big smile stretched across Oliver's face as he took another drag of his pipe. Charles sat down next to him and pulled out a pack of Pall Mall cigarettes and a book of matches. He fanned away the cloud of smoke from his pipe as Ollie asked, "Well, when did you start smoking?"

He struck a match, lit the cigarette that hung from his lips, and quickly fanned his hand, putting out the match. He blew a cloud of smoke from his lips and held up his pack of cigarettes, saying, "Shorty's brother was rolling around with some gal and forgot these in the barn, so we got them and give them a try." He looked down at the cigarette and took another drag as he added, "You know, I like these. Think I'm gonna keep smoking them. Shorty is still smoking, too. Ol' Dan won't try them, but that's all right." He pushed Oliver on the shoulder lightly as he added, "Hell! I never thought you'd be smoking, let alone a pipe! You look all older and stuff." Leaning over, he tried to pull the dark peach fuzz on his top lip. "Well, looky here! You got some hair growing on ya."

Ollie pulled away from him, laughing, and advised him not to touch his "man hairs." The two sat there smoking away until Charles heard his name being called. He quickly snuffed out his cigarette in the dirt. They both looked back toward the house, fearful of being caught. They heard it again and scanned the landscape for the voice. Relief set in as they saw Dan coming through the fence. The two boys jumped to their feet and ran to him.

Once they reached him, Oliver placed his hand on tall Dan's shoulder and said, "Man, am I glad it was you instead of our daddies!"

He looked down at his hand as it held the wooden pipe, then tossed his head back in laughter. "Y'all smoking that nasty tobacco stuff? You know I don't think that's good for y'all. From the looks on your faces, you don't want to get caught either." They shook their heads as he laughed at them, adding, "So what are y'all up to besides sneaking around smoking?"

Charles quickly changed the subject and grabbed Dan by his shoulders. "Have you seen Mrs. Creel's apple tree?"

He grabbed him back by his arms and said, "No, but Mama had some the other day from her tree and, man, were they good!"

Oliver popped up with a light jump and said, "Let's go get a few. Nobody will know." Without hesitation, the boys then headed out to the apple tree. They walked up the road toward her house, checking carefully to see if she was truly gone. As they got closer, Dan advised, "It'd be better if we go around behind the church through the woods to get to the tree. It'd provide us a better chance of not being seen."

After a slight detour, they stood before a fully-loaded, large apple tree. The limbs hung low due to the weight of the abundance of apples. Three large branches sprouted from the tree's trunk. Climbing it would be easy. The trio scrambled up the tree, then stretched out, balancing carefully on the strong but thin limbs.

Once the apples were picked, they each bit into them. The boys nodded as if to compliment the apples' flavor and juiciness. At that moment, the sounds of church music gracefully fluttered through the tree where the boys were perched. Upon hearing this, Charles whispered, "Oh, shit! I forgot about the church people."

The churchyard was connected to Mrs. Creel's property. There was no way they could get down without being seen, for that apple tree's life began on the property line. The boys could see people starting to walk around outside, but the foliage from the tree was thick enough no one could see them. They began to whisper to one another, discussing their predicament. Some time had passed, and their bellies were full of apples. They had no choice but to stay put, stretched out on the tree limbs. The church crowd bowed their heads in prayer and ended in a unanimous amen. Some people began to eat as others sang hymns. Children were running around playing. Charles lit a cigarette, and Oliver dug around in his bag looking for his pipe. Immediately, Oliver looked at Charles, grinning from ear to ear, with his hand still in his bag. He spoke a little too loudly, "Oh shit! I almost forgot!"

Dan shushed him. Oliver was always looking to impress Charles, just knowing he would be amazed. Oliver pulled out a long red stick with a string hanging from it. Charles quickly snatched it from his hand, questioning what it was as he investigated it. Oliver's chest poked out with pride as, with a sideways smile, he said, "Homemade dynamite. I made it. And yes! It'll blow some shit up."

They inquired how he had made it, and he told them that he'd learned it from the same old man who had given him the pipe. "All I did was take a bunch of M-80s and empty the powder out of them. I got a heavy cardboard tube and capped off the ends. Next, I made a small hole in the side. Then I poured the M-80 powder in the small hole and stuck a fuse in it. For the finale, I sprayed it with some red paint that I snuck from my sister. " He adjusted himself, giving his chest an extra boost, "Looks pretty good, don't it?"

Dan advised to be careful with it. He knew what one M-80 could do.

Charles was startled at first, hearing his seriousness, but quickly blew it off. "You didn't make no damn dynamite. Oh, he's just bullshitting us." Twirling it through his fingers, he smugly added, "This thang ain't real."

At that moment, an offended Oliver quickly reached out with one arm to take it away from him, dangerously balancing on the thin limb on his tiptoes. This move caused him to overreach and lose his grip with the other hand. In that instant, he lost his footing and screamed out as he fell to the ground. Charles looked down to see him lying on his back. As he studied him to make sure he was okay, he didn't realize that his cigarette was too close to the fuse of the dynamite.

The words "oh shit" loudly rang from the tree yet again.

Meanwhile, the church folks were looking around for the source of all the curse words and saw Oliver sit up from his fall. Charles was still holding the lit tube as he watched the sparks and the fuse burn down. Dan yelled at him to do something, but he was frozen.

Finally he yelled, "Holy shit! This thing is real. Let's get out of the tree! But what do I do with this?"

Dan reached over, grabbed the burning tube from him, wedged it between two branches, and said, "Jump!" They both jumped from the tree, scrambled to their feet, and ran.

A loud BOOM rang through the air behind them. All of the boys fell to the ground. The church people had no idea what was going on. As whole apples turned into pulp scattered with leaves and branches, the people were grabbing their children and ducking for cover. Finally, the last few leaves flickered to the ground, and dead silence fell on everyone's ears. The boys looked over at the church again to make sure everyone was okay. Once they gathered their bearings, they stood up.

Charles began to think out loud: "Oh man! What have we done?" He knew right then that he didn't want to go home.

With this thought tumbling in his head, Oliver began to get angry. He turned to Charles and yelled, "Why?"

Dan jumped between them and held them apart with his long arms and said, "Just wait a minute!" They ignored him because they were mad. "Guys, guys! Come on! Stop this!" he yelled again.

As he tried to hold them apart, a hand touched Dan on the shoulder. It was Gordon, standing there in his Sunday finest on a Friday. He had on a black rayon button-up with a dickey and black corduroy slacks.

Looking him up and down, with beads of sweat rolling down his face, Dan said, "Aren't you hot in that getup?"

With a blank look, Gordon asked, "What's going on?"

That couldn't be answered because he had spotted what was left of the once-bountiful apple tree. All that was left were a few stray limbs on a four-foot stump with apples and branches littering the ground. Seeing this caused his jaw to drop, and all he could say was "Oh God."

Upon hearing his words, all the boys looked in the direction of the apple tree. Once they saw the disaster they had created, they joined in repeating those same words.

After a few minutes, Charles looked at the other boys and spouted out, "Later," leaving a trail of dust as he ran away from them all.

Oliver looked at tall, stiff Dan, and without saying a word, he bolted after his cousin. Left standing there was the smart one with the good one, and the smart one quickly realized he needed to be somewhere else. He spouted out quickly, "Bye, good one. I'll phone you later, if I can."

Dan went home as the other two slowly walked back home. Once the boys reached the house, they could see Oliver's sisters at the swing.

As they got closer, Cathy Jo asked, "Did y'all hear that loud bang?" The boys looked at one another as she continued, "I don't know what it was, but Aunt Stella went to find out."

Here it was lunchtime, and the boys were already in deep applesauce. They slowly opened the screen door to the kitchen, hoping no one would say a word about the tree. Just about that time, Prunella said from behind the door, "Oh, Charles! You done it now. I'm sure glad it wasn't my mulberry tree. I, well, I..."

49

***

While Charles Jr. told his daughter of his apple troubles, he started laughing so hard that his cough became uncontrollable. Prunella quickly ran to the kitchen and got a glass of tea for him. As he swallowed the tea and regained his breath, he said, "I'm sure glad it wasn't the mulberry tree, either." He sat quietly for a minute, then asked, "Did I ever tell you I spent eight years in the army?"

Chapter 6

The Family Loss

Prunella sat back down next to her father. He began telling her more about his earlier years.

Charles patted her on the leg, then began. "Yep. When I finished school, I chose to go into the military. I was gonna do like my father: leave a boy and come back a man. That's where I got all my knowledge about mechanical things like working on jeeps." He looked in her eyes and said, "Girl, I'm telling you, don't ever buy one of those jeeps because they ain't worth a sh—" Stopping just before cursing in front of his daughter, he cleared his throat and rephrased: "Well, them things just ain't worth dealing with."

He looked up at the ceiling as if he could see his memories there.

After a few moments, he continued, "Yep, I went in the army. I was sent to Fort Benson, North Carolina, in 1954. They trained me for about a half a year, then I was sent to Hong Kong in 1955. You know, that was the same year James Dean died in a car wreck. That crazy boy was only twenty-four years old. Hmm, sure is a shame. Now, let's see...I was sent to Singapore for a year. After that I was in Korea from 1957 to 1959. I was just about to come home for the Christmas holiday when I got the call about Daddy being killed." He stopped, turned his head to her and asked, "Did I ever tell you about your grandpa being killed?"

She replied with a nod of her head as she picked at the white blankets. Then she shrugged her shoulders as if she didn't know.

He proceeded: "Well, Prunella, Dad left out for work on December 9, 1959. It was foggy that morning when he arrived at the job sight out on Highway 42. He and a couple of other men were standing on the side of the road. A truck hit my father, killing him instantly. The person didn't stop. With the fog as thick as it was, the other men only heard the truck and saw the taillights."

He looked away from her as tears began to well up in his eyes; then he cleared his throat and continued this sad memory.

***

Charles was standing with Prunella Jackson and Stella at his father's funeral, fighting back tears. As the service came to a close and people started leaving, Stella hugged him. She said to them, "Everyone will be coming to the house, so I'm going. I'll see you two there."

Prunella stood strong and quiet just staring at Charles Sr.'s final resting place. Charles Jr. placed his arm loosely around her shoulder. They both stood there like that until she broke the silence. She began stroking the long stem of the flower that she held and said, "You know, lilies are life's miracles. They represent purity and refined beauty. I look at them like Mother Nature's narrators for our feelings, spreading about their passion of pinks, gratitude of yellows, reds for love, and white for the sophistication of it all." She paused and leaned her head on his shoulder.

Peering through her velveteen netted hat, she looked up at Charles Jr. "You know there is over 200 families or so of lilies and well over 3,000 species of them. You know what? None of that matters to me as much as their beautiful colors." She bumped him with her elbow as she grinned, adding, "Kinda like you and me. We belong to the same family, but we are different."

He pulled her close to him, and she said, "Charles, I have wondered where I would have grown if I wasn't planted in your family's flower bed."

He squeezed her tightly and gave her a smile as he replied, "Prunella, I know that no matter where it might have been, you would have shown them all of your beautiful colors that I know you carry...but you're my personal rainbow."

They stood quietly embracing, soaking up their love for one another. She turned to him, wrapped her arms around his, and looked deep into his eyes. She then leaned into him and spoke softly, "You know I had a chance to leave and see the world. Your father, bless his heart, brought back a bouquet of tiger lilies. Then he handed me a nice-size bar of solid gold. He told me that if I ever felt like I was suffocating here, I should leave and travel the world or something."

Charles heard the word *gold* and perked up, interrupting her softly, "Well, Prunella, what did you do with the gold?"

She got quiet as she turned back to face the grave. She then turned her head back to Charles Jr. and whispered, "I planted it down with the tiger lilies." She looked back at the grave, then back at him and said, "Well, child, once you were born, I thought you was a good reason to take up root here."

She walked toward the grave and placed the red lily that she held down on the ground. As she did this, two men in suits walked up to Charles Jr. One of the men reached out to shake his hand and said, "Hi. Are you Charles Thomas Richards Jr.?" He nodded yes. "Well, sir, we are from the Mississippi Department of Transportation, and we are truly sorry for your loss. Your father was a great man." As he said this, the other man handed him a medium-size black box. The first man continued, "On behalf of the department, we would like to give this to you as a token for the hard work Mr. Richards put in with the department."

He looked down at the small black velvet box with his father's name in gold letters. It was bound with a beautiful red sash. As he opened the box, he was unable to speak. Inside was a cross made from 200 grams of gold with two carats of rubies encrusted on the four ends. Prunella stepped up and thanked the men for him, as he was speechless.

When they left, he looked at her with wide eyes and said, "Where do I hide this?"

Charles clenched the box in amazement as he watched the men walk away. He looked past the men, and there, standing in his line of sight, was a beautiful, petite strawberry-blonde woman. His heart skipped a beat. Recognizing the man that this beautiful woman stood by as his neighbor and childhood classmate, he thought, *Wow! He sure landed him a nice-looking woman.*

With that thought, the woman turned and made eye contact with him. In that moment when her eyes met his, a warm fire of desire sparked in him. It warmed him so much that he forgot that he was at his father's funeral and gave her an ear-to-ear smile. At that moment, Prunella let out a deep cry, and Charles turned his attention back to her. He held Prunella until a dainty, soft hand touched him on his lower arm.

He looked down at the hand as the consoling words "I'm sorry for your loss" came from the owner. He slowly looked up this arm, thinking intently, *Oh my. It's her, the beautiful elegant woman who was with the neighbor.* The sensual sound of her voice sent quivering shivers up his spine as she spoke to him, saying, "Hi, there. You probably don't remember me. I'm Sharon Shaw. My brother is Mark Shaw. Surely you remember him," then flashing a beautiful smile.

Stuttering in his head, his nervous words finally came forth: "Oh. How is Mark?" Not that Charles really cared at that moment.

Charles had seen a fair share of women, but never had he seen one so beautiful. As he looked into her bright green eyes, he wondered where she had been all his life. Then, as if she heard his thoughts, she said, "I was about four years behind you and Mark in school. I was just a young, scraggly thing then." She lowered her head with a giggle.

He didn't remember her, but he was sure not to forget her now. Charles found her very exotic and intriguing. He used his military experience to pay close attention, gazing across her hand for signs of marriage or engagement. She possessed great qualities that made her so pleasing to him. He didn't hesitate in asking her out once she showed no signs of entanglement.

Not very long after that, he and Sharon were married in 1960. They had a beautiful wedding at the church. Smiles and love filled the room. Sharon stood there model-ish and chic, and he was handsome and debonair with a full blond head of hair combed over and back just like Elvis.

Later that year in December, Prunella Jackson passed away. The loss was unbearable and heartbreaking to him. It was rumored that Prunella grieved herself to death after losing Charles Sr. As he stood at her graveside, just a couple of feet from his father's, he couldn't bear his own feelings and regret. He fell to his knees as he yelled out, "Prunella, I'm so sorry. I should have been there for you!" Grief rang through his heart, and loud cries wailed from him as his hands forcefully grabbed the Mississippi dirt. Stella came to his side, placing her hand under his arm as if to lift him to his feet.

Charles's bloodshot eyes looked up at her, and she looked deep into him and said, "We all die, son, but the life we lived and the love we put into those lives live forever. Now she went on to look after your father, and she will always be looking after you. She was a good woman, and you know what she would be telling you right now: 'Stop wallowing in this mud. It will be a pain to get that mud out of those britches.'"

He lifted up, never losing eye contact with his mother. A huge smile broke out across his face. That was the nicest thing he had ever heard her say about Prunella. She then reached into her purse and pulled out an envelope. As she handed it to him, she said, "Here. I found this in her Bible. It had your name on it, so I thought you might want it."

He took the envelope from her. Stella turned to the grave and placed an orange tiger lily on top of the stone, then walked away, giving him a smile. Written in Prunella's handwriting was Charles Jr.'s name. He flipped it over and opened it. Inside was just a picture of her favorite mulberry tree. Written on the back of the photo were the words "Tiger Lily." He smiled as he placed it into his coat pocket. After the funeral, he had to go back overseas. He only had a few more months of service until he would be able to retire.

***

Haggling coughs strangled Charles and brought him back to the present as he held his hand over his mouth. He suddenly felt dejected as the profound hopelessness of cancer continued to slowly close in on him. He knew it had passed a judgment that would bring him to his last days. He loved his cigarettes, but if he had really known it would bring this ill fortune, he never would have picked them up and drawn in their sinful pleasure of smoke.

He gently caressed his daughter's smooth younger hand and said, "I want to show you something. Go over to my closet and look in the pocket of my old army uniform."

She walked over to the closet door, opened it, and walked into the small space. She looked around at all of the stuff before spotting the uniform hanging last among the abundance of clothes. Prunella struggled to pull it from the closet, causing a few other items to fall to the floor. She removed the old plastic and tossed it aside. Laying the uniform on the bed, she began searching the pockets. She ran her hand along the inside pocket and found a photo of three golden calla lilies.

With her head tilted to the side studying the photo, she questioned, "What's this about, Daddy?"

He replied with a smile, "Child, that there is worth more than you could imagine. Now look up in my closet and see if you can find a small black box."

She placed the picture on the nightstand, then stepped back into the closet. Standing on her tiptoes, she finally spotted it under some old board games Charles had hidden from her when she was little, as she liked to flush the small pieces down the toilet.

At first touch, the soft velvet made her caress it, mesmerized by the beautiful softness. Prunella ran her fingers lightly over the dazzling gold lettering of her grandfather's name. As she started to speak, she was interrupted by his coughing. He was trying to answer the question he knew she had, but was unable to get control of the cough. After attempting to speak, he finally just waved his hand, giving a silent command to open it.

She lifted the top, finding that it opened like a book. She ran her fingers around and down the inside of the box. Tracing her fingers along a cross-shaped empty space about four by six inches, she looked at her father in confusion.

Charles just looked at her with a sly grin, flashing a decaying, chipped-tooth smile, and said, "It's a melting mystery. Makes you wonder."

He cleared his throat and then said, "I'm feeling like I just might be able to eat a bit. How about some soup and crackers? I know there has got to be a can of something in them cabinets besides that turkey deal."

She gave him a smile as she placed the box down on the nightstand with the picture of the lilies. She went to the kitchen, leaving Charles along to his thoughts. As he lay there quietly, his eyes became very heavy and his mind crept off to dream of his days with Sharon.

***

Chapter 7

A New Life

Charles's dream took him back to a cold Monday morning in November 1961. He was sitting at the breakfast table with Sharon. He reached into his pocket and produced a box and placed it on the table in front of her. She excitedly picked it up and gave him a huge smile. When she saw the contents, she gasped, "Oh, Charles! This is unbelievable!"

Even though he knew the answer, he asked, "Do you like it?"

She responded with tears of joy, nodding her head yes. She motioned to him to help her put it on. He took the box from her and removed an emerald necklace with twenty-nine stones and a pair of matching earrings. While he placed the necklace on her dainty neck, she asked, "How much did this set us back?"

He could not answer, for he was fumbling with the clasp. Just as he was about to answer her, she yelled out in pain. She was in labor. He jumped to his feet and helped her to the car. They raced to the hospital. After five hours of labor, Sharon gave birth to a beautiful baby girl, Charleen Richards. Once Charles held her, he knew life would never be the same. Although he had originally wished for a boy, this baby girl did away with all thoughts of a boy. She was his princess. He was filled with joy and kept saying, "She is so precious. The most adorable baby girl I've ever laid my eyes on, and she is mine!"

Charles's mind flew through Charleen's infant and toddler stages as his dream took him to her first day of school. She was so beautiful in her cute blue sailor dress with her strawberry-blonde hair tied back with a bright red ribbon. Sharon and Stella fussed over her outfit. According to Stella, Charleen should be wearing a red plaid dress that she had picked out. Those quarrelsome two never could agree. Living with her mother-in-law was at times too much for Sharon. They had lived with her ever since they were married, but the living situation had to change.

His dream was interrupted when his daughter's voice echoed down the hallway, "Hot chicken soup on its way." He groaned as he struggled to pull himself up by the wooden bed frame. Just as she turned the corner with the soup, she started fussing at him for not waiting on her to help him. Charles became hostile and expressed that he didn't like the implication that he was helpless. He had always been hard-headed and prideful and had never been the type to ask anyone for help, but he knew his strength was deteriorating. He was losing muscle mass at a significantly fast rate, and it was turning him into a fragile and frail old man. His mind contained cherished thoughts that made him want to be alone with his soup. Placing the bowl of soup on the nightstand, Prunella helped him sit up. Once he was sitting up comfortably, he looked up at her and said, "Honey? Could I please try this on my own?" Not saying a word, she just smiled understandingly and handed him the spoon. Pulling the door closed, she left Charles alone. He looked over at the bowl of soup, turned slightly to it, and dipped a spoonful to his mouth. He took another spoonful and looked around the room as he savored it. As he was looking around, his mind went again to his memories.

***

He saw himself standing with a man and shaking his hand after signing a check to Vergel Hill Construction in 1967. Charles had built Sharon her dream home. It was built far enough away from Stella on the family land that it made Sharon very happy. He chose the place where Prunella Jackson had loved to disappear—next to a tall, twisted mulberry tree. He had the house built close enough to the tree that it was only a few feet from the back door. The house was a beautiful three-bedroom red brick with four white columns on the front porch. There was a double carport attached to the side of the house. All of the appliances were straight off the showroom floor. Beautiful light-oak paneling lined the inside walls, and the floor was a unique golden-flaked quartz with granules of what looked like pearl. It seemed to change color as you walked on it and had the highest epoxy shine as the overhead lights reflected on it. Hanging in the formal dining room was a stylish gold-finished chandelier with six lights formed to look like candles. Pearl accents draped stylishly on it, adding that fancy look that Sharon loved so much. Pendulum octagon crystals from the chandelier cast prisms of light around the room that moved and danced as they dangled elegantly from its bottom. Sharon favored the color pink, so Charles indulged her by having bathrooms built with pink tubs, showers, toilets, sinks, and even pink-tiled walls. There was a large mirror hung on the pink-tiled bathroom wall to reflect her beauty. The house was perfect in every way for their new family. He could see the joy in her eyes.

Charles had bought a milk truck and leased it out for deliveries. He had freedom most people didn't, for he could pick and choose when he wanted to work. Although usually he worked it himself, Dan would earn some extra cash and take on a few routes for him from time to time. One particular day, when he was stretched out in his chair, reading the newspaper and sipping his coffee, and Sharon was flipping through the latest magazine, the phone rang, and she answered it. Hanging up, she yelled, "Oh my, Charles! We've got to get Charleen from school!"

She was scrambling around, gathering her purse, and he questioned her urgency. "Dear, slow down. What's happened?"

Her panicking caused her words to quiver, taunting her lips as she tried to tell him. "She passed out in class. She asked to go to the restroom and fell once she got up to the teacher's desk. Oh, hurry please! My baby!" No more had to be said. He jumped into action and knew he had to get to her quickly. He wished Charleen could have attended the school where he had attended, but it only stood for one more year after he graduated. He raced down the highway to the small town where her school was located.

Once they made it to the school, he asked no questions. He simply scooped up his angel, put her in the car, and sped to the local doctor. As they waited for the results from the tests, he watched his little girl slowly come back to herself again. She gave him a smile that warmed his heart.

The doctor came in the room and began asking a series of questions. "Has this ever happened before? Does she urinate a lot? How much does she drink in a day or night? Have you noticed her being extra tired?"

Sharon answered, "Well, yes, I have noticed she is going to the restroom a lot, and she seems to stay thirsty. Also, when she's tired, her speech fumbles a little bit. What does that mean?"

The doctor placed the clipboard down on the counter, crossed his arms, propped up against the counter, and said, "Mr. and Mrs. Richards, I am afraid your daughter is a diabetic. I have run some tests; she has a severe case." He picked up the clipboard again and looked at it. "Okay. She is twelve now, and I know it seems like this will mess up her life, but I assure you this can be maintained and controlled." He then looked directly at Charleen and said, "Your body does not produce insulin as well as it should." He looked at her parents and admitted, "This is a real serious illness, and I have not had someone as young as her, but I do know how to treat this." Turning his attention back to Charleen, he stroked her head and said, "You can go on and do anything you want to with a few little adjustments in your life." He then turned his attention to them again. "One of the goals of treatment is to maintain her blood sugar. By controlling this, it prevents or delays complications." He lowered his voice and his head as he added, "Problems could arise such as heart problems, kidney failure, blindness, and even amputation." He gave them a smile of hope as he raised his head. "A proper diet and exercise and certain medications will lower her risk. So what we are going to do is give her an injection now and a prescription for insulin she can inject at home. The bottle of insulin needs to be stored in the refrigerator."

***

Charles was sitting on the edge of the bed, lost in thought when Prunella knocked on the door, causing him to drop his spoon. Upon entering the room, she saw the bowl and drops of soup splattered all around him.

"Well, Daddy, did you get any soup in you?" As she sat down on the side of the bed, she giggled and said, "Your blanket won't be hungry for a while. Did you eat the whole bowl or did it?" She patted him on the leg as she added, "I'm just kidding, Daddy."

"I'm sorry I made such a mess," he replied.

Prunella waved her hand at him. "It'll be fine. I'll just take this top blanket off."

He reached up and stroked her hair back. "You know, you are as beautiful as your mother. I love you. Toss that blanket aside and come sit with me. I want to talk to you about your mother."

"What about her, Daddy?" she asked as she tossed the blanket into the hallway and sat down on the bed next to him.

"I want to tell you about the first time I saw her," he began the tale that would take them back over thirty years.

***

The sun's bright glare reflected off of Charles's milk truck's window as he pulled up to the Quick Pack. The store was just a county over from his home. The clatter of the diesel engine came to a quiet stop as he happily leaped from his truck. He opened the cooler door, pulled the dolly out, calculated the order, and then wheeled the milk to the front door. He pressed his back against the old, scuffed wooden doors and pushed. The door opened and a sexy, raspy female voice said hello.

Charles turned around to see a tall, exotic, beautiful female helping him with the door. She bore a striking resemblance to Uma Thurman in her younger years. She had long, gorgeous creamy pale legs with silky brunette hair that was fashioned into a beehive. Her baby-blue eyes sparkled like amethysts. Then the exotic woman spoke, "Hi. My name is Geraldine Rogers. This is my first day working here. Let me help you with this." As she opened the door further, their eyes met with intriguing indulgence. They couldn't look away. Geraldine aroused his curiosity. She seemed to be the most interesting, beautiful woman; her appeal strongly captivated him, so much that he began to fancy her. He wanted to entangle himself with her. He knew it was an illicit idea to take her on the milk route, but giving in to his desire was all he could think about. After many months of flirting, he took the infidelity leap.

On one of her days off, she rode on the milk route with Charles, the two of them sharing their life stories. The more they talked, the more they felt a connection. They were born ten years and one week apart, for he was thirty-nine and she was twenty-nine. Both were married with one female child. Charles deeply loved Sharon, but there was something about Geraldine he loved also, for they were complete opposites. Geraldine told Charles of her husband, Berry Rogers, and how he loved to go to the bars; telling him of the time that she had to kick a woman out of her house because Berry had forgotten that she was off that day. Soon she stopped talking and began to stare out the window watching the white line steadily trace the right side of the road. She added resignedly, "My daughter, Christine, has some issues because of his drinking. I would divorce him, but I can't afford it. Berry won't keep a job, and my little check don't go far."

Charles pulled into a small store just off the beaten path where he was to deliver. He tossed his brown coat to her, saying, "Here, duck down and put this over your head. John Mize might recognize you and run his mouth. Sometimes he follows me out to the truck." Then he got out and went inside.

Geraldine hunkered down under the coat. A storm was brewing; thunderous rain loomed overhead. Lighting struck as she peeked from the safe cover of the coat. Frightening shivers ran through her crouched body, causing her to have a plaguing thought: *This is not a good start to our new friendship.*

***

Chapter 8

Rethinking it All

Prunella stayed completely quiet as Charles told her of this. She didn't know what to say. This was a lovely memory, but he had been married to Sharon at the time. She didn't approve of his sneaking around. He could tell by the look on her face, and he hung his head in embarrassment. "I think I could take a nap now, love," he said as he shifted down into the bed.

"Yes," she replied, "that would probably be a good idea. Do you need to use the bathroom?"

"Nope."

He was not using the bathroom as much as he should, and this worried her. She kept her concerns to herself so they wouldn't upset him. She picked up the spoon and bowl and left him to rest. Charles drifted off to sleep worrying about the look in Prunella's eyes.

***

His dreaming began again as he returned to a sunny spring day when he had received a call from Oliver. "Heya, Charles. It's me, Ollie. I've got some folks for you to meet." Charles was so full of excitement, for he had not heard from him in years.

"Bring them on!" he exclaimed. "Damn! I ain't seen you in forever. Where the hell have you been? I can't wait. Hurry up and come on and get here. Where ya at?" He couldn't get a word in edgewise because Charles was spitting out question after question.

"Hey, hey...I'm at your mama's," he tried to tell him, laughing. "Oh, you ain't changed much, from what I can tell from this here phone call. I'm trying to tell you I'm at your mama's."

Charles hung up the phone without replying, gathered up Sharon and Charleen, then raced over to his mother's. Ollie was standing on the porch puffing away on his pipe when they pulled up in the blue Ford truck. He was so excited that he jumped from the driver's seat and high-stepped it onto the porch. He observed that Oliver the boy had been replaced by a man, taking note of his thinning salt-and-pepper hair and slightly wrinkled olive-colored skin. The only thing that had not changed was his deep, rich-brown eyes.

Oliver spoke first, "Well, look at you! You still got all your durn hair, you old lucky dog. You can't even tell if you got a gray one or not with that blond nap of yours." He grinned as he stepped closer to him. Then he looked him up and down. "You always were a styling fella. And look at them britches! I'll bet them thangs could stand up on their own." He gave him a larger smile, exposing what teeth he had left, and wrapped his arms around Charles, giving him a big bear hug. "Well, I want to introduce you to my wife, Mary." He placed an arm around his shorter, lovely wife and reached over and scrubbed the top of a little boy's head, adding, "And this is my son, Russell Jr. Yep! I named him after Daddy."

He released his wife and bent down to a basket, pulling back a small blue blanket revealing a baby boy. "And this little fella is Gregory." He stood up, wrapped his arm back around his wife, and said, "These are my pride and joy. They are the best things to ever happen in my life." He was grinning from ear to ear as he asked Charles, "So, who you got there with ya?" Charles proudly introduced his daughter and wife.

Once the ladies started talking, Oliver said, "I want to take a walk around here and reminisce. Come on." The men stepped off the porch, leaving their wives and children to visit. As they walked around the house and toward the barn, he noticed all the repairs that were needed. He then asked, "What are y'all going to do with the place?"

"Well, we have thought about tearing it all down. I don't have time for all them critters we had, and Mama don't either." He kicked a board as he added, "I think this place died with Prunella, Ollie. It's hard for me to come over here sometimes. Shit! I miss her."

Oliver interrupted him, "Oh, I don't curse anymore. Ever since I met Mary, my world has gotten better. She don't like that kind of language around her."

Charles gave his apologies and from then on refrained from cursing. He began to ramble on, "I bought a milk truck and took up delivering to the stores around here. That took care of our dairy needs. Mama went to work for the state school. It's hard to believe she's been there for a little over thirteen years. She's sixty-three now, and I keep telling her to retire, but she refuses. She took it bad when Daddy died. All she does now is work. Sharon and I lived with her for some time, but when Charleen came along, I had to do something. You know how Mama likes to get her way. Well, let's just say she found out a time or two that she wasn't getting her way when it came to Charleen. I thought at one time Mama and Sharon were going to become unladylike." He then pointed over Oliver's shoulder, saying, "You see right over there through those trees? You can just see the roof of my house. You'll have to come over and take a look." He paused to look around, making sure there wasn't an extra set of ears that would hear what he was about to unload. Seeing they were alone, he drew in a deep breath, then exhaled. "I met a woman about a year ago, and I've been seeing her romantically."

Oliver was visibly shocked at his confession. He then gave him a stern look and stated, "Cut it off now! You have a beautiful wife and daughter. I'm sure this woman you are seeing is lovely, but what you're doing is wrong!"

Charles took a long pause as he tilted his head up to the sky. He knew he should not be seeing someone else, but this other woman had such a pull on him. He looked at Oliver and gave him a sly grin. "Oh, Ollie. If the circumstances were different, you'd really like this one. She's the kind of woman that likes to hunt and fish," he said with a wink. "She gives me a run for my money. Feisty!" He pulled a pack of his favorite cigarettes from his pocket and lit one. He added with a grin, "Well, I see you are still pulling on that pipe. Yep! I ain't put these down either. What can I say? I like to smoke. Sharon don't care for it none, so I try not to do it around her." About that time, they heard Stella yell from the back door of the kitchen, "Y'all come eat! I got a pot of black-eyed peas and a pone of cornbread."

When he heard this, Charles turned toward the house. He loved his mother's cooking. Even though she could see they were coming, he yelled, "Yes, ma'am! We'll be right there." He turned to Oliver and placed his hand on his back, urging him slightly toward the house. As they walked to the house, he felt a strange feeling of separation, and he began to shift through time and space with vivid lights. They were flickering and fluttering all around him. Their beauty brought him a sense of calm and comfort. Before long, he was sitting on a church pew with his family.

The sun's rays pierced the stained-glass windows intensely and embraced the beautiful Sunday morning. As they sat there receiving the Lord's love, he felt the presence of his deceased father speaking to him: "Charles, my son, look next to you."

He turned his head to his beautiful wife and daughter; then he heard his father speak again: "What you are doing is unfavorable in my eyes. You must stop."

Lowering his head in shame and silently making a promise to his father to stop seeing Geraldine, he reached over and placed his hand on Sharon's, giving it a gentle squeeze. As he looked into her bright emerald eyes and gave her a smile, he mouthed silently, "I love you."

When the service ended, the Richards family went home for lunch. Charles changed into his old jeans and a t-shirt and house slippers. He plopped down on the couch as Sharon prepared lunch with Charleen's help. Sharon poured a glass of sweet tea for him. Charleen was honored to deliver it to him. When he sat up to reach for it, he found that his hand passed right through the glass. He couldn't grasp it, but this appeared not to bother Charleen. She let go of the glass, and it landed in his lap. Once the cold liquid touched his skin, he awoke to find that he had urinated on himself.

***

Awake and feeling the warmth of his urine, he yelled out, "Aw bull-sh-larky!" Shaken at the loud, halfhearted curse word coming from her father's room, Prunella ran down the hall, flung open the door to his room, and asked, "What's wrong, Daddy?"

He looked at her with his eyebrows lowered, poking out his lip like a petulant child, and flipped his cover back. His baggy pin-striped pajama bottoms revealed what had happened, but he said, "I wet my durn self. I hate to ask, but could you please help me out of this wet mess?"

"No problem," she simply replied. "Would you like to sit in the shower and rinse off while I change your sheets?"

He gave a simple nod, and she stepped into the bathroom to prepare the shower. Charles pulled off his urine-soiled pajamas and tossed them aside. He put on his robe, then shuffled toward the bathroom door. Once he reached it, he had to prop against the doorframe to catch his breath. Prunella bit her tongue to keep from fussing with him for not waiting for her to help him. After all, it wouldn't have done any good to fuss. He was going to do what he wanted to anyway.

So she only gave him a loving smile and said, "The water is ready, and your stool is in there." She gave him a kiss on the cheek and continued, "If you need me, I will be in here putting on fresh linens."

He blew her a kiss as he closed the bathroom door. The steam from the hot water rapidly filled the small bathroom. The warmth of this steam soothed his weary bones as he stepped into the shower. He began to ponder his dream. Once he was on the stool, his mind went back to the day he had ended it with Geraldine.

**

It had been a warm Wednesday morning as he had pulled into the store where she was working. Even though he knew it was the right thing to do, he dreaded entering the store. He could see her behind the counter. Pushing his feelings aside, he put on a smile as he walked up to the register.

He handed her a dollar bill from his wallet and said, "I'd like two packs of Pall Mall filter shorts." While her boss was looking over the delivery form, Charles signaled for her to meet him outside. She nodded in response to his gesture, then turned around, giving him a good look at her backside. She was very flirty and looked back over her shoulder as she did this. Before her boss could see this, she quickly composed herself.

Charles let his eyes flow over every detail of her clothing. She was wearing a blue-and-green flowered blouse, which lightly caressed her breasts. Two buttons were undone, giving him a glimpse of her bra. Her blue jeans had that novelty red-and-white stitching that ran up and down the legs and across her butt, giving her a taller, more slender look. The wide belt loops accented her beautifully contoured shape.

Geraldine handed him the smokes, and the store owner okayed him to wheel the milk to the cooler. Once the delivery was complete, he returned to his truck. As he climbed in the seat, she opened the passenger door and slid in, giving him a huge smile and a kiss on the cheek.

He was cold and unresponsive to her kiss. With concern on her face, she asked, "What's wrong?" He placed both hands on the steering wheel and lowered his head to them. A deep groan escaped his lips, for in his mind he wanted to break it off with her, but his heart wouldn't let him speak the words.

Finally he found the strength to say, "Geraldine, we have got to stop this."

Much to his surprise, she nodded in agreement and spouted out, "Yep. I agree. You're right. We do need to stop." She slung her hair around to cover her face as tears began falling down her cheeks. He heard soft sobs coming from the bunched-up hair, and he reached to pull it back to see her face. "I can't do this!" she snapped. "I'm falling in love with you, and we are both married." She lit a cigarette and puffed it strongly. After about four strong puffs, Geraldine blew out painful words with her smoke: "Honestly! It sickens me knowing you are lying in the bed with her." She leaped from the truck and ran inside.

Charles knew he couldn't go inside after her, so he cranked his truck and pulled away. From that day forward, he was going to focus on his wife and daughter. He decided to drop the route to that store to prevent any impulse to connect with Geraldine. The days seemed like they would brighten as he made his decision, but darkness was on the horizon.

Chapter 9

Going to the Show

It was an early Friday morning in 1975, and Charles wasn't feeling well. But he went to work anyway. As the day went on, he still felt ill, so he threw in the towel and went home. He knew how quiet the house would be, for Charleen was staying with Stella for the weekend.

Pulling into the driveway, he could see that Sharon was not there. He figured she was out for the day, gathering groceries or running errands. He was looking forward to taking it easy in the peace and quiet.

He walked in and turned on the TV. To his surprise, it was only noon and the midday news was on, so he sat back on the couch and listened to the forecast. Scattered storms were on the way, with strong winds and rains throughout the weekend. He shook his head and grunted as he lay down on the couch and covered his eyes with his hand. The TV began to disturb him, so he turned it off.

After napping for about an hour, he woke up when keys were tossed onto the countertop. He opened his eyes only to catch a glimpse of a blurry figure going down the hall. "Hey, Sharon? That you?"

"Yes, dear, it's me. I'm going to change real quick. I'll be right out."

As he held his head in his hands, he realized the nap had not eased his headache. Painfully, he called out again, "Hey! Do we have anything for a headache?"

"Look in my purse on the table. I think there are some aspirin in there." He slowly got up from the couch and made his way to her purse. As he dug around for the bottle of aspirin, he saw a small envelope. The front of the envelope had bold decorative print: "The Saenger Theater." The envelope was open already, so he investigated the contents. Inside were two tickets stamped "The Arthur Harper Show, George Jones impersonator, accompanied by the comedian Jug-A-Bob. Saturday at 7:00 p.m." That was tomorrow night! Knowing he would be free to attend this event, excitement overpowered his headache and he yelled, "When did you get these?"

Sharon was still in the back room and yelled back, "Get what, dear? The aspirin? Oh, I got them the other day."

Charles chuckled, "No...no...these tickets to the Saenger Theater in Hattiesburg with Arthur Harper and some fella named Jug-A-Boob. Don't know him, but I do love some George Jones. So where did you get these?"

She took a long pause, then said, "Hmm...it was the darnedest thang. I happened to luck up on them at the grocery store. As I was making my way back to the car, I looked down and there they were in the parking lot. I picked them up. I thought you might like them." She was walking into the living room where he was as she was answering him, placing an earring in her ear, saying, "So I didn't turn them in as lost." She walked over to him, placed her arms around his neck, and whispered, "Surprise."

Still holding the tickets, he wrapped his arms around her small waist, gently lifted her up to his lips, and kissed her passionately. As he returned her to the floor, she looked up at him with a large, benevolent smile and said, "By the way, the other man on the ticket that you called Jug-A-Boob is Ross Jug-A-Bob. He is a heavy-set hillbilly that likes to make wisecracks that I understand are tacky and tasteless jokes about liquor and girls, but he is really funny, from what I've heard."

"Well...he sounds like a boob to me."

The next day, Sharon fancied herself up in a casual white evening dress that elegantly hugged her curves. She wore a large green belt that accented her tiny waist. Matching dark-green knee-high zippered suede boots finished her stylish ensemble. She was exquisite. Her loose strawberry-blonde shoulder-length curly hair bounced when she walked into the living room. Charles was giving his full head of blond graying hair one last swoop of the comb as he looked in the mirror. He was wearing a dark-blue polyester leisure suit, and stood there looking at his own image until she walked into his line of sight. He turned around grinning joyfully and said, "Oh, Sharon! You look ravishing." He slipped up behind her and wrapped his arms around her and said, "You look too good. Let's stay in."

She pushed back on him as she said, "Oh no, mister! I'm fixed and ready for the night." They stood there together looking at themselves in the mirror, posing as if to take a picture.

Then he said, "You know what would really look good?"

It was as if she had read his mind, for she pulled away from him and spun like a ballerina, saying, "I know exactly!" They both smiled as she pranced down the hallway to their bedroom. Seconds later she returned with the box that he had given her the day their baby was born. The emerald necklace with the diamond clasp and earrings looked as beautiful as the day it was given to her. She removed the necklace and handed it to him, then scooped up her hair with both of her hands. He delicately placed the expensive jewelry around her neck. Once the necklace and earrings were in place, he grabbed his keys from the counter bar and said, "Let's go."

The sound of thunder rolled, warning that rain was on its way. Sharon relaxed her stance, then crossed her arms as she looked at him and said with a smile, "We are taking mine."

He grumbled, reaching for her keys on the bar. "Oh, all right! I guess I could drive your car this time." Charles had bought her a 1972 bubblegum-pink VW Beetle for her thirty-third birthday. He had only driven it one time before, as its color most definitely indicated it was a woman's car. She nudged him on the arm for the face he was making as they walked out to the car.

Charles went to the edge of the carport and looked up into the threatening sky and said, "We had better get on. Looks like it's fixing to come down." After a short drive, they arrived at the theater. The building was composed of a large theatrical auditorium. Seats numbering around a 1,000 were on the floor, while the balconies contained 100 seats reserved for customers who had paid extra. There was a full bar suitable for smoking in those balconies. Sharon handed the tickets to the usher. As he tore the ticket, he pointed down an aisle. Walking in the direction indicated by the usher, he leaned into her and said, "I think we are going to have great seats."

They sat down and settled in to enjoy a wonderful night of entertainment. The excitement consumed them as the lights lowered, indicating the show's beginning. After two hours of beautiful country music and comedy, they stepped out of the theater. The moon was full and exposed the hues of the night as they walked to the car, but ample folds of wind began to stir. It seemed the storm was not over. Clouds began to mystically cover the moon's bright appearance, darkening their walk.

They began to pick up the pace as large raindrops fell onto their heads. Once in the car, they adjusted their clothes, shaking off the droplets. Suddenly, a set of headlights ran across the pink beetle as squealing tires screeched out of the space behind them. Charles grumbled, "What an idiot!" He then cranked the car and slowly pulled out. As they rode along, he began to get hungry. "Are you hungry? I want something new. There's a place on the way home called Old Red Barn. People say it's the best place to get whole catfish."

She gave him a simple nod. "Sounds good."

The amount of rain on the windshield was enough of a hindrance without the blinding lights of a car in the rearview mirror rapidly approaching. "Dadburn it!" Charles complained. "I wish whoever that is behind me would dim their lights. It's hard enough to see the road with all of this rain streaking up my view!"

Sharon peered out her window, searching for the restaurant sign. "Slow down. It's just up here on the right."

He leaned his head to the side so the blinding lights wouldn't be in his eyes. At that moment, the car behind them revved its engine and passed them as he turned into the restaurant. He slowed down to catch a glimpse at the impatient car, but was unable to see it because of the dark night's rain. He then let out another grumble as he looked for a parking space, "What an idiot!"

Charles expressed his delight at finding a parking spot close to the front entrance. While exiting the car, she pointed out the wagon wheels mounted on the red walls and what looked to be a horse hitching post. Around the outside were bushes and trees next to the building, giving it an unkempt look. She expressed how much the place made her feel like she was in the old West. Entering a set of solid black doors, they saw a sign: "Welcome to the Old Red Barn. We have the best catfish fresh from the back door ponds. Come on in and getcha a bite." They soon realized the outside was a bit deceptive in its appearance, as the inside was neat and tidy. The tan walls were a deep contrast to the extravagant deep-red carpet. Old farm tools hung on the walls, which immediately reminded Charles of his troubled days as a youth, for those same tools had hung on the walls of the shed he'd spent so much time in.

A young female approached them at the door and said, "Hello there! Welcome to the Old Red Barn! Would y'all like smoking or non-smoking?" He left the answer to her, and to his surprise, she replied, "Do you have a well-ventilated room for smoking?"

"Yes, ma'am. We have a covered patio. Would you like to sit out there?" Sharon gave her an accepting nod, and they followed the hostess. Charles took in every detail as they walked through the restaurant. While he was looking around, he almost ran into a man standing next to the door to the patio. He looked up just in time and started to give his apologies before realizing it was only a life-sized wooden statue of an Indian. Doing a double-take, he shook his head and walked past the statue. Country music played from the speakers as the hostess placed them at a round wooden table. As they sat down, he pulled out his cigarettes, leaned in, and thanked Sharon for choosing the seating that allowed him to do so.

Enjoying his cigarette and the company of his wife, he noticed the beautiful wooden beams forming a pyramid to the center of the ceiling. A disco ball was slowly spinning as it hung from the top. Directly below the ball, on the floor, was a large wood carving of fish seemingly swimming around two cows' feet as they stood in the water.

Charles's back was to the door, and Sharon could see all who came onto the patio. As they were talking, she recognized a couple walking in. Her eyes followed the couple to their table. As she watched them walk, her eyes spotted the all-too-familiar face of a man sitting alone at a table in the corner. He shocked her, for she hadn't even seen him come in.

The man was of slender build with shaggy, long brown hair and deep-set brown eyes that appeared almost black. He seemed to be deep in thought as he gripped his Budweiser in one hand and chewed the fingernails of the other hand. The man was staring at her husband, and this made her very uncomfortable. The glare in his eyes sent chills down her spine. She looked away as he made eye contact with her, and didn't bring him to Charles's attention. Deciding to ignore this man, she continued to discuss the concert and their dinner. The sound of thunder clattered the windows, and the lights in the restaurant flickered as the storm raged on outside.

Sharon had not looked over in the shaggy man's direction for a little while. The urge to check if he was still there kept pulling at her. Finally, she could resist no more. She looked at the table where he had been, and thankfully he was gone. She searched the room quickly for him, leaned into to Charles, and said, "I'll be right back. I'm going to the restroom, and then I'll be ready to go."

She was in deep hope that the man had left the restaurant. Every step she took was fearful, for the last thing she wanted to do was run into him. The lights continued to flicker, making her feel even more haunted. Once she made it to the restroom, she went into a stall, sat down, and put her face in her hands. As she sat there shaking her head from side to side, she let out a long sigh. After a few minutes, she washed her hands and looked deep into the mirror. She twirled the beautiful emerald necklace as she spoke to her reflection: "What have I got myself into?"

Chapter 10

The Picture

Sharon was still standing in front of the mirror as Charles paid the bill. She opened the spring-loaded door, and as it screeched open, she stuck her head out. After carefully looking around, she left the doorway and entered the light-flickering hallway. In that instant, Charles and Sharon ran into one another. Her eyes were fearful. He gently held his nervous wife and said, "It's okay. We are leaving." He could feel the tension from his wife and watched her eyes scan the restaurant. With a look of concern, he asked, "What's wrong, dear?"

She shook her head and, out of concern for him, replied, "I'm fine, dear. This storm just has me disoriented, with the lights flickering and all." She gave him a smile as she rubbed his upper arm.

As they walked out of the restaurant, Charles could tell something wasn't right. He quickly opened the car door for her, then ran around to the driver's side and climbed in. She shook the rain drops from her clothes as he cranked the car. Sitting there for a moment, he wondered what could possibly be wrong with her. They had enjoyed such a lovely evening, but he just had to know. The sound of rain was deafening on the car's roof, so he had to speak loudly: "Seriously, Sharon. What's wrong?"

Turning to him, she flashed a smile and replied loudly, "Nothing is wrong, dear!"

Charles backed up from the parking space. Thunder was rolling loudly and lightning was flashing violently as he turned his windshield wipers on high, then pulled out onto the highway. About a mile down the watery road, he could no longer accept that nothing was wrong with Sharon. She'd been completely silent, and he spoke up again: "Darling, I know something isn't right. I just can't ignore it. You've been acting strange ever since you went to the restroom. Are you feeling well?"

She had been looking out the passenger window ever since they left the restaurant and had hesitantly turned her head to answer him. As she did, a flood of lights filled the car. Charles struggled to see the dangerously slick road. The lights were coming from a car behind them, so close it looked like daylight inside their car. Sharon turned in her seat as he asked, "Can you see who that fool is behind us?" Her eyes opened wide as the intense brightness of the light coming from behind them revealed a car whose shape was too familiar. The shock and fear kept her silent, so he had to ask again strongly, "Can you tell anything?"

She turned to him, sitting sideways in the seat. "Charles, I've got to tell you something."

He knew by her demeanor that her news couldn't be good and had to have something to do with the car throttling behind them, seeming to want to push them off the road.

She took a long pause, then said, "I've been having an affair. The tickets I said I found? Well, I lied, but I love you. I really do. I always have, ever since I was a little girl, but I know what you have been doing, too."

An enraged Charles asked, "Just what exactly are you talking about?"

"Oh, come on! Charles, don't do that."

"Do what? Tell you I've been seeing someone else? Is that what you want to hear?"

"Well...yes and no. Yes, I know, and no, I don't want details," she answered, ducking her head down slightly to avoid the bright lights in her eyes.

"Well, right now, Sharon, all that is irrelevant! I don't have someone stalking me with their car!" He slowed his speed and turned on his blinker, tapping his brakes. As he turned, the car went around them. Tensions rose as they both realized what had just been admitted by them both. He drove on calmly and silently, watching the rain beat the pavement through the vigorous swiping of the wipers. He knew he was wrong for having an affair, but the thought of her... Well, that had cut him to the bone. He was deep in thought and told himself, *I'm a man. We are supposed to do stupid stuff, but not my lady.*

Mixed emotions continued to fill the car as he drove them through the storm. He just wanted to get home. Suddenly, the interior of the car began to light up again, getting brighter and brighter. "Is it that car again?" he asked. She turned around in the seat to look. "Do you know who that is?" She let out a deep sigh because she knew it was the same car.

The fear of her secret began loosening her speech. "I know about you and that woman, Geraldine, I think her name is. I found out from my brother, Mark. He saw you two together all hugged up at that store next to where he works." She paused as she looked back over the seat at the blinding lights and revving engine sounds. She then looked back at a silent and shocked Charles and added, "Mark thought he was telling me something, but all along I was really the one holding a secret. I love you, but sometimes you can be so square!"

He gasped at the thought of him being a square, and this forced him to ask, "Where did you meet this fella, 'cause I take it that is him behind us." The loud car behind them pressed close, threatening to push them off the road again. As Charles tried to make sense of both of their mistakes, the other vehicle swooped up beside the small VW beetle. He stared straight ahead and kept his eyes on the road, attempting to speed up and get away from this car.

Sharon yelled, "Oh my God! It's him." As she was shouting, the car bumped the left side of the Volkswagen. The shocking jolt caused the car to fishtail and disoriented Charles as he tried to gain control of the vehicle. The rain prevailed with its fury as the angry, violent drops vigorously filled a small dip in the road, forming a puddle. The Beetle's right tire caught the puddle and sent the car sailing out of control. He struggled to regain control, but his struggle was in vain. The car went off the road and ramped up a small embankment before flipping and rolling into a row of small pine trees. The other car lost control and slid into the ditch on the other side of the road, barely missing a large oak tree, before plowing into a parked tractor in a field. The impact to Charles and Sharon's car was so damaging that the windshield was knocked out and one of the doors broke in half. The passenger side was completely destroyed, and the force was so intense that the eight-track tape player was in the back glass. Sharon hadn't been wearing her seat belt. It hung loosely outside the car. Charles was fighting unconsciousness and could see emeralds rolling around on the roof of the car. He called out for her, for he was pinned underneath the steering wheel and couldn't move. She didn't answer. With a slight turn of his head, he could see her lying limply across the roof of the car. She was bleeding from her nose and ears, and he could plainly see that his beloved wife's neck was broken. He then faded away into unconsciousness.

***

95

A chest-clinched memory of his wife's death broke Charles as he sat there on the shower stool. His salty tears were disguised as they indiscriminately mixed with the shower water. His injuries had been mild in comparison to his wife's. He thought, *All I suffered was a broken collarbone, broken ribs, and a ruptured spleen.* His tears fell harder as he raged to himself, *Why did I survive? Why did she have to die? I wish it had been me.*

With a knock on the door, he heard Prunella's voice: "Are you okay?" He answered as he turned off the shower, "Yes, I'm fine. I'm almost done." He sat there for a moment as the last beads of water rolled from his body to the shower floor. He wiped the remaining tears from his eyes and adjusted himself on the stool. He had composed himself by the time he opened the clear shower door and took a steady step out onto a white shaggy rug. The rug felt good on his worn, calloused feet. After putting on his robe, he slowly opened the bathroom door.

Prunella was standing at the foot of his bed replacing the plastic cover over his military uniform. She had the bed freshly made for him. As he looked over at the nightstand, he could see she had carefully placed the picture of the three lilies on top of the black box. He smiled, for he knew of the lovely meaning. She realized her father was standing there as she put the uniform in the closet. "I've got the bed all ready for ya. I didn't know if you wanted to put that picture—"

"No, you need to put this picture up for safekeeping," he interrupted her as he picked up the photo and held it out to her.

"Daddy, why is the word *mulberry* written on the back?"

"I have faith that you will figure it out." He waved the picture at her he continued, "But until then, put this here up." The phone began to ring as he stood there with the picture extended to her.

She took the picture from her father. "I'm going to get that. I'll be right back."

He yelled out as she left the room, "Put that up now!" He then put on a fresh pair of pajamas. He felt his body was on the verge of collapse after fighting to put them on. Once the pajama battle had been won, he lay back in exhaustion. Weak and out of breath, he allowed the reflections of his life to circulate in his mind once again as he awaited Prunella's return. He pondered Sharon's death and his physical recovery. Deep sorrow was felt in his soul as he caught a chill from the thought of how cold and empty the house had felt after her passing. Having to look his daughter in the eyes, knowing what he knew, rendered him quieter. The memory of that night turned him almost to stone. They had unspoken truths about the accident. She couldn't hold anything against her father, because she had knowledge of the rumors. They both set aside the facts and rumors and contained their fears. Both were strong on the outside, but full of tears on the inside. No one would have ever known that these two had fallen asleep many nights with tears drying on their cheeks.

The struggles of trying to balance work, home, and Charleen's medical needs had been a strain on him. He couldn't do it alone, and he had buckled under the pressure. She stayed with Stella while he tried to regain control of his life. Two months after Sharon's death, he had been taken to court over the incident and was found not guilty of any wrongdoing, although some people continued to believe he was guilty. And he was to receive a large sum from a life insurance policy on her. His heart began to race now as he recollected Mark Shaw coming to his home.

***

It had been a beautiful sunny day, and he was cleaning out his truck. Mark pulled up and got out. Rather cavalierly, he walked over to Charles. "Where is Charleen?" He then spit on the ground and added, "Let me guess! She's at your mother's again." Mark tried to stay calm, but his words seemed to carry a vicious tone. Realizing his remarks hadn't gotten a rise out of Charles, he stepped closer, taunting him, and said, "So now that my baby sister is gone, you gonna try to get rid of her baby girl?"

"You just stop right there!" Charles barked loudly.

Mark stepped forward despite his warning and pointed his finger at him. "You had better not spend a dime of that money that I know you got a comin' to you! You had better give every last drop of it to Charleen." He then stepped closer to him, adding loudly as he poked him in the chest, "It's your fault her mama ain't here no more."

Before he realized it, Charles recoiled his right arm, clenched his fist, and hit Mark square in the nose. Under the force of his fist and the command of gravity, he involuntarily fell to the ground and was now lying on his back in the dirt. Charles towered over him and said, "Now let me tell something to you! That's my baby girl, too, and with every day that goes by, I give myself hell about all of this. I wake up every day in this house that I built for your sister. Her essence and memories are the very fabric of this house, and I will not stand here and let you try to make me feel guilty. It wasn't me who killed her! If you want to lay blame on someone, blame the guy

98

who took her from us both. I do feel ashamed for my wrongdoings. I'll never get to fix them. I've heard the rumors that you've been spreading about her life insurance, and yes, I have a policy...and it just so happens, she is the beneficiary!"

When he finished speaking, Charles stretched his hand out to a bloody-nosed Mark, who took his hand and pulled himself up. As he wiped the blood from his nose with his shirttail, they both nodded at each other, and Mark left.

***

Prunella came back into the room. "That was the doctor. He has some new medicine that he wants you to take. He said it should be ready around 3:00 or 4:00—"

"Don't worry about that stuff right now," Charles interrupted her. "Come over here, and let me talk to you some more."

Chapter **11**

Under the Tree

Prunella sat on the bed as he took comfort in his pillows. Once his head nuzzled in, Charles began to talk about his life again, taking her back to the early years of being with her mother.

***

The hot, sticky Mississippi heat brought out more than sweat from people. The hateful rumors in town continued for years. Half of them thought he had killed Sharon on purpose just to be with another woman, and the other half believed he was telling the truth. Months turned to years, and the rumors kept coming. The word around town now was that Geraldine and Berry had divorced, and Charles was the one who had paid for it. Unbeknownst to them all, that rumor was true.

She moved in with him after the divorce was final. They became inseparable—hunting, fishing, and camping. They did everything together, spending many hours talking about their lives. He shared his memories of his father's and Prunella Jackson's deaths, his time in the military, and even his mischievous days as a child. She told him that when she was growing up she was a no-nonsense person who had to endure inappropriate touching from a family member. He gave her his promise that he would never let anyone hurt her again. He had found more than just another wife. She was his best friend as well. This marriage was a perfect fit—or so it seemed.

The summer's beauty of a Sunday morning compelled Charles and Geraldine to sit outside under the oak tree that grew tall in the front yard. The thick abundance of leaves provided a perfect shade from the heat. Charleen had left early that morning with Stella to attend church. Christine, age eight, waddled around the yard in her pink swimsuit, which seemed to be a bit small for her. She was pretty pudgy, weighing ten pounds at birth. Christine could not escape the inevitable fact that she was going to have weight problems. Her chunkiness formed pudgy rolls of fat that spilled from her swimsuit. It looked tight enough to cut off the circulation from her legs, but it didn't seem to bother her as she happily played with the water hose.

There was a slight breeze, but not enough to truly keep them cool, so Charles went inside and got a brand-new Lakewood twenty-inch box fan, which he had bought for his workshop. He placed the fan on a milk crate, stretched out an extension cord, and plugged it in. Aiming it at Geraldine, he said, "How's that?"

He sat back down in his lawn chair, sipped his sweet tea, and watched the cars go down the highway. Soon Stella's car pulled up, and a happy Charleen, now fifteen years old, jumped from the driver's side door, grinning from ear to ear. Stella emerged from the passenger side and gave him a smile. Charleen's inner glow seemed to brighten her light-blue Sunday dress. Her blonde shoulder-length hair flicked back on the sides took on the look of wings. She skipped over to him. "Hey, Daddy! Did you miss me?"

"I sure did." He held out his arms. "Come give your daddy a hug." Giving her a squeeze, he added, "So you're driving on your own now, huh? You'll be moving out soon." Pushing her back from him and giving her a wink, he said, "I ain't gonna let ya go."

Charleen squeezed her father, wrapping her pale freckled arms around him. "I met a boy, Daddy."

He gasped as he held up both hands in surrender. "Hey...hey! I was just kidding." She giggled as she turned to Geraldine. Concerned about the boy, he unleashed a series of questions in a deep voice: "What do you mean, you met a boy? Who is this fella? Where did he come from?"

She ignored his questions as she leaned down and gave Geraldine a hug and a kiss on her cheek. "Oh! He is so cute, too. He has long, curly black hair and big puppy-dog brown eyes, and he looks real strong, too. Oh! He looked so smart in that light-green polyester knit suit today."

"What's his name?"

"Frank," she giggled shyly.

"He ain't good enough," Charles piped up, "not for you."

"Daddy, you haven't even met him!"

Geraldine grabbed her arm and gently pulled her into her lap as she said, "Oh, come on! Don't get all defensive. She is getting to that age to date."

He laughed and sat back in his chair with a serene composure, knowing he wouldn't allow her to date until she was seventeen. "Well, she ain't but fifteen," he said. "She got two more years."

"Ha!" Geraldine gasped.

He started to say something else, but Stella stepped in behind him and placed her hands on his shoulders, giving them a squeeze.

"Oh, give it a rest, you two! She is a smart girl, and if she wants to see this fella...she's gonna see him." She then patted him on his shoulders with her large, gentle hands. "Everyone missed you at church today. When are you going to come back?"

He twisted around in his chair, tilted his head, and looked at his tall mother, making eye contact with her. "Really?" Charles wrinkled his forehead and released his thoughts: "How can the Lord hear my prayers if the room is clogged with judgmental, gossiping folks? I heard the rumors around town. I know what some of those church people say about me. It's funny how when I'm in town they talk like the devil. Oh, but on Sunday morning they speak with angel's tongues." He turned back around in his chair and huffed, adding, "Mama, I feel like they cloud my prayers."

"Okay, son, I see. Well, just as long as Charleen can still go."

He quickly turned around and grabbed her hands. "Mama, I would never stop her from it. That I promise."

"All right, son. Well, y'all enjoy the rest of your Sunday. I'll catch y'all later. I'm going to the house to prop my feet up." She started to walk away but stopped and turned back to him. "Oh, yes, she done real good driving today. A little nervous at first, but she kept it between the ditches." Giving him a smile and a wave at everyone, she drove away.

Charleen trotted off into the house to change her clothes, and Charles took the opportunity to give Geraldine some good news. He was feeling fully committed to her as they relaxed in the shade. With a sweet, gentle smile, he whispered, "Well, you are a landowner."

She had been lying back with her sunglasses on but quickly sat up and removed them, "What exactly do you mean, 'I'm a landowner'?"

"Yep! And that's not all. You're a wealthy one, too."

"Now, come on! Stop playing with me. What are you talking about?" She propped herself on the arm of the chair and leaned toward him.

He reached into his back pocket, pulled out an envelope, and handed it to her. Meanwhile, Charleen came back outside and found a milk crate under the tree, pulled it up close to her father, and sat down. She wasn't feeling well. Her face had turned pale, and she slumped over, propping her elbows on her knees while holding her face in her hands. She felt weak but hoped it would pass, not wanting to bring it to her father's attention and interrupt his conversation.

Christine pulled the water hose over closer to her, then began to spray at her feet. Charleen calmly tried to stop her from spraying but couldn't stop. Christine's laughter became harder, for she was enjoying aggravating her.

Geraldine opened the envelope and read aloud: "Mr. and Mrs. Richards, oil was located 5,000 feet below the property of 19 Dove Road, Arua, Mississippi." Her tear-filled eyes bounced from the words "Mrs. Richards" and "property owner." Choking words cracked from her lips: "Is this for real?"

He reached out his hand to hers. "Well, yes, it's ten acres real. I had seen where some land was for sale on Dove Road. Well, I noticed there are about three oil rigs pumping around here, so I bought what was for sale and had it tested. There on the paper are the results, and yes, ma'am, it belongs to you."

She jumped up and latched onto him, wrapping her well-built arms around him. As they held each other in excitement, Charleen slipped off the milk crate, falling by his feet onto the ground. He pushed Geraldine aside and picked Charleen up, then ran in the house, yelling, "I'll bet she hasn't ate! Quick! Get a glass of orange juice!"

He laid her on the couch and ran into the bathroom to get a damp cloth. As he sat down on the couch, he lifted her head while pulling her into his lap. He took the glass of juice from Geraldine and held it to Charleen's thin, faded-pink lips. While slowly pouring small sips into her mouth, he begged her all the while, "Come on, baby girl. Take a sip for Daddy."

She began to take in the juice; then her eyes fluttered open. Geraldine took the washcloth and dabbed around her mouth, removing the juice that hadn't made it. She could hear Christine outside, screaming, "Charles, let me run out and see what's going on." Leaving him the cloth, she ran outside.

He stroked her hair. "Baby girl, you can't do this to Daddy. I can't have you leaving me, too," he said as he leaned down and gave her a kiss on the forehead.

Once she felt her father's lips on her skin, confusion caused her to ask, "What happened, Daddy?"

Tears began to well in his eyes as he replied, "You passed out, baby. You haven't ate, have you? If you aren't going to eat a good breakfast, then you're going to have to at least eat some toast in the mornings." Handing the glass of juice to his daughter, he said, "Here, drink the rest of that."

Geraldine came in with a soaking wet Christine. "How is she?"

"She's gonna be all right. I'm gonna fix her a sandwich," he said, sliding out from under Charleen. "Now you just stay right there. Lie back and rest. I'm getting you a sandwich."

He wandered around the kitchen as he fought back tears. Geraldine sat Christine's round body in a chair at the table, then joined him in the kitchen. She could see the watering of his eyes, but didn't address it. Knowing he needed space, she gave it to him. She couldn't imagine the pain he was feeling. Although she had a child, hers was not sick. Charles completed the sandwich and took it to her. He didn't believe in eating or drinking in the living room, but this was one time he ignored his own rule.

In the meantime, Christine had spotted a pack of cookies on the counter. As her mother was completing her sandwich, she huffed, "I want some cookies!"

"You can't have them until after you eat this sandwich I'm fixing for you."

"No! I want them now!"

Charleen calmly sat the sandwich plate in front of her. Just as she turned her back, Christine pushed the plate so hard that it slid off the other side of the table. Charles looked up as he heard all of this and saw her push the plate.

Geraldine spun around with a snap. "Just what do you think you're doing, missy?"

Charles instantly yelled out, "Do something with your child!"

His words took her by surprise, but as she was about to address his comment, Christine yelled, "I want cookies!"

"Hey, now! That's enough, little girl!" he yelled back. "Now your mama done told you no!" Then he looked over at his wife, giving her a cross look. "She is gonna have to get under control." Turning back to Charleen, who was still lying on the couch, he said, "Sorry, darling. Are you feeling any better?"

"Yes, sir. If you don't mind, I'm gonna go lie down in my room." Charles gave her a kiss; then she walked slowly to her room. Christine continued to sit at the table, soaking up every detail of their emotions and how they handled the illness. She didn't understand the severity of it, and jealousy began to fill the young girl's mind. "Oh, Mommy, I don't feel good," she whined, grabbing her stomach. "I think I'm sick."

Her mother took her by the hand and led her to the bedroom that she shared with Charles. After removing her swimsuit and replacing it with one of her t-shirts, she told her to go lie down on the couch.

"No, I want to stay in here," the child argued.

"No, you go lay on the couch."

"I want to stay in here!"

Now wanting to argue with her anymore, Geraldine gave in. "Fine! Whatever will make you happy."

Charles was seeing a side of her that he wasn't too sure about. He shook his head as he told Geraldine, "I'm going back outside." Then he retreated to his chair under the tree to rest his mind.

As she tended to Christine, Geraldine felt the fit-throwing had upset him. "Christine, why are you acting like this?" Tucking the blanket under her, she said, "Now, you get your nap out, and when you get up, you'd better act right."

Christine jerked her head around to her mother and gave her a squishy-faced grin, saying in a high-pitched voice, "Okay, Mommy." The sound of her voice with the look of delight on her face made her seem as if she was playing, so Geraldine gave her daughter the evil eye as she slowly pulled the door closed and returned to her husband outside.

Chapter 12

Makes You Wonder

Geraldine walked out to a more peaceful Charles relaxing in his lawn chair under the shade tree. She was hoping that their day would not be completely ruined by the chaos. Instantly, she gave her apologies for her daughter's behavior as she knelt at his side. "I'm so sorry; sometimes she can be such a handful."

He chuckled and patted her arm. "I can see that."

Feeling him relaxing more, she began to relax as well. What they didn't know was that their patience was about to be tested once again. As they rested in the shade, Christine wasn't snug under the covers in the bed as they thought.

Her young blue eyes wandered around the room, taking in all the interesting things scattered on the dresser top. Then she focused her attention on the bifold closet doors and began to wonder what could possibly be behind those thin wooden panels. She laid still and quiet, listening for any sound of movement in the house. Feeling the need to check, she slid off the bedside and tiptoed to the cracked door, then peeked out. After hearing and seeing no one, she quietly tiptoed over to the closet. She pulled at the closet door, squinting her eyes as the small rollers squealed a high-pitched tone as it rolled open. The loud noise prompted her to avoid making any more noise for a moment.

Christine only opened one door, as it gave her enough light to see if the closet needed further investigating. She looked around at first, seeing only clothes, shoes, and boots neatly placed together. Recognizing some of her mother's belongings, she pushed them aside. Once some things were moved around, she spotted something interesting on the floor in the back of the closet. Excitement ran

112

through her. No longer caring if she made noise with the door, she quickly pushed it open to let in more light.

The light grew brighter, showing more of the closet's contents and highlighting the dark-shadowed metal box. She sat Indian-style and pulled the metal box closer to her. Pulling at the top of the box, she found it was locked. Now uninterested in the box, she pushed it aside and looked around for something else of interest. Moving a small bag of sewing materials to the side, the corner of a shoebox lid came along with it. Looking around for what the lid went to, she saw the shoebox. Christine scooted closer to get a better reach and comfortably placed the box in her lap. Handfuls of gold, silver, and pearl necklaces, earrings, bracelets, and rings filled the box. She pulled at the wad of necklaces, lifting it in the air, and a couple of large-stoned rings fell from the tangled mess. Dropping the wad of necklaces back into the box, Christine picked up a few of the stone rings and placed them on her plump thumbs, oohing and ahhing at their beauty. She continued to fumble her hands around in the box of treasures, slipping several bracelets over her fists and letting them fall past her wrists and settle on her forearms, for they were too big and fell off as she reached for another handful of jewels.

Smiling and cooing over the satisfaction of her find and digging in her treasure chest, Christine thought to herself, *What else could possibly be in this bifolding heaven?* Standing up and turning around, she saw four shelves built permanently into the walls on each side of the door. She pushed aside what was junk to her, until she ran across a beautiful black velvet box with a ribbon. She pulled at the top of it, thinking it would remove like the shoebox lid, but it was hinged on one side. This caused the contents to fall to the floor. Standing still and quiet, she slowly looked down. Next to her foot was a huge gold cross with rubies inserted at its four ends. Although the bright, shiny object lay at her feet, she took no interest in it. She placed it back in its box and onto the shelf. Her hand slid across the dusty shelf, and a key fell off onto her naked foot. *That's the key to the metal box!* she thought.

Excitedly, she spun around, plopped on the floor, grabbed the metal box, and then inserted the key. Fighting her excitement as her pudgy fingers tried to unlock it quickly, she no longer cared that she was now being quite noisy.

Charleen emerged from her room to find the source of the noises. She walked across the hall to her father's room. Christine was oblivious to the fact that she was about to be discovered as she continued to fumble in the metal box. It was open now, and she was running her hands through old collectable coins, diamond rings, and a small handful of unique emerald stones. She was so engrossed in the lovely contents of the box that she didn't hear Charleen walk up behind her. Then she heard, "Oh...I thought Daddy was in here, but oooh...I'm telling!" Not giving Christine time to speak, Charleen ran out to her father and Geraldine.

"Daddy! Daddy! Christine is in your closet in your box!"

He jumped to his feet. "What do you mean in my closet?"

Geraldine didn't say a word. She just jumped up from her chair and flew into the house. Before they made it to the bedroom, Christine had put everything back and was lying in the bed, tucked under the covers. But what she didn't know was that she hadn't put the key back on the right shelf.

Her mother flung open the bedroom door with such anger that it bounced off the stopper and slowly began to close. She scrambled to the bedside where her daughter lay pretending to be asleep, looked at her, and then walked over to the closet door. As she slung it open and looked around, the coin box was slightly out of place. Charles was a creature of habit and always kept things in the same place, but the key was on the wrong shelf, and that's all she needed to know. Turning to the bed where Christine lay, she said, "All right, missy! Just what the hell have you been doing in here?" Beet-red splotches of anger appeared on Geraldine's face as she aggressively asked her again, "What the hell have you been doing in here?"

Christine sat up and rubbed her eyes as she gave an innocent reply: "What is it, Mommy? I was sleeping."

Geraldine scampered over to the bed and snatched her up by the arm, lifting her from the bed, yelling, "Get the hell up!" As this took place, Charles walked into the room. Looking at him while still holding Christine by the arm, she said, "Charles, she has been in here snooping around in the closet. I give you permission to spank her ass right now!"

He looked at Christine and asked, "Is this true?"

With puppy-dog eyes, she looked up at him, standing too tall and strong for her to fight, and gave him a deliberate lie. She thought she was in the clear because she just knew everything had been put back right. "I was sleeping, Papa."

Geraldine was unable to tolerate her lying to his face. This caused her to draw back with her masculine hand and swat her on the backside, protected only by panties and a t-shirt. This provided her ample opportunity to turn her chubby white butt crimson red. They spun around in a circling dance of discipline as Charles struggled to understand what was going on.

He'd soon had enough of seeing them in a screaming fit, so he said, "All right, that's enough!" The command was heard clearly, and she released the child's arm, which was now ruby red from the wringing of her skin. He blankly looked at them both, then turned to leave the room, saying, "I'm going to check on Charleen."

Just as Charles left the room, Christine screamed, "I want my daddy!" She fled to the living room, pushing past her mother with huge crocodile tears, and flung her body on the couch, then yelled again, "I want my daddy!"

Geraldine had had enough of her crazy shenanigans. The decision to let Christine stay with her daddy for the weekend would come sooner than she knew. Not saying a word, she just picked up the phone and called him. She extended the cord, stretching it to its extreme, as she walked closer to the couch where Christine lay. She tapped her foot and stared at her with a cold, hard look. The stare told her that if she opened her mouth, her mother would fly over and close it. Just as she was about to give up on the ringing phone, Berry answered the call.

"Well, it's about time."

"Oh, damn it, don't start with me! What do you want?"

Christine's bluff was up. Not really wanting to go to her daddy's, she sat on the edge of the couch and begged, "No, no, Mommy! I'll be good. Please, Mommy! No! I want to stay here."

No longer caring, Geraldine quickly snapped her fingers at her and pointed for her to stay seated on the couch. Christine slammed her body onto the couch, crossed her arms, tightened her lips, then arched her eyebrows down and looked at her mother with an evil glare. In return, Geraldine rolled her eyes at her, then turned away and barked at Berry, "I've had it with her. I'm going to bring her to you, and you can just keep her for a couple of weeks. I don't give a damn. She don't act like that with you, so I'm bringing her today!" She slammed the phone down, pointed at Christine, and said, "Puddin, go get changed! I'm taking you to your daddy's!"

Christine started crying as she jumped off the couch and ran to the back bathroom. Geraldine let out a cry, "Oh dear God, help me!" and lowered her head and shook it from side to side.

Charles came out of Charleen's bedroom and down the hall to his distraught wife. He now understood what had taken place after talking to her. "You've got to do what you've got to do." He put his arms around her and gave her a loving hug.

They stood there relaxed until she said, "Well, I'd better go see if she is getting her stuff together." Leaving the comfort of his arms, she went down the hall to the bedroom. As she stood outside the door, a feeling of dread fell over her. She didn't want to fight with her daughter anymore, but to her surprise, she opened the door to find her packed and ready to go, dressed in a Winnie the Pooh sundress. "Puddin', I'm very disappointed with your behavior."

Christine stuck to her ruthless lie as she made tiny circles with her bare foot on the floor and gave her an innocent look. "Mommy, I don't know why you are so mad at me."

"Puddin', get your sandals on and get in the truck. I'm taking you to your daddy's."

"Fine! I don't like it here anyway!" she grumbled, grabbing her sandals and running out.

Geraldine walked out to find her sitting in the 1970s Ford truck, ready to go. Eager to get this over with, she quickly jumped in the truck and headed down the driveway.

Once she had cleared the driveway, Charleen sat back in her chair under the shade tree and looked at her father and asked, "Daddy? Are you all right?"

He ran his hands over his wavy, slicked-back hair and said, "Yeah, I guess so. You know, I haven't ever worried about anything in my house before, but with that one around, I ain't so sure I won't have to. I don't know, I just don't know."

They both sat there quietly thinking on the subject until she spoke up: "You know, Daddy, it will be okay. Maybe it's just curiosity, like all young kids have."

He slowly looked over at his fifteen-year-old daughter, chuckled out loud, and repeated, "Those kids? Well, listen to you sounding like you are turning thirty-five instead of sixteen!" Laughing excessively, he added, "Child, you aren't far from a chicken speck yourself. So tell me about this boy who has you feeling all grown up."

"You would like him. He is so funny,"

"Where is he from?"

She sat up in her chair and pointed over his shoulder. "Well, his name is Frank, and his family moved here from Greens, Mississippi. They live right down the road, not too far from Uncle Mark." She then sat back in her chair with delight, as if she were painting the sky with her smile. When Charles saw this look, he knew his baby girl was entering into a new phase in her life.

Their conversation soon came to a stop, for Geraldine returned. They could see the golden top of Christine's blonde hair still sitting in the passenger seat. He thought, *Oh, Lord. What now?* She leaned up in the truck seat to look out the window. As her eyes met his, she released a cold, calculated, evil stare, as if she had magical powers and wished to set him on fire. In that moment, he feared what was behind her icy eyes of fire.

Chapter 13

Shocking News

Charles continued to tell Prunella his thoughts and feelings of that Sunday in 1977. Not only had Christine's eerie stare stirred up emotions in him, but thoughts of Frank had churned inside his mind, then. He nuzzled further down in the bed and began to tell her more of that day.

Geraldine had pulled into the open carport's empty space. Once she got out of the truck, she slammed the door angrily and stomped over to the lawn chair. Slinging her purse to the ground next to her feet, she plopped down in the chair. Christine, who still sat in the truck seat, turned completely around to watch her mother walk away. Charles could clearly see that Geraldine didn't feel like talking.

He looked at Christine sitting in the truck and waved to her, beckoning with a positive, silent message. She didn't budge, so he gave her a smile, then waved to her again, but she stayed put. He wouldn't give up on her, and they became engaged in a staring contest, for neither would look away. He knew that she despised him, for the hate seemed to ooze from her eyes. He was stunned and couldn't understand why she was sending him such a strong message.

Charleen tugged on his sleeve, breaking the uncomfortable look, as she asked him, "Can I phone him to come over? He can ride his bicycle down and you can meet him."

Charles mindlessly replied, "Yeah, go ahead," and she quickly ran into the house. He'd been so preoccupied with Christine's strange behavior that he answered without giving it a thought. He could tell Geraldine wasn't worried about trying to get her out of the truck, so he leaned toward her and said, "Okay, so tell me what's going on."

"I got all the way over there with her, and Berry wasn't there," she spat. "His buddy, J. J., was there and relayed a message for him, telling me that he wasn't gonna bail me out every time I had a problem with her." She snatched up her purse, rummaged around for her cigarettes, lit one, and drew in a deep pull. Then, exhaling a cloud of smoky words, she said, "Well? What do you think about this?"

His mind had wandered as she told him of this, because he was thinking he had just said yes to meeting Charleen's first boyfriend, so he didn't respond to her question.

"Charles? Hey?" She waved her hand in front of his face and asked, "Did you hear me?"

"Oh, yes, dear. Okay. Well, she will just have to stay here. We will make arrangements." About that time Mark Shaw pulled into the driveway. Charles turned to Geraldine and said, "Could this day get any worse?"

Mark opened the door to his black Chevy pickup, walked around to the front, and leaned back against the grill, crossing his long legs at the ankles. Charles knew he had to keep cool even though he detested him, for Charleen and Christine were there. So he spoke up calmly, "Well, how ya doing there?"

He kicked a couple of rocks with his Western-style boots, looked at the old rusting truck by the shed, and glanced at the milk truck sitting in the open sun. Then his eyes slowly roamed over to the two trucks under the carport. Ignoring the blue Ford with the huffy child still sitting in it, he focused his attention on the new red truck. "What you got there? A new 250 four-by-four, huh? Hmm...

it's a Ford. Yep! I sure hope you're not spending all that money on your new toys and land. I heard you bought that land down on Dove Road. Y'all planning on moving or something?"

Charles tried to keep his composure, for he knew the point of this questioning, but anger began to well up inside him. Geraldine could see the sparks coming from his crystal-blue eyes surrounded by a beet-red face that had nothing to do with the warmth of the sun. She felt the tension between these two, so she turned to him. Still sitting in the lawn chair, she asked, "Can we help you with something today? Surely you didn't stop by just to talk trash."

Charles was not the kind of man who believed you should talk about people's money or business, and Mark's inquiry into his finances was not his business. So he stood up to walk over to him, but Geraldine grabbed his arm. In a gentle but stern voice she said, "No, Charles. The children."

Mark pushed himself off the truck grill. "Is there a problem?"

Charles shook his head and sat back down. "Naw...but I think it's time for you to leave."

He turned to get into his truck. "Well, I'll tell you what. The day she turns eighteen, she'd better get that money from my sister's death. Maybe you won't spend it all in the meantime."

Fury started to rise up in him again, so much so that he stood up from his chair, but in that instant Charleen came running outside and flew past the truck that Christine was sitting observantly in and ran to her uncle Mark, giving him a big hug. Charles sat back

124

down in the midst of his anger, wishing he could lash out at him, but he choked it all back for her.

They shared a moment of family love; then he slowly drove off, passing her fella on his bicycle as he rode up the driveway. Charles's impression of Frank wasn't favorable. He was not one to judge a book by its cover, but this cover looked mighty suspicious. He could see the playboy in him as he flung around his long black hair, strutting around in his flared-leg jeans and sleeveless t-shirt. It made Charles sick to his stomach to have Frank's small, muscular frame stand so close to him. Stepping back from Frank, he spoke through almost clenched teeth: "So...she says your family is from Greens?"

Frank slung his long black hair from his eyes. "Yeah. We moved here 'cause my daddy got a job with the industrial chicken plants that they are going to build. They're working on one now."

"Are you thirsty?" Charleen interrupted.

"Yeah, I could use a swaller of something."

"I'll go get you some sweet tea. I'll be right back."

Once she was out of sight, Charles began to grill him. "So how old are you?"

"Seventeen."

"She ain't but fifteen," Charles gasped, "and it'll be about five more months before I start letting you take her off."

"Yep, that's right," Geraldine spoke up. "She is still a sweet flower, and you're not gonna do anything to disturb that, now are ya?"

Frank sat back on the milk crate, nervously rubbing his hands on his legs as he gave her a reply, "Oh, no, ma'am! I would never do that."

Charles leaned up in his chair and into him. "Hell, I don't really want her dating until she is thirty-five, but I know I can't do that to her. I don't mind y'all meeting up at church, but I'm not too keen on you two going off alone anywhere. I mean anywhere. Not even behind doors. There is no such thing as private time with the two of you right now, understand?"

Frank nodded his head in agreement. Then Geraldine signaled to him to quiet down because Charleen was returning. As she walked up to him with the glass of tea, she asked her father, "Daddy, do you mind if we go walking?"

"Where are y'all wanting to walk to?"

She pointed down the road toward the same area that he had blown up the apple tree. "We're just going to go down to the creek."

"Now, darling, that's too far. How about y'all circle around here in the yard?"

Charleen was disappointed in her father's answer but replied, "Okay, Daddy." She grabbed Frank by the arm and led him around the front yard.

Geraldine sat with a large grin on her face as she looked over at the unsmiling Charles. Once he looked at her, she said, "She's so smitten with him."

"Oh, hush up!"

She tossed her hands up innocently, shrugged her shoulders, and said, "What's the matter? He seems harmless."

Suddenly, their attention was taken by the sounds of Christine opening the truck door and slamming it. She slowly walked over to her mother, dragging her feet every step of the way. Geraldine didn't say a word. She just turned back around to Charles. Christine took her time getting over to them, for she was intently watching Charleen and Frank walk around the yard. She took so long that Geraldine turned again to see if she was still walking toward them.

When she saw that she was getting close, she grabbed a milk crate and pulled it closer to her and said, "Well, puddin', you finally decided to get out and come over here and sit with us. Here, sit down next to me."

Christine didn't say a word as she sat down, crossed her arms, and poked out her bottom lip, never taking her eyes off the pair walking around in the yard. Her curiosity finally got the best of her. "Who's that with Charleen, Mama?"

"That is her boyfriend."

"He is cute," she shyly replied, dropping one shoulder and giving her mother a smile. Before they knew it, she had jumped up full of energy and run over to the lovebirds.

Charles witnessed this entire act and said, "If she's going to be staying here from now on, we can fix up that other bedroom for her. I hate to say it, but I'm gonna have to buy some kind of safe to put my things in."

Geraldine didn't say a word. On one hand, it hurt that he felt that way, but on the other hand, she understood his concern. They stopped talking and continued to relax under the large shade tree. They watched the two smitten teenagers become separated by Christine. In their silence, his heart began to break as he watched his baby girl fall in love for the first time.

***

Charles stopped talking to Prunella and turned his head away from her. She touched his upper arm, then swept a gray strand of hair from his face. "Daddy, are you all right?" Tears welled up in his eyes. He didn't reply, so she just gave him a tight smile and lay down next to him. Prunella stretched her five-feet-five body next to him, placing one arm around her father and nuzzled into him. "I love you, Daddy. Tell me something about Mama."

It took no time for him to remember things about her. He soon began to prattle on about her in detail.

"You know I don't drink alcohol. I ain't ever liked that stuff, but I got to thinking about my first wife, Sharon, while I was out on my milk route. Well, it just so happened that it was the anniversary of her death. I decided to get a small bottle of whiskey. Of course, the first few swigs burnt my goozle, but I continued to nip on it. As I was going home, hell, I felt pretty good. You know me. I was having fun with everybody—ya mama and Charleen's goofy boyfriend. Dang, Prunella! I was even enjoying Christine."

She gasped, covering her mouth, then muffled through her hand, "How did you?"

He chuckled at her reaction. "Hold on. I ain't done. Once I got to the house, they all wanted to play a game of monopoly. So we all gathered up there at the kitchen table. Christine was about ten years old, and she ain't never been a small child, ya know. Well, she was developing in places that it didn't seem time for. It made me sick watching her prance around trying to get Frank to pay attention to her places." He tossed his head around from side to side in his pillows as if trying to shake off that memory and said, "Aw! I don't want to think about that right now..." He then turned his head up to look at her and added, "You know I don't like talking business without it being the proper time. All right...well...I be danged if Charleen didn't bring up that subject. Her uncle Mark took it upon himself to tell her about her inheritance when she turned eighteen. I tried to get her to talk about something else, but your mama tried to pry into it for her. I had to shut your mama down because I didn't feel comfortable talking about that with a bunch of young 'uns there. This was the first time me and your mama argued, so I done something stupid. I went out to the truck and finished off that bottle."

"Oh Lord, Daddy! What did you do after that?"

"Prunella, I drove to the cemetery where Sharon is and sat there drunk, just thinking." He poked himself in the chest with his pasty, wrinkled finger and added, "This here old man you're looking at went to expressing how much I loved and missed her. My drunk, staggering butt got down on my hands and knees, buried them in the dirt in front of that cold hard-marbled stone, and cried my eyes out. Your mama had followed me and was standing right behind me the whole time, watching and listening to me. Needless to say, Geraldine Richards let me know about myself. She said, 'Charles, I should have known. Here all this time I thought you really wanted me, but if she was here, I wouldn't be. Would I? Well, never mind that! Get up off your knees. I'm pregnant!' I sat there stunned, and then it hit me. I loved your mama and I definitely wanted to be with her, so I jumped up and ran after her."

She chuckled out the words, "So...how did you survive Mama's wrath, Daddy?"

He twisted his head around to her. "I did a lot of running!" They both burst out in laughter as he added, "You know, I've seen her mad plenty of times, but let me tell you, your mama's manners go out the window when she is scared or mad. Boy, let me tell you about your uncle Oliver and me causing just that."

***

Chapter 14

Camping Cannon

Oliver and his family were coming to town for the Fourth of July in 1983. The heat had been scorching everything in sight, so they planned to take their families camping. There was a beautiful creek perfect to camp by and celebrate that hot weekend. It provided plenty of fish that loved to hang around the edge of the water, as it was sheltered by large oak trees that canopied over it. For those who wanted to swim, there was a perfect spot of gently swirling cool water that flowed into a small sand cove just off its bank.

Charles told Geraldine that Oliver and his wife didn't curse and asked her to refrain from swearing. She knew it would be hard, but gave her promise. Everyone gathered all the essentials for camping, eating, and fishing for the weekend. Once Charles and Frank completed their deliveries, they would meet them all down at the creek. He had never missed a day of work since Sharon passed away, so this meant the Richards family didn't ever go too far from home.

Charleen was all grown up now, and he kept true to his word. She turned eighteen and inherited not only her money but also the passion of wanting to own her own business. After graduating in 1980, she spent two years in college learning how to run a business. In that same timeframe, she and Frank had married. With her diabetes, they knew children weren't possible. Although she would love to have them, they knew it was for the best.

Charleen could handle anything thrown her way. She pressed on no matter what and pursued her dreams. With her inheritance, she bought into the new wave beauty sensation of indoor tanning. This was something she could sink her teeth into, for she had been admired for her beauty in high school and in college as well as for keeping up with the latest fashionable styles and giving the best beauty advice. Finding a nice vacant building next to a beauty salon in town only a few blocks from their new home, she opened a shop housing tanning beds with lotion products, perfumes, and purses. Her business was booming, and she now made plenty of money of her own.

With Charles resting in the knowledge that she was financially sound, he paid her man to work with him. He didn't like his style, but the girls went crazy over him. Most of them said he looked like Bo Brady from the daytime soap opera *Days of Our Lives*. He always kept an unshaven face with long black hair and wore faded blue jeans, which were so tight he looked to be poured into them, and a Hawaiian-style shirt unbuttoned to expose his chest hair, with the collar popped up like an urban Dracula. Charles couldn't or wouldn't ever see what those turned heads saw.

The sun's continuous heat blazed throughout the day, causing the truck's air conditioner to work overtime to keep them cool. They were finally on their way to the creek where their families awaited them. Once they made it there, Frank grabbed a small brown sack of beer from the floorboard, then disappeared down the sharp hill that sloped to the creek. Charles took off his uniform, neatly draped it over the truck seat, secured the door, and followed Frank, watching him strip his shirt and shoes, leaving them where they fell, while never letting go of the brown sack of beer. Frank ran to the water's edge where he saw Christine and Prunella splashing about.

"Where is everybody, Christine?"

She pointed upstream where her mother was sitting with Mary and her two boys, fishing. About that time, Geraldine looked up, saw him with the girls, and waved. Charles made it close to the water, and Frank pointed upstream, then jumped in the water. He gave her a wave, blew her a kiss, and then walked up to the campsite where Oliver was relaxing in a lawn chair.

"Well, it's about time you got here, old man!" Just as he reached into the large cooler for a cold drink, the sounds of a horn constantly blowing and a vehicle with a powerful engine roaring loudly as it crossed the bridge startled Oliver. "Who is that, making all that racket up there?"

"Well...it sounds like Charleen in that new Corvette she bought."

"Corvette!" He sat up in his chair. "You let that girl get a what?"

"Well now, I can't tell her what to do with her money."

"But that's one powerful car for such a frail young lady."

Meanwhile, as they talked, she pulled up in her dream car, a 1981 special pearl-white T-top Corvette. She switched off the engine and looked in the rearview mirror at herself, pulling down her overly large sunglasses to expose her beautiful green eyes. She blew herself a kiss, then threw her stylish beach bag over her shoulder, balancing a small radio and a Styrofoam cup filled with vodka and orange juice.

Charles looked up to see her coming down the hill, lighting up the dark green forest as she pranced down the hill wearing a soft-yellow one-piece bathing suit with a yellow-and-white paint-splashed wrap tied neatly around her waist. "Oliver...I want you to look at that. Ain't she the most beautiful thing you've ever seen? Why, she's as pretty as a golden calla lily!"

As she got closer to them, Oliver stood up and said with a big smile, "Dang, Charleen! You so skinny, if your head fell through your butt, you'd dang sure hang yourself!" He ran over to her and gave her a hug.

Laughing at her uncle's joke, she wrapped her arms around him tightly, saying, "Oh, I ain't that skinny."

"I'm just joshing with ya girl. You really look wonderful," he said, flashing her a big smile as he sat back down in his chair.

Charleen sat down across from him and placed the radio at her feet. The ground was uneven, and it toppled over, causing the batteries to fall out as it rolled toward her uncle's feet. He leaned over to pick it all up and became excited at the feel of the batteries in his hand. He jumped up from his chair, exclaiming, "Charles! C batteries. Ha! It's perfect. Come on! I've got something to show y'all!" Holding up the batteries, he looked at Charleen and asked, "Can I have these?"

"Well...I guess so," she snickered, giving him an arched-eyebrow look of wonder.

Once they started up the hill, they heard Oliver's oldest boy, Russell, calling out to them, "Where y'all going?"

They all motioned for Russell to follow them up the hill. Charles had fallen behind but quickly caught back up to Oliver. Then he began to rattle on about his job in Alabama supervising in a metal fabrication shop. He told him about some projects they were working on, which made no sense to Charles. Once they were on top of the hill, he rolled the batteries around in his hands, repeating, "Oh, you're gonna love this!" He took up a faster pace, almost jogging to his small black truck. He looked back at them and yelled, "Come on!"

He flipped down the tailgate and jumped up into the back, and they all stood around watching him. Giving them an overly expressive, joyful smile, he leaned down and snatched back a green army blanket, revealing a small black cannon. Oliver slid the heavy cannon to the edge of the tailgate and hopped down. With a loving touch, he ran his hand down the short barrel, then traced his fingers across the imprint of a large, circled "OL." He continued to run his hand along the barrel, circling his fingers around the hole at the end of the barrel, saying quietly, "Perfect. The C batteries are just perfect...yep! This will work." He spoke louder, "Oh, man! Charles, I just made this at work last week. I got a pattern and made a mold in some sand, then poured hot metal into it. I did the same with this stand."

Charleen and Charles were stunned at this creation. As they leaned on the side of the truck, Oliver looked over at them with a big grin. "Pretty neat, huh?"

"So that's why you were flipping out over my batteries?" Charleen asked.

He slid one of the batteries into the hole, then dropped in the other one as he replied, "Well yep, they're a perfect fit!"

Charles swiftly asked, "Have you fired it before?"

"Nope. But we fixing to!"

Intrigued, Charleen and Russell grinned at one another as they listened to him tell about this new toy. Oliver placed the cannon on the ground just behind his truck and pointed it toward the woods. He closed the tailgate, got his toolbox, and pulled out a spool of wick along with a Prince Albert can full of gunpowder. Charles just stood back and watched him prepare the cannon as he clung uncomfortably to the truck's bed. "Ollie, are you sure about this thing?" he asked.

Squatting beside the cannon, Oliver turned his head to give him a look. With that look and based on past experiences with him, Charles knew they needed to back up. He pulled Charleen gently by her arm as they moved over by the milk truck. "Hey, Russell, I'd advise you to come on over here with us." Russell didn't hesitate and ran over to them.

Oliver lit the fuse and ran over with everyone else. He placed his arm around Charles's shoulder and said, "Okay, let's watch this thang blow!"

The sparkling of the fuse grew closer to the cannon's gunpowder. They covered their ears to prepare for a loud bang. Within a matter of seconds, a loud bang rang out from the cannon accompanied by a flash of fire at its end. A storm of smoke engulfed their surroundings. The sounds of the world were closed out for a moment, and no one could hear Geraldine and Mary screaming as they ran up the hill. All eyes were on the cannon as they stood stunned by its blast. The smoke floated up from the cannon and drifted into the air, temporarily blocking the sun until dissipating into the wind.

Once the air had cleared, everyone's mouths fell open as they stood looking at the unexpected damage the cannon had caused. Geraldine and Mary finally made it up the hill and stopped at the top once they saw everyone was safe. Gregory, Oliver's youngest boy, had run up with the ladies, but he didn't stop with them. He ran past his mother to his father.

Geraldine stomped her foot at the sight of everyone now standing at the back of Oliver's truck. Placing her hands on her hips, she exclaimed, "Charles Richards, what in the world are y'all doing up here?" He couldn't say a word, for he was speechless. The other women couldn't see what they were looking at.

Suddenly Gregory shouted, "Daddy! Your truck!"

Due to the cannon being placed in close proximity to the back of the truck, the powerful force of the explosion had kicked off the back metal plug of the cannon, making a fist-sized hole through the tailgate.

The women could tell from Gregory's expression that they were missing something. Mary walked around and grabbed her face as she saw the tailgate's gaping hole. Geraldine stomped over to them, saying, "Well? Is anybody gonna say something?" Charles saw her coming toward the back of the truck, so he quickly stood in front of the gaping hole. She looked confused, looking from face to face, wondering what she was missing. All eyes were on Charles.

She stomped her foot. "Okay, what gives?"

Oliver spoke up, "Go on. Show her."

138

He stepped aside for her to see. Geraldine took one look at the back of the truck, stood quietly for a second, then unleashed: "Damn you, Charles! Why were y'all messing around with that damn thang? What the hell were y'all thinking? Oh, Lord! What if..." She couldn't complete her sentence. Frustrated, she placed her hands on top of her head, then began to use every curse word possible as she spun in circles. She stomped her foot at them again. "I got to get away from all y'all and get my bearings back. Y'all are damn crazy...damn crazy!" She then started flapping her arm as if orchestrating a symphony and using colorful curse words as she stomped off down the hill, back to camp.

Everyone stood there unsure of what to say until Mary said, "Oh my, she sure has a way with words." Turning to the men and shaking her finger at them, she yelled, "It's y'all's fault she cursed like that. I'd better go check on her before she teaches the critters down at the creek a new language."

***

Chapter **15**

Pocketing a Memory

It was 10:30 a.m. on June 15, 1985, the day before Stella's seventy-eighth birthday. The heat adhered their clothes to them as Charles and Geraldine worked through the early morning in the garden. Christine, now in her teen years, was complaining about picking the corn. As for little Prunella, she gave her ambitious assistance to her father as she followed in behind his every step. As he looked at her, a huge smile stretched across his face. Seeing those little sleepy sky-blue eyes fighting to stay open as she carried a small armload of corn through the rows just warmed his heart.

Once they were done, they all sat under the oak tree. Little Prunella excused herself to chase the exotic country additions around in the yard. Geraldine wished she had known how stupid guineas really were. She thought they would be glamorous for their homestead. They were the perfect fowl for ridding areas of snakes, ticks, and rats. Eventually, through the years, they all ignorantly walked slowly out to the highway and to their deaths.

The fervent heat continued to torture them as they sat in the shade shucking the freshly picked ears of corn. Just then, a bright glare from a windshield twinkled up the highway, catching Charles's eye. Prunella's keen senses recognized the roar of the Corvette's engine. She knew it was her big sissy coming down the drive.

Leaving the guineas to their frantic state of confusion, Prunella, full of excitement, ran over to her daddy, yelling, "It's Sissy! It's Sissy!" He reached out and grabbed her to keep her from getting in the way of Charleen's low-riding Corvette. High-pitched squeals rang from her at the sight of her big sister. She watched intently as Charleen climbed out of the car and walked toward her. Charles let her go, and she ran for her. The soft bounce of her long blonde curls flowed to her face, tickling her nose. Charleen picked her up and held her on her hip. Prunella's tiny silver teeth sparkled in the bright sunlight, for she was grinning widely. She wrapped her tiny dirty arms around her. "I've missed you! I've missed you!"

"I've missed you too, sweetie!" She turned to their father. "When is she going to get these silver teeth off?"

"Well, they gonna have to just fall out on their own. She has lost about two so far."

She let out a grunt. Seeing a strain on her face, he immediately took the little six-year-old from her arms. "Come here, child. You're getting too big for Sissy to hold you like that." As he reached out to his disappointed baby girl, she tucked her head down to pout. Charleen assured her that she loved her and missed her too, and she was soon smiling again.

Charleen gave her father a hug as she spoke to Geraldine, "Hey, pretty lady! How are you today?"

"Honey, this old thang sitting in this chair ain't been pretty since 1940 something."

Charles spoke up, quickly correcting her, "Pardon me, Mrs. Richards, but you will always be a pretty woman to me!"

"Is Grandma Stella home? I've got a birthday present for her."

Prunella ran up to her. "Sissy, I'll take you over to see her." She then placed her dirty little hand in her sister's clean, smooth hand and gently pulled her across the yard.

Christine saw an opportunity to escape the corn shucking and quickly jumped to her feet, dropping ears of corn everywhere. Geraldine frowned as she said, "Chrissy, you get all that picked up, and then you can go over there with them."

She picked up the scattered ears of corn, then took to jogging so she could catch up with them just as they reached the edge of the carport. Stella opened the door before the girls reached it. She looked over at a few boxes that were next to the trailer and began waving her arms around, clapping her hands, and yelling loudly, "Get on outta here. You ain't brooding under my darn porch!"

Charleen jumped aside as two guineas ran under her feet, honking and flapping to get away from her. "Well, Grandma, they're just looking for some shade."

She placed her hands on her hips. "I can't stand them stupid birds. Every time I step out here on the porch, I step in their crap!"

Prunella took it upon herself to help her get rid of the birds. She started whooping and hollering at the birds, "Get! Get! You better get on out of here before Grandma gets ya!"

Stella took pleasure in her six-year-old vocabulary. She was a tough little girl. Upon entering the trailer, Prunella ran over to a small wooden toy box in the corner of the living room and snatched out some crayons and two coloring books. She plopped down beside the coffee table and demanded that her big sister sit down and color with her. Charleen always aimed to please her little sister, but before she sat down she handed her grandma a small box.

"Happy early birthday, Grandma,"

"Oh, thank you, dear!"

Prunella continued to color as Stella opened her present. Christine stood there looking at all of the things she had and asked if she could go to the bathroom. Stella didn't look up as she pointed down the hall. Christine walked toward the bathroom. She could see that the bedroom door was open. Glancing around to see if anyone was looking, she went into the room and pushed the door halfway closed. A beautiful jewelry box caught her eyes as it sat on the dresser. Feeling the urge, she opened it and rummaged through its contents.

Shining in the box was an Edwardian eighteen-karat-gold ring with diamonds and rubies from 1922. She was so fascinated that she placed it in her bright-yellow shorts pocket and closed the box. Just as she was about to leave the bedroom, Prunella yelled out, "I'm telling! You ain't supposed to be in here!"

She turned around and snatched her by the arms and, gritting her teeth, said, "Shut up!"

Prunella tried to yell out, "Grandma!" but Christine covered her mouth.

Meanwhile, in the living room, Charleen passed out in the living room floor. When Prunella heard the commotion in the living room, she was eager to get back in there, but there was still a tight grip on her arm and mouth.

"Let me go, Chrissy!"

She let go of her and instantly slapped her small face. Feeling the sting on her face caused her to stand there in shock. Christine realized only too late what she had just done. Prunella quickly ran out of the bedroom to tell on her, but once she saw Charleen lying limp on the floor, it was no longer a thought. Stella's long body kneeled beside her trying to shake her awake, but there was no response. Seeing this caused her to instantly run out the door yelling, "Daddy! Daddy! It's Sissy!"

The surprising sounds of her running out, yelling caused Charles to jump up, not caring about the corn that fell to the ground. He grabbed her and ran inside to Charleen. Huge tears were falling from her little blue eyes as she begged, "Sissy! Help my Sissy, Daddy, help Sissy!"

Once inside, he sat her down. "What happened?"

"I don't know what happened," Stella replied. "One minute we were talking; then she just fell down."

"Mama! Do you have any orange juice?"

"Yes. Yes, I do. I keep it around just for..." She scrambled to the kitchen and returned with the juice, and he gently tilted the glass to Charleen's lips. Without having to be told, Prunella ran into the bathroom, grabbed a washcloth, wet it, and ran to him.

Geraldine walked in the door, and Christine ran to her, letting out a fake cry. Stella had witnessed her standing there with an uncaring look while the chaos was occurring, and now she was acting as if she was frightened. This caused Stella's stomach to turn.

Charleen slowly came to and realized what had happened, then began to apologize. Charles stroked her hair and soothed the words, "Baby girl. You have no need to apologize."

Prunella joined him in the stroking of her soft hair, twirling her tiny fingers around one of her sister's curls, and repeating, "Now, baby girl, you have no need to apologize."

She turned to her to give her a smile, but noticed the red slap mark. "What happened to your face?"

She pointed over at Christine. "Chrissy slapped me."

Charles's eyes darted over at her. "Did you slap your sister?" She didn't respond to his question; she just slid in behind her mother. Geraldine moved to the side to expose her for him to ask her again, "Did you slap her?"

"No! She did that herself."

He jumped up from the floor, walked over to her, and bent down to look directly in her eyes. "Chrissy, that's clearly a hand mark on her little face, so you're telling me that she chose to slap herself?" She didn't respond to his question, so he straightened up and crossed his arms. He bent down to Prunella and looked closer at her face. Looking back at Christine, who stood only five feet tall, he snapped, "Do you think we believe you?" She continued to hang her head. He turned back to Prunella and asked, "What happened?"

Swinging out her arms, pointing, and then folding them in a huff, she replied passionately, "Chrissy was plundering in Grandma's room, and she didn't want me to tell!"

Christine lunged at her, but Charles grabbed her. He was so mad at her that he looked at Geraldine and said, "Please get her out of here." So they quickly turned and walked out the front door.

After Stella helped Charleen sit up on the couch, she went in her bedroom to see if she had messed with anything. She looked over the room, scanning it in detail, and stopped on her jewelry box, thinking, *That would interest her immensely.* She opened the box and scratched around, observing all of its contents. Suddenly everyone heard a loud cry from the end of the house, "OH...NO! Nope! No way! Charles!" She flew into the living room like a raging bull. She was steamed. "Where did she go?"

They all looked toward the front door. She stomped toward it and flung it open. They were standing under the carport. "Where is it? You give me back my darn ruby ring! My husband gave that to me for my fifteenth birthday, right after he started courting me!" She stepped closer to her as she continued to question her.

Christine shyly hid behind her mother, as if her large, short body could hide from Stella's anger. Geraldine put her hand up. "Stop right there. How do you know she has your ring?"

Stella stopped, settled into her aggravated stance, pulled her shoulders back, and replied, "Now look here. Despite what you may think, I may be old, but there ain't nothing wrong with my eyesight or memory. I know what is missing, and that child knows what's missing!" She made eye contact with Christine as she pointed at her pocket. "Turn it out now! Let us see what you just might not have!"

Christine, unable to think of something, scooted behind her mother once more. Charles had come out and grabbed her by the arm. "Answer your Grandma and do as she said!"

She cried out as if she were in pain. Although he had a grip on her, it wasn't as tight as she made it out to be. "You're breaking my arm! Let go of me! Mama, tell him to let me go!"

Geraldine was frantic and didn't know what to do. She yelled out at him, "Let her go!"

In that moment, he turned his attention to her as Christine quickly ran behind her mother again, but Geraldine turned with both of her hands and grabbed her. Looking her straight in the eyes, he asked, "Chrissy, do you know what they are talking about?"

"Why, yes, she knows!" Charles interrupted. "That's why she slapped Prunella; she got caught!" He let go of her. "Empty your pockets—NOW!"

Christine hesitated because she knew the beautiful heirloom was stuffed in her pocket. She lowered her head, reached into her pocket, pulled out the ring, and handed it to her mother. Then she began to cry, for she realized she was caught. Geraldine clenched her teeth as she spoke to her, "Go to your room, and don't come out until I say so!"

Christine ran across the yard to the brick house. She handed the ring back to Stella with her head lowered slightly in shame of what her daughter had done. She looked at them and apologized before leaving to deal with her.

They went back into the trailer as she walked away and sat down on the sheet-covered couch. With all the chaos, he had been temporarily distracted from Charleen. Now he turned his attention to her. "Baby girl, you might need to go to the hospital and get checked out."

"I'm fine, Daddy!" she argued. "It will be all right."

"No, not this time. I'm gonna call Frank to take you to the hospital. If he don't, I will."

"Okay, I will go." She looked over at her Grandma. "I'm glad you got that back."

Stella looked down at the ring. "I'm sure glad, too. Oh, thank you, Lord!" She smiled as she looked over at Prunella. "Well, I've got to thank my baby for looking out for her old grandma." Everyone sat quietly; then she added, "I know you love that woman, but that girl of hers ain't no good. You'd better keep a close eye on that one."

***

Charles paused to point to the large upright safe in his bedroom as he said to Prunella, "Now you see why I bought that big thing. You know it took six big boys to get that in here?"

"Well, there ain't nobody gonna walk out with that," she laughed.

"It's reinforced, but it's still just a lock with a magic number. You know I ain't gonna make it, so that's in my wallet."

"Don't talk like that," she said, as she adjusted herself to sit up further on the bed.

Charles shifted into a more comfortable position as well, and they began talking more about the past.

***

Chapter 16

A New Family

A few months after Christine's thieving escapade, Stella pulled Charles aside and told him that she wanted to move into a rest home. She expressed that she'd had her fill of country life and needed to be around others her age. She didn't tell him, but deep down she knew there wasn't much more time left for her on this earth, and the thought of the girls or him finding her departed in her trailer was too much. This prompted her to make the decision to move to a rest home nearby. He reluctantly arranged for her to have a private room at the Golden Meadows Rest Home, about twenty minutes away in town. Charles, Geraldine, Charleen, and Prunella never missed a visit to see her.

It was a Friday, only five days before Christmas. They all came in to see Stella, but as they walked in, Charles could see her at the nurses' station with her arms folded in a superior stance. He looked at Charleen and said, "Looks like your grandma is fussy today."

Stella spoke loudly to the nurses, "Well, you girls wouldn't know anything about taste...even if it was paid for you!" As she turned to walk away, she flipped back around and added, "You know it's over?"

The two nurses looked at one another, confused. Then one of them asked, "What's over?"

She pulled at her hair as if it were large like theirs, placed one hand on her hip, and stomped her foot as she said, "Halloween!" Turning sharply around, she stomped back to her room, waving her hands in the air and loudly adding, "Oh, it's the '80s! Yeah! So much color, and they want to wear them all!" Once she reached the door, she gave it a slam, causing it to echo throughout the building.

The family walked up to the nurses' station, towing Prunella by the hand. Once they got closer, one of the nurses turned to the other and said, "Man, talking to her is like swallowing a bundle of briars!"

Just as she released those words, Charles, smiling, replied, "Amen!"

"Oh, I'm...s-sorry, Mr. Richards."

"Oh, you stop that, hun. I know my mama is a mess," he reassured her, leaning on the counter. He complimented their inflated hair, all the while delivering a sophisticated, charming smile, and added with a wink, "My mother has always sought after perfection in people, and if she thought they were lacking...well, she tends to blow sour compliments up their backsides like a hot air balloon. I personally think you girls look great."

Charleen bumped her father on his back, for she could see Stella looking out her door, listening to every word he said. Stella had impeccable hearing, and the family always joked that she could hear gnats when they crossed their legs.

At that moment, she yelled, "Charles! It's Christmas time. Leave the Halloween teens alone, and get in here before all that color they have on explodes and turns you funny!"

Charleen covered her mouth to keep from bursting into laughter. She looked down at little Prunella, then pulled her to the room. Charles apologized to the young ladies as he walked away. J u s t as he got to her door, Stella spouted, "Those crazy girls just don't know I've worked in here darn near all my life. I know how this works."

"What is going on, Mama?"

She turned around, mumbling under her breath, sat down, and slapped the top of her legs. "Them girls want me to wear one of those gowns. I told them I ain't gonna put that paper dress on. Besides, you think they know anything about fashion? You know I've always wore these polyester-cotton short-sleeve dresses." She stood up and twirled, adding, "I love the lightweight feel, and they make me feel pretty. Them girls don't know anything about fashion. Just look at 'em. They all painted up like they going to war. I know it's the '80s, but shoot...you see all that black stuff around their eyes? You know it wouldn't hurt them to thin out some of those caterpillar hairs from over their eyes either. Horrible...just plain horrible!"

Charleen giggled at her grandmother's sense of humor. Stella was always sure to be up before dawn and prettied up for the day, so no one had ever seen her without makeup.

Prunella ran up to her, tilting her head as far back as it would go because she was so tall. She gave her a large smile, forcing her to pay attention to her, as she started wrestling with her coat, crying out, "Help! Help me, Grandma. I want this off." Stella sat back down on the side of the bed and helped her take it off. As she removed the coat, she noticed the scratches, bruises and bug bites all over her young arms. "What have you been doing? Sweetheart, it looks like your arms have been unconsciously aware they're on your body. Goodness gracious, child!" Then turning her attention to Charles, she asked, "Where is Geraldine? It's not like her to miss a visit."

Charleen answered quickly for him, "Oh, she is back at the house with Christine. Grandma, we have something to tell you..." She paused to look at her father for permission to continue talking. He nodded in agreement, for he knew Stella was like a firefly that liked to flutter around other people's dirty laundry. She'd buzz around waiting for the opportune moment to light them up with a critical response and send them on their way.

She drew in a deep breath. "Okay. Well, I got to Daddy's house today, and I could hear yelling. I took my time walking up to the door 'cause I didn't want to get involved with the dispute. I wasn't going to go in, but when I heard Prunella screaming, I rushed in there. That fat-butt Christine was blocking the doorway. I asked her what was going on, and she told me to mind my business. I then stepped up to her and looked her in the eye and said, 'Look here, Sister! This is my father's house, and what happens in it will always be my business!'"

Charles interrupted quickly, spitting out, "Mama, Christine is pregnant!"

Her eyes shot over to him. "Oh, dear Lord! She's what?"

Charleen jumped back into the conversation: "And that's not all. She wants to move herself and her man over into your trailer."

Stella jumped up as if she were a spring chicken and barked, "I don't think so! I might want to move back. No ma'am! I'll light it up with a match before she moves in my place. As a matter of fact all my stuff is still in there. Keep her away from it!"

Charles reached up and placed both of his hands on his mother's shoulders and assured her she had nothing to worry about. She sat back down on the bed as Prunella bounced on it.

"Charles, that Christine gal ain't right. She's trouble...trouble, I say. So that's why Geraldine didn't come with y'all. That heifer has her on a leash. Well, so what if she is pregnant? Why is that stopping her from coming to see me?" She shook her head, then looked back up at him, who stood at the foot of the bed watching his little one jump around on it. Squinting her eyes slightly, she said, "If I was you, I'd keep my eyes on that one. You hear me, son?" She then grabbed up little Prunella and pulled her into her lap. Pushing back her shiny blonde hair, she looked her straight in the eye. "Child, listen to me. I know that's your sister, and we should not be talking about her, but you need to pay close attention and not get caught up in her mischievous games."

Prunella really didn't understand, but she gave her grandmother a nod.

After that visit, the Richards family's holidays turned to grief, for Stella passed away on Christmas Eve. Charles kept silent, but frequently large tears filled his eyes. The sense of sadness over losing his mother rendered him completely speechless. When he would try to talk, it was as if his tongue were made of cement. Charleen stepped in and helped her father with the funeral arrangements. She became his rock, helping him cope with the loss. Planning the funeral also helped her to deal with the painful loss.

The church was filled with white lilies, for they were Stella's favorite flower. She had frequently claimed that they were the most beautiful things God ever placed on this earth. She often complimented Charleen by telling her she contained the same qualities. Geraldine and Mary had acquired several different kinds of flowers. They were both crafty and used their talents to skillfully arrange them with pink accents around the casket.

Stella was placed to rest beside her husband, Charles Thomas Richards Sr. This was the first time eight-year-old Prunella saw her father cry, so as the funeral went on, she never let go of his hand. Geraldine would pry her small hand from him, but within a matter of minutes, she was right back at his side, holding his masculine hand. After the beautiful service, friends and family gathered at the Richards' home. They expressed their sympathy with scads of food in decorative dishes. While everyone sat around talking and enjoying the food, Charles slowly came back to himself.

He pulled Oliver aside, and they walked around in the yard as he questioned him about what kind of work he did. While they were walking, Prunella clung to her father. Little did she know, the conversation between her daddy and uncle would make a lot of sense in later years.

The oil well was pumping plenty of oil for them. Now with Stella out of the picture, Christine's home invasion continued to disrupt the family. They had explained to her that living in that trailer was out of the question and that they didn't want another trailer on their homestead. The subject of a place to live always caused many arguments.

They discussed the situation and came up with a solution. They decided to buy her a trailer and put it on two acres of the ten that they had on Dove Road. She had a family now, as she'd married Jerry Lott after high school, and had a son named Donovan.

In her mind, Christine felt like Geraldine was her own personal bank because of the oil well. One day she approached her mother about building a house for her, and Geraldine told her there was nothing wrong with the trailer they'd purchased for her little family.

Christine complained that she hated the trailer, that it wasn't as nice as a house, throwing out wishes for it to catch fire and burn to the ground.

Lo and behold, the trailer did burn to the ground. Geraldine was in shock when she found out it had burned. Terrified, she was constantly saying, "If they'd been in there when it caught fire... What happened?" They claimed they didn't know how it had happened. Christine cried on her shoulder, saying over and over how they'd lost everything. Charles and Charleen knew that she'd probably burnt the trailer down, but getting her mother to see that was just not in the cards. Now Geraldine feared their living in another trailer.

In 1989, she built them a nice Jim Walter house on the same two acres where the trailer had been. It was a beautiful three-bedroom home with new carpet, furniture, and appliances. All of this was done with the full agreement that they would pay the house note. Jerry worked out of town from time to time with an oil company in Louisiana, so money would not be a problem.

They let them live with the family while their house was being built. During this time, Christine went to cosmetology school and received her license. After eight months of training, she landed a job at the beauty shop next to the tanning salon. Charleen used to go in the beauty shop and talk with the girls who worked there. However, once she started working there, she stayed away. The thought of her right next door sickened Charleen, but she quietly maintained her thoughts and feelings.

From time to time, Frank would go over and have her trim his hair and catch up on the latest gossip. Christine was a beautiful girl, but she was lazy, ballooning up to an enormous size. She would flirt with any man who walked by. The sight of her flaunting around town sickened Charleen because she knew how atrocious she really was. Jerry worked in another state, leaving Christine and the baby alone for weeks at a time. Geraldine and Charles tended to her needs and wants just so she didn't have to struggle. Her mother tried to keep her pleased in every way possible, but one day she snapped.

Chapter **17**
Labor Day Pains

September 1990, on Labor Day weekend, rolls of sweat ran down Geraldine's face as she set up the backyard for a barbecue. The loud sound of locusts screeching from the tall pine trees drove her crazy, and she fussed at their sounds.

Eleven-year-old Prunella was running around the house, singing to the country music that played loudly. She jumped on and off the furniture, for she was a naturally high-strung little girl. Geraldine had given up trying to keep her from doing such, for it kept her entertained enough to stay out from under her feet.

At 10:30, Oliver and Mary and their two boys were expected to help her start cooking. Charles had a short route to do, so he let Frank have the day off. The phone rang, and it was Charleen, saying, "Hey, does Prunella want to stay with me this weekend?"

"You want me to put her on the phone?"

Suspecting that she was talking to her big sister, Prunella swung over the back of the couch and leaned for the phone. "Hey, Sissy!"

"Hey, little bug, do you want to stay with me this weekend? Janet will be with us. You remember her, don't you?"

Not thinking, she just nodded her head yes, as if Charleen could see her.

"That's my little cousin. Remember? Uncle Mark's daughter?"

Prunella finally answered and was so excited, knowing she was going to stay with her big sister that weekend. The room filled with energy. Her little body was like a flesh bullet bouncing in a rubber room.

Time passed and soon everyone was there except Christine and Jerry. Geraldine had called her several times, but there was no answer. She hung up the phone for the last time and turned to everyone. "I don't know where she is, and I'm tired of calling."

Charleen had been holding some information that she thought Charles would want to know, but she didn't want to express it to anyone else. She waited until her father was at the grill, maintaining the heat on the sizzling meats. She eased over to him and whispered, "Daddy, I've got to tell you what I heard the other day."

He gave her a smile and whispered back, "What is it?"

"I heard they have not paid a house note in six months. I also haven't seen her at work for about two weeks now."

"What?" Realizing he was loud, he waved her into the house where no one could hear them.

Once they were inside, she began, "Well, Julie and Karen at the beauty salon where Christine works asked me if I knew what was going on. Julie told me she'd gotten a few phone calls from a loan company looking for her," she exhaled a sigh as she placed her feminine hand on his shoulder. "I hope she hasn't messed up and lost the house and the land."

Charles's face turned blood red as thoughts stirred in his mind. He shook his head, saying, "Oh, that conniving bitch! Sorry for the curse word."

"No need to apologize for that, Daddy. Besides, she is one."

He was chomping at the bit to tell Geraldine what he had just heard, but he looked at her and decided not to tell her yet, for she was having a wonderful time playing dominoes with Oliver, Frank, and Russell. He turned back to Charleen. "Are you sure?"

She placed her hand over her heart, saying, "I swear that's what they told me. I hope it's not true."

As they walked back outside, Charles said, "Don't say anything to anybody. I've got to figure out how to tell her mama that she just might be losing those two acres with the house."

Both gave a half smile as they parted from one another. Frank had been watching the expression on both of their faces as they came outside. He was curious about what they'd talked about, but she assured him it was of no importance. She then went to play with Prunella, Janet, and Gregory on the swing at the edge of the yard as Frank went back to his chair.

Dusk was falling on the Labor Day gathering, and Oliver and his family were pulling out of the driveway just as Christine and Jerry were pulling in.

Charles looked at Geraldine. "We have got to talk."

The door of the truck squeaked open, and Christine adjusted her heavy body in the truck and called out, "What do you have left to eat?"

"Well, just where have your butts been? Almost everybody is gone already except Charleen and Frank, and they are about to leave with Prunella."

Just as she spoke, they walked out of the house with a happy Prunella and Janet. Christine saw them and sat back down in the truck seat. Charleen walked over to Frank's car and placed two wrapped plates of food on the seat. She then went over to her daddy and gave him a kiss and a hug. "I love you, Daddy. I'll see you later. I'm going to get these girls to the house. I promised them that we would play some board games and dress up like rock stars—you know, act silly!"

Suddenly Geraldine remembered. "Wait! Wait one minute." She ran into the house and returned with an envelope in hand. As she started to hand it over to Charleen, she quickly pulled it back. "I know it's early, but I just couldn't wait. When I heard she was gonna be close by, I jumped a pair."

Charleen's eyes lit up as she looked in the envelope and gazed at two tickets to a Melissa Etheridge concert in Mobile, Alabama, on November 4, just twenty-three days before her birthday! She was so excited that she began to jump up and down. "Oh, *you* are coming with me!"

Giving her a big smile, Geraldine said, "I was hoping you would say that. I love the raw sound of her voice. It just seems to fix my spirit. There's passion in them vocals."

Prunella squeezed into the crimson-red passenger seat of the Corvette with Janet as she said, "I'm gonna have a car like this one day." She grinned, exposing some new teeth and some of the leftover silver teeth. Charleen, who now sat in the driver's seat of the Corvette, pulled a Tinkerbell keychain from her bright-yellow purse and placed the key in the ignition. Then, peering over at Prunella, she repeated, "I'm gonna have this car one day, ain't I Sissy?"

Charleen tossed her head back in laughter as she looked at her father, who'd heard what Prunella had said. "What can I say? She has the Corvette fever. You're gonna have to get her one, Daddy." She gave him a big smile as she cranked the car and pulled away.

Frank followed right behind her. Christine didn't want to get out while they were there, so she and Jerry stayed in the truck until they were gone. Geraldine spotted her grandson Donovan in the middle of his parents. Reaching her arms out to him, she said in her sweet, raspy grandma voice, "Come here, my little boo-boo."

Charles wanted to jump in and ask them questions, but he thought to himself, *I'm going to take some time and feel these two out.* He then put on a hospitable face and turned on his charm. "Get out. Y'all might have missed everyone else, but there is plenty of food in the house."

Christine slid her hefty body around in the truck preparing to get out and asked, "What was that all about, Mama?" When Geraldine acted as if she hadn't heard the question, Christine pulled her stretchy green shorts down from around her thighs and huffed, "Whatever!"

"Come here, my baby boy. Mama is taking too long to get you out of this hot truck," Geraldine said as she lifted him up, giving the two-year-old boy slobbery kisses.

"Oh my God, Mama. You can have him. He's been getting on my nerves. So are you going to tell me what that was all about with Charleen? What did you give her?"

"Oh, it was nothing," she answered nonchalantly.

"Oh really! So she has just started losing some screws and jumping up and down at the sight of white paper?" Her face became red.

Charles spoke up, "It was concert tickets to see Melissa Etheridge." Christine didn't want to say anything derogatory to him about Charleen, but she knew she was going to badger her mother about it later. "Oh, okay. Well, that's nice." She then turned her frustrations to her mother, who had accidently bumped into her as she shifted her grandson on her hip. "Oh my God! It's too hot, and your sweaty skin keeps touching me. I can't stand that feel. Yuck!"

"Get over it," Geraldine spouted over her shoulder. "Come on in here and get you something to eat and cool off that attitude."

Jerry got out of the truck and told her to calm down as he followed her toward the house. Just before Geraldine stepped in the door, Charles called out to her, "Come here a second."

She mumbled to them to help themselves to the food and stepped to the edge of the carport saying, "What, Charles?"

In a loud whisper, he said, "I heard they ain't paid a house note in six months."

"Oh! Come on now! You know you can't believe rumors."

He tried to shush her by waving his hand, and whispered, "Charleen told me."

She then took the news seriously. She looked back at the house and stepped closer to him, saying, "Now say what?"

"Yes. She told me the girls at the salon said she is supposed to be working, but she ain't been, and a loan company has been calling them, looking for her."

Her face turned red as the anger rose inside of her. "I'll kill her! After all we've done for her!"

"Now, calm down. Don't get crazy. Let's find out first."

They both walked in the house where the others were stuffing their faces. Geraldine sat Donovan down in the living room and gave him a few toys as she said, "Oh yeah, Christine. I was going to come by the shop this past Thursday and get you to fix these gray curls of mine." Jerry choked on his bite of chicken at what she had said. "What's the matter, Jerry? Y'all starvin'? You might want to slow down before it kills ya."

Christine paid no attention to the comment and displayed all-too-much interest in the care of Jerry as he coughed up the chicken. As she continued her deceptive display of concern for her husband, Geraldine could see right through her twenty-one-year-old daughter. She had not grown up any. She walked over to the refrigerator, plucked a can of soda from the door, popped the top, and sat it down in front of a skinny, pale Jerry. He was sweating profusely, and it wasn't from choking. "Here! Drink this. See if that will help wash down some of that bullshit you two were gonna tell me."

"Mama, we have only missed a couple of payments. I was gonna tell you...Who told you?"

Her mother sat across from her at the kitchen table, folded her arms, and huffed. "What does a 'couple' mean?" It was as if Jerry had lost his appetite. He pushed his plate back, staring at his wife, who could no longer look at her mother. He hung his head in shame. The only thing he was thankful for at that moment was that Charles's view of him was obstructed by Geraldine.

"So what about work, you two?"

"Fine! I quit my job, and he works on and off now. I quit because my feet hurt. I can't stand on my feet all the time, and them girls wouldn't let me sit down. I don't know why they did it."

She continued to make one excuse after another, but her mother couldn't hear her because her ears were numb from hearing her nonsense. Charles continued to keep silent, for he let his wife handle these dealings.

Geraldine came back to her senses. "What about them foreclosing on the house?"

Jerry got up from the table to walk out, and Christine yelled, "Where the hell do you think you're going?" He turned to look at her with a knowing look, for he knew of the many trips to McDonald's and everywhere else their money had gone. It was not an argument he wanted to have, so he turned back around and walked out.

Geraldine didn't try to stop him; it was Christine she wanted to hear from. She gave her a cold, hard stare and lowered her head as if she were a bull about to charge. In a deep baritone voice, she asked, "Are you being foreclosed on?"

Christine jumped from the table and shouted, "It's none of your business!" She ran over and picked her son up from the living room floor. When she got to the door, Geraldine blocked her path with a poked-out chest, as if she could wrestle her to the ground. She looked down at her short, hefty daughter. "I can't believe you! I go out on a limb for you, and this is how you repay me? You know we lose those two acres of land when they foreclose on the house!"

"Well, y'all have enough money, and y'all still have eight acres. You two have done more for Charleen and Prunella anyway. Y'all don't ever do nothing with me anymore."

"Look here, missy—" she began.

"Oh, get out of my way!" Pushing past her, they stormed out the door.

"Don't bring your little family here!" Geraldine yelled out the door.

Christine stopped and turned around. "Well, where will we go?"

Placing her hands on her hips, and in a stance reminiscent of Stella, she spoke loudly, "Your daddy's! I don't care. I'm tired of your shenanigans!"

"Well, I'm going to college in the fall to get my nursing license."

At that, Geraldine stopped, then shouted out, "Now, you know you'll have to be on your feet!" Then she stepped back, grabbed the door, and slammed it as she turned to Charles. "Where did I go wrong?"

Chapter **18**

Opening Old Wounds

The sound of the phone ringing traveled down the hallway to Prunella and Charles. She left his bedside to answer it. She would have to leave him to go pick up his medication. She had asked him if he wanted her to call someone to sit with him. Not wanting to be considered feeble, he had declined her offer, asking her to leave him there alone. All he wanted was to lie down on his couch in the living room. She reluctantly left him alone and raced to the pharmacy to pick up his medication.

She had only been gone for a few minutes when he heard the metal carport door rattling. At first he thought it was Prunella, but she never came in. This startled him, so he got up from the couch and shuffled slowly over to the door. As he looked out, he saw a familiar pair of blue eyes and bright blonde hair. It was Christine.

"What do you want?" he said gruffly.

"Open the door. I just come to check on ya."

"I'm all right. Prunella is taking care of me," he answered sternly.

"Oh, come on now. I just want to check on you."

"You've checked. Now go away!"

There was the sound of the metal door slamming shut, then silence. He was afraid to look out the door's window again. His mind raced, remembering the back door was unlocked. Though weak, he found enough strength to pull himself as quickly as possible toward the back door. After balancing on furniture and counters, he finally got there, locked it, and leaned up against it to rest. Knowing his legs were on the verge of collapse, he had the thought, *Oh, man. What have I got myself into? I've got to make it to the couch.*

He pushed himself from the door and started taking small steps. Just as he reached out for the arm of the couch, Charles fell to the floor. Unable to move on the golden quartz floor, his piercing blue eyes slowly closed. A familiar voice called him from above. He thought, *Oh, no! I can't go now. What about Prunella? I can't leave her.*

***

Charles could feel November's cold nipping at his ears. He was standing outside his home watching Geraldine skin a deer. She turned to him. "Well, are you gonna light me one?" He pulled a pack of cigarettes from his coat pocket. Lighting two of them, he placed one between her lips. She took a drag of it, then removed it from her lips with her bloody fingers.

Charles cringed. "Yuck! I don't know how you can do that." He loved to hunt and eat the game, but he could not stand the sight or touch of the innards of his kill. He was glad she could clean what he killed.

At that moment, she said, "You had better be glad I don't have a problem with this, 'cause then you'd have to give up hunting."

"I don't think so, woman, 'cause I'd just get some little fella to do it and pay him in meat." He then gave her a laugh. They got a kick out of taunting each other.

Over his shoulder, she saw a car pulling into the driveway. With her cigarette dangling from her mouth, she nudged him with her elbow and nodded her head in that direction. He turned around and said, "Who is that? I don't recognize that car."

When it pulled up to the house, the door opened and Christine stepped out. She removed the cigarette from her lips and yelled out, "Where'd you get that nice thang?"

"Come look at it!" she yelled back with a smile.

Geraldine slung the knife into the tree that the deer hung from. Charles was taken aback and smiled remembering Prunella Jackson doing that same thing while cleaning his kills. Christine looked a bit slender in her colorful nursing scrubs. She seemed fashionably in tune with herself for once. A newfound happiness dwelt inside her, for she was working at Golden Meadows and renting a small two-bedroom home in town. And now she had a nice car to drive.

She proudly ran her hand down the opened, ice-cream-white car door and patted the dark-blue vinyl top, saying, "Daddy gave it to me when I started my job." She sat back down in the white buttery leather seats and ran her hands around the dark-blue steering wheel cover and added, "Check this luxurious Lincoln out. I love this car."

Geraldine leaned down to look around inside the car. She wanted to reach out and touch it, but her hands were still bloody from skinning the deer. Unable to see inside well, she walked around to the passenger side, using one clean finger to open the door. She gazed across the blue dash and said, "Hmm...not one crack. Not even a stain on the carpet or a tear in the seat. Just look at that wood-grain paneling. How old is it?"

"Like six years, I think."

Charles walked around the car taking a good look at it. About that time, Prunella came outside. She was thirteen now and had developed into a beautiful girl. Her face was tastefully made up, and her clothes were as stylish as Charleen's. They both possessed the same beautiful, petite, model-ish natural beauty.

Christine saw her and curled her lip in disgust. "Well, aren't you just the cream of the crop? Look at my car."

She could feel the tension coming from her, but to pacify her, Prunella replied, "Oh, you are looking beautiful today." Then she opened the back door and sat down. She looked around, then stretched out on the large back seat. As they talked, she interrupted, "Wow! You could sleep in this car!"

Christine turned around and snapped, "Just what's that supposed to mean?"

Prunella sat up quickly. "What's your problem?"

"YOU!"

Prunella jumped out of the car and marched back inside the house. Their mother tried to diffuse the situation, telling her to calm down, that it meant nothing. In the same breath, she asked if she was coming to Charleen's birthday supper tomorrow.

"Damn!" Christine snapped again. "I can't have good news because y'all always want to tell me something about Charleen. Can't I be of some importance?"

"You are important to me."

Charles didn't stay to listen to her anymore. She offended his good taste and moral sense, so he just turned and walked back to the half-skinned deer. Christine cranked the car and told her mother to get out, so Geraldine pulled her body back and, uncaring of her bloody hand, thrust the door shut.

Christine rolled down the passenger window. "You think he loves you? Hmm...Everybody talks about y'all in town. You're just a rebound to him, Mama!" After boldly speaking like that, she quickly backed out in fear of what her mother might do, casting dust and rocks as she took off around the small circular drive to the highway.

The next day was Charleen's thirty-first birthday. It was 4:00 a.m. and Charles was sitting at the kitchen table, fully dressed in his uniform. While drinking his coffee, he called her so he could be the first to cheerfully say, "Hey, sugar plum, happy birthday!" giving her a laugh as he added, "Did I wake you up? I would apologize for it, but I'm your daddy. I wanted to make sure you heard "happy birthday" from me first."

She gave him her sleepy appreciation and assured him she was just about to get up. He reminded her that she was to come to his house around 5:00 p.m. He chuckled as he hung up the phone, saying to his wife, who had just walked into the kitchen for a cup of coffee, "You'd think Frank would take off today. Hmm...I guess she is keeping him on his toes."

Charles knew Frank had used Charleen before as an excuse to skip work by saying she was sick. He was quite happy with him taking off when it came to her—even though it wasn't always true.

Delighted, he arrived at the enormous, sprawling Milk Company. As Charles passed through the gates and made his turns, he continuously tried to look at himself in the large truck mirrors to check his silvering Elvis hairstyle. Although the darkness of the early morning prohibited a good look, he knew his hair was still in place. Singing along to the country music playing on his radio, he backed the truck up to the loading dock, jumped out, and started talking to the guys standing on the dock.

Meanwhile, Frank had spotted him as he sat in his warm car in the parking lot. He got out and began walking to the dock. Hearing the scuffs of Frank's boots on the pavement, Charles turned to see him walking up bundled in a brown leather coat, holding a Styrofoam cup in one hand while the other hand was stuffed far down into his tight faded-out jeans pocket. He struggled in the cold draft of the wind as he clung to what heat he had soaked up from his warm car and fussed over the November winds, which tossed his long, curly dark-brown hair around his face. Charles just shook his head as he watched his son-in-law go into the office.

The truck was loaded, so he climbed in and waited for Frank. As he sat there, the sun started to light up the morning. The glimmering sparkles of the morning light reflected off the frosty dew of the grass. It was peaceful staring out the window, gazing at all the milk trucks sporting a large smiling cow on their sides. He loved that cow. She seemed to make his day brighter. His thoughts drifted to his birthday present for Charleen. She loved horses, and he had bought her a solid-gold horse statue. It represented the strength she possessed in her life and in her business. Lord knows he had spent a lot of money on it, but he couldn't wait to give it to her.

Frank brought Charles's thoughts back quickly as he opened the truck door. He didn't make eye contact with him; he just looked straight forward. Charles felt something wasn't right, for he noticed the distinctive colorless look on Frank's face. "What's wrong?"

He turned slowly to him. "Charleen didn't answer the phone, and I've called like three times."

His smile dropped as he yelled, "Get out! Go home! I'm right behind you."

Within minutes, Frank pulled into his driveway, screeching into their carport next to the Corvette. Charles pulled up in the milk truck and slammed on the brakes in front of the brick home and saw the Corvette under the carport. A gut-wrenching feeling hit him, like thirty-one knives piercing him at once. "Oh, no! God, no!" The worst fear cast lightning speed into his fifty-seven-year-old body. He quickly switched off the engine, grabbed his keys, and ran to the front door.

They always had a key to one another's houses. He opened the red front door, shaking the fall wicker wreath as he slammed it behind him. He leapt across the soft, light carpet of the living room like a professional dancer whose feet never seemed to touch the ground, because he knew how she felt about shoes on the carpet.

As he entered the hall, he could see the bathroom where Frank held a half-wet, limp Charleen on the floor next to the tub. Her long, bouncy blonde hair was now darkened by the tub water. The loud sound of water being vigorously sucked down the drain echoed off the light tiled walls of the small bathroom. He had begun CPR, pressing furiously on her small-framed chest. Beneath her damp nightgown top, her heart lay still and unresponsive. Charles ran to the yellow telephone that hung in the kitchen and dialed 9-1-1. He stretched the long cord into the narrow hallway so he could see the bathroom.

Frank, now out of breath, looked up at him and stuttered, "She... she..."

Charles fell to his knees, allowing the phone to slip from his hands. He crawled to his baby girl's side as Frank picked up the phone. He gently touched her face, blistered red from the hot water in the tub. He yelled out, "What happened to my baby?"

"I don't know. It looks like she had a seizure. Guess she was cleaning the tub and fell in. I turned the hot water off when I got here. There was a washcloth clogging the hole."

Charles looked over into the tub, where the last bit of water was circling the drain. As he held her lifeless body, he felt his whole body being pulled down, as if the drain were sucking him down with the last drop of water. A cloak of darkness covered him as he began to feel squeezed and compressed. He felt the struggle in his eyes to find a source of light. Panic began to run through him, and he found it difficult to breathe. He whispered to himself, "This is it. I am done for."

Once he released the words from his ghostly lips, he began to see light again and thought, *Yep, I'm done.*

***

The light grew brighter, and he began to hear his daughter Prunella calling him.

He couldn't see her and kept asking, "Where are you?"

"Oh, Daddy! Please open your eyes."

Chapter **19**

Learning the Truth

Charles was still lying on the cold floor with Prunella kneeling beside him. He struggled to come to, and when he finally did, his voice merged with his body again. He mumbled, then sputtered until a loud cry rang from him, "My Charleen died too young! She was supposed to be burying me!"

Prunella burst into tears, for she knew where his mind had taken him. She latched onto her father, hugging him tightly, as he lay folded unconventionally on the floor. His right arm had lost all of its color, as the weight of his body had been on it. She quickly released him and rolled him over slowly. "Are you all right? Are you hurt?" She was so afraid that he had broken something that she demanded, "Daddy, don't move. Lie still!"

He huffed and puffed with determination to get up as she shifted him around on the floor. "I'm fine," he said. "Help me sit up, love."

"What happened, Daddy? Why are you on the floor?" She lifted him up with her small but strong frame and placed him on the loveseat. "Daddy, what were you thinking? I should have called someone to stay with you." As she sat next to her father, Prunella hunkered over and put her face in her hands. With her elbows braced on her knees, her long blonde hair covered her face and hands.

He lifted his hand to her hair and gently pulled it back to expose her face, and said, "Look at me." She turned to look at him with her moist, swollen blue eyes. "What do you think about Frank?"

It was as if lightning had shot up her back and down her legs, causing her to jump to her feet. Nervous thoughts ran through her head as she scampered to the kitchen to fix a glass of sweet tea.

"Prunella, do you think I should leave him any money?"

She quickly returned to him with a glass and his new medication. She handed him the glass, then fumbled with the medicine bottle cap. She was in such deep fear of telling him what she knew about Frank. Being overly focused on not wanting to tell him what she knew caused her to aggressively press on the bottle cap, spilling red capsules all over the floor.

He looked at her as she stood there with her hands shaking, and said, "What in the world is wrong with you? Look at your hands, child. You are trembling."

She shook her head and said, "Oh, look at me. I've made a complete mess of your medication." She bent down and began to pick up the pills and put them back in their bottle.

Charles leaned over and touched her on her back. "You know something, don't you?"

She couldn't hold it in any longer. Seething the words through her teeth, she said, "I hate him! Yes, I do, Daddy!"

Charles felt the power behind the look in her eyes. He took a big swallow of his tea, then said, "Okay, Prunella. Spill it!"

She scooted her legs out from under her and sat Indian-style with her arms straightened, tightly gripping her knees, then said, "Okay. It makes me sick to have to tell you this, but here goes." She took him carefully back to the night of September 1, 1990.

***

They had left the Labor Day barbecue at Charles's house and headed to Charleen's for a sleepover. Shimmering light from the Corvette's curves streaked down the highway. Prunella's hot, sticky, bruised-up legs kept touching thirteen-year-old Janet Shaw's fuller legs. As they sat tightly together in the passenger seat, Janet complained, "Move over. You're taking up the whole seat." But Prunella couldn't sit still, especially with the sounds of Melissa Etheridge playing loudly from the radio. Finally, they arrived at the house.

They walked through a breezeway to the backyard where two fully grown dogs were fenced in, greeting them with happy barks while Charleen unlocked the back door. When they went over to pet the dogs, Frank pulled up and walked around back to where they were. When the dogs saw him, they began to bark happily again. Without speaking a word, he snapped his fingers at the dogs, commanding them to be quiet. They hushed and obeyed perfectly as they lay down.

After not finding any further joy in the dogs, they went in the house. When it started to get dark and everyone was settling in for the night. Prunella jumped up and suggested loudly, "Let's play dress-up rock stars!"

Charleen happily agreed. The girls pulled out the makeup and some crazy clothing that she no longer wore. The sounds of loud music bumped in the house as they laughed, played, and sang until it was bedtime. They went to sleep in the spare bedroom.

About 3:00 a.m. Frank came tiptoeing into the spare bedroom where Prunella and Janet slept. He carefully placed his hand over Janet's mouth, for her eyes popped open instantly. She looked wide-eyed at him. "Shush...come with me," he whispered.

188

She felt scared and confused as he led her from the comforts of the bed, down the hallway, through the living room, and unlocked the back door. Not turning on any lights, Frank opened the back door and went outside with a frightened Janet. Just as she said, "Where are we going?" the dogs barked loudly. He instantly snapped his fingers, giving the command to be quiet. As usual, the two dogs obeyed, circled around and lay down quietly. He led her into the dog yard and told her to get into the large blue doghouse that sat in the middle of the dog yard. She refused, saying, "No. It's dark in there. There might be spiders and snakes." Frank shushed her once more as he looked back at the house for signs of movement. Seeing it quietly resting in the wee hours of the morning, he pushed her to the opening of the doghouse. Janet began to cry, for she knew this was not normal. She began to beg him to not make her go in there. He just pushed harder to make her get in. Once she was in, he took one more look at the house, then climbed in with her.

She sat there in the dark with him breathing heavily next to her, and she could feel the dry hay poking her bottom. She only had on a large blue t-shirt and cotton flowered panties. "What are we doing in here?"

As she released that question, he reached up to her flat chest and began to rub. He then rubbed himself. "You know what we are doing in here." Now he was rubbing her between her legs. "Take your panties off."

Janet shrieked with fear and began to cry heavily, pleading, "Please. Please, I don't want to."

He grabbed her face and gave it a squeeze. Only a slight hint of light came through the square opening of the dog house. He became more aggressive as he snatched at her panties, pulling them off. He returned his hand back between her legs and forcefully gave her sloppy, wet kisses on and around her mouth. The foul stench of alcohol replaced the smell of the dogs in the small space, for his breath and sweat reeked of it.

Prunella and Charleen slept soundly in the house as he pulled his manhood from his pants and forcefully took her childhood.

Two years of carrying around the unreasonable guilt of his contemptible pleasure twisted and disrupted Janet's psychological well-being. He had crushed her childhood dreams, leaving her struggling to understand relationships and sex. After much consideration, Janet decided it was time to confide in someone. It was Prunella's sixteenth birthday, and Janet told her everything. She released the horrible, foul truth about Frank. After telling her of his vulgarity, Janet added that he had tried to touch her again the day of Charleen's funeral. Sickened by what she had been told, Prunella knew he was capable of doing this, as he had overstepped his bounds with her also.

***

Charles wept as Prunella told him of those filthy things. He struggled to fully comprehend the false perception he'd had of Frank. His baffling, morbid behavior disgusted him, and with dread he asked, "Has he ever put his hands on you?"

"Daddy, I didn't want to tell you this, but you really need to know what kind of man he really is." She took him back to a couple of months after Charleen's untimely death. Charles had told Frank on several occasions to come eat supper with the family so as not to be alone.

***

One day Prunella was sitting at the kitchen table playing cards with Frank and Geraldine. Charles was outside in his shop. Geraldine excused herself to go to the restroom, leaving the two of them alone in the kitchen. He leaned over and placed his hand on her inner thigh. Prunella pulled away from him, then stood up next to her chair to leave. Just as she was about to step away, Frank pulled her close to him and rubbed his penis on her leg, saying, "Oh, come on. Charleen would have wanted us to be together."

She instantly jerked away from him, saying, "That's gross!" She left him sitting alone at the table, but turned back and said, "You are sick!"

***

Prunella assured her father that, as far as sexual contact, he had never had the chance to do that again. She refused to be alone with him after that day. She then began to tell him of the meanness in Frank, giving him details of him blackening Charleen's eye one weekend and how he controlled her every move. He was a cheater, and Charleen had made Prunella promise never to say anything to their father. She didn't wanted him to know that she had made a mistake by marrying him. And knowing their father was a man of his word, "until death do you part" fell hard on her life.

All of these horrible things came to a conclusion in his spinning mind, and he turned to her again. "Do you think he could have killed her?"

She was unable to answer the question and just began to cry again. Finally she answered, "I know she was sick, but she was fine the day before. I overheard him telling Christine that he was tired of taking care of a patient. Daddy, I don't think he really loved her. I think he was all about her money and yours. I personally wouldn't give him air to breathe."

Charles burst out in tears. He ran his fingers through his already disarrayed gray hair, tangling it and flicking it with anger. He cried harder than he ever had. Prunella saw her father crying these painful tears, and it wrenched her heart. Angry fumes began to build up in him as he sat there bawling like a baby. He then quickly straightened up. "That sour bastard!" His tremulous thoughts of Frank formed into a deep hate for him. She could see the veins coming to life in her father's forehead as they bulged and pulsed with fury. He puffed up, spouting, "Damn it! Get my gun. I'm fixing to kill that..." As he scrambled to get up from the couch, furiously and truly intending to get his gun, the unsteadiness of his feet rendered him unbalanced, causing him to fall backward onto the couch. It momentarily knocked the wind out of him, and he struggled to catch his breath.

"Now, you need to slow down, Daddy, and take it easy. You're not going to kill anybody."

"If I wasn't on my deathbed, I'd sure try!" After sitting there in deep thought, he turned to her. "I should have pushed for them to do an autopsy. They ruled it as natural causes. Hell, I'm the one that told them she fell out a lot..." He paused, then added, "I know what it feels like to be looked at like that. I had thought about it before, but I shut myself down. But Prunella, what if..." He started feeling the effects of his new medication. "I think I need to go lie down in the bed."

She helped him up, and they slowly headed down the hallway to the bedroom. She asked him, "So what were you doing on the floor?"

"That spiteful sister of yours came over and wanted to check on me. I don't think it was me she was trying to check on," he answered breathily.

After slowly and carefully walking back to Charles's bedroom, she put him to bed and tucked the covers around him. She sat down, saying, "I remember the day I found out that Charleen died. I knew something was wrong by the look in your eyes, but Christine didn't give you time to tell me. She just blurted it out so cruelly, 'Charleen is dead.' All I could do was climb up the mulberry tree and cry."

"I remember that, Prunella," as he reached for her hand. "If it wasn't for your mother, I'd have slapped her, but I turned my attention to you."

"Sometimes I wonder if she didn't help him get rid of Mama. I do think that they fooled around, and she knew it. Daddy, it's possible that they did. She hated her and wished her dead before."

"Well, it makes sense to me now why Jerry beat the shit out of her the night of the funeral. They were whispering with one another at the funeral, and from the look on Jerry's face, he was suspicious of them. Your mama wanted me to go over and help her that night, but I refused."

They fell silent with their thoughts. She looked at the vintage 1950s brass alarm clock and saw that it was 4:30 p.m. "Daddy, I'm going to fix a little supper. You rest. Let that medication do its job. Do you want me to wake you if you fall asleep?" She stood up and started toward the door, turning around for his answer.

"I doubt I'll be falling asleep. My mind is too twisted."

She hung her head, then added, "I know, Daddy. Mine too. Charles lay there drifting in and out of consciousness, for the new medication brought him a little peace.

Chapter **20**

Changing Careers

Charles fell fast asleep thanks to the new medication. His mind took him back to April 1994, two years after Charleen's passing. He had found it more difficult to work the milk truck, for it carried a bad memory. Prunella had taken Frank's place with him on his route, but it didn't ease all the pain of losing her. His long-time friend Dan had opened a coffee shop in town close to Charleen's old tanning salon, and within the year, Frank closed the tanning salon and Dan gave him a job. Charles would go to the shop and check on him from time to time, but seeing him became difficult. Along with the loss of Charleen, memories began to resurface from that fatal night in 1975 when he lost Sharon. Deep down, he was suspicious about that morning he found her. He fought the thoughts, for he knew what it felt like to be scrutinized after losing a loved one. He kept his visits to the coffee shop to a bare minimum.

***

One day, he had a short milk route and made it home before 1:00 p.m. Geraldine had left a note for him that said, "Gone to town. Not sure when we'll be back. Love, Geraldine & Prunella."

He looked at the note, placed it on the table, and looked out the window into the backyard. The mulberry tree was loaded with berries, so he grabbed a bowl from the kitchen and headed out to the tree. While picking berries, he heard the sound of rocks crunching in the driveway, indicating that someone was pulling up. Loud music accompanied the sound, and he knew exactly who it was. It was Frank pulling up in the Corvette. He parked the car and got out. He looked horrible! His hair was a mess, his jeans were baggy, and his shirt was completely unbuttoned. He stumbled toward the carport door.

Charles called out to him from the backyard, "Hey! I'm back here!"

Frank instantly stopped, then spun around on his bootheels and followed his voice to the backyard. As Charles continued to pick mulberries, he noticed the wobbling of Frank's steps and the slur in his speech.

He turned to him and asked, "What have you been up to? Have you been hitting the bottle?"

Frank lowered his head, then nodded yes, while his lips said no.

Charles turned to him and, almost spilling the berries, said, "Boy, don't lie to me!" He walked over to Frank and leaned in to smell. He quickly pulled back to protect his nose. "Oh my goodness! You try to tell the police that, and I promise they ain't gonna believe you. Come on in here, and let's get a cup of black coffee in you."

He made them each a cup, and they sat at the kitchen table together. He leered at Frank and leaned closer to him, saying, "What in the hell are you doing out in that car drinking for, son? You know how dangerous that is? Well, you might be grown and can do what you want, but let me tell you this: my wife and daughter are in town somewhere. That means you could have met them on the road with that intoxicated vision of yours! Now, dammit, I've done lost both, and I ain't aiming to experience it again. Accidents happen. Don't let yourself wake up and regret things that you have done. Sometimes you can't take that shit back. So get to drinking that there cup of black joe." He then sat back in his chair, relieving Frank from the uncomfortable closeness of his face, and said, "Well, I'm going to get off my soapbox. So tell me: What have you been up to lately?"

Frank took a nervous sip of his coffee, lowered the mug carefully to the table, and slowly sat back with his arms folded. Charles looked at his hairy arms and his shirt, which strayed from his body loosely, squinted, and looked away from him. "Son, please button that shirt up and cover up that forest of fur."

He cleared his throat and buttoned up his shirt. "Is there any way I could pawn you the Corvette? I'm in need of a couple thousand dollars. I'll pay you back, I promise! If I don't, for some crazy reason, you can just keep the car."

Charles wanted to pry, but he felt that he shouldn't get into his personal business. He had to trust him to make a good decision, so he answered, "No problem." A large smile emerged from under his thick, graying, bristly mustache. Charles let him know right then that the car would be staying with him until he paid him back. "Well...how fast do you need this money?"

Frank took a deep breath and exhaled. "As soon as possible."

Charles placed his hands on the table. "Okay, let's go get that right now."

He quickly sat up straight in his chair and asked, "Are you serious?"

Charles slid his chair back, stood up, and gave him a wave. "Come on. Let's go get it."

They walked out to the beautiful 1981 metallic-pearl-white Corvette. Charles took a long look at the dazzling color. Charleen had had it custom-painted by a friend. Its once-shiny coat was now dulling with the days. He ran his hand along its side, streaking his finger along the crimson pinstripes. He walked around it. "Charleen surely loved this car."

Frank hung his head and climbed into the driver's seat as Charles walked over to the passenger side, not saying a word. Just as he was about to open the door, he saw a large, long dent down the side of the door. He sat down and, just before shutting the door, he looked over and asked, "So what happened to the outer door panel?"

"Accidentally slid up against a pole," Frank answered, adding no more detail.

"Seeing as how you downed two cups of black coffee, I'm gonna let you stay in that seat, but if you cross either the white line or the yellow line, I want you to pull over and get your ass out of that seat."

He cranked the car, forcing the gas pedal to the floor in order to give an extra roar to the powerful engine, grinning from ear to ear. He quickly backed up, and the spinning tires cast a cloud of dust as he flew out of the driveway and down the highway. Just as the guys disappeared out of sight, Geraldine and Prunella returned from their day in town with a car full of discounts. It didn't take them long in town, and after they conducted business, he dropped Frank off at his house.

Driving the Corvette for the first time, Charles slowly rode through town to get back home. He pulled out onto the highway and, first making sure no one was around, stomped the gas pedal to see what the car would do. This caused him to fishtail in the highway, almost landing in the ditch. He gasped as he quickly recovered the car back onto the road.

He thought, *Oh my God! There is just too much engine under this hood. If I'd known this, I'd have fought harder for her to find another car.*

Charles carefully made his way home. Upon his arrival, Prunella came out the door and asked, "What are you doing in that, Daddy?"

"It's mine for a little while. Frank will be back for it, though."

She climbed in the passenger seat with a smile and said, "You can just give it to me for my sixteenth birthday."

He took in a quick breath. "No way in hell! I can't in my right mind give you something like this. Shoot! If I'd known what power it had, well, I'd have told Charleen to find something else."

She looked down with disappointment. He reached over and placed his hand on top of her platinum-blonde hair. "Baby girl, it would make me a nervous wreck if you were in something like this."

"Okay, fine. I get it," and she changed the subject. "Oh, you have got to come see what me and Mama found today!"

He rolled up the windows and sighed, thinking, *Oh man! What now?*

Prunella ran inside the house ahead of her father. As he walked in the door, he saw box after box scattered around the kitchen and spilling over into the living room. Charles looked confused. He began to look in the boxes, picking up dented cans along with boxes of crackers, chips, and beef jerky. Some stuff was out of date but still good to eat.

"What is all of this?" he called out.

Geraldine came from the back room, and when she saw him hovering over the boxes, it made her smile. "Well? Did I do good or what? You wouldn't believe what I paid for all of this," she spoke proudly.

"How did you find this deal?"

She pulled a card from her purse and said, "I ran into a friend of yours that went to school with you." She handed him the card from Steven Miller.

"Old Shorty! How did you run across this cat? I ain't seen him in years!"

"Well, me and Prunella saw a new store in town that has sprung up since the last time we've been there, so we stopped to check it out." She paused to point at the card and continued, "That fella there asked me where I was from. Once I told him, he asked if I knew you. I laughed and told him, 'Sure, I know him. I married the old coot.' Well, he was so dang happy that when he was helping me load this stuff up—Oh yeah..." She ran to the back room and returned quickly with a medium-sized white box. She handed it to Charles, kissing him on his cheek and smiling. "I hope it still works. Like I was saying, that fella knocked that box out of the car seat pushing my boxes in while he was digging in his britches for that card you've got there."

He looked at the box. There wasn't a label on it. "What is this?" As he pulled at the ends opening the box, he pulled out a conventional scanner. He turned the two little black knobs, then flipped it around to read the writing in small black print.

201

Watching him squint to see the words, she blurted out, "It's a scanner. Now you can hear and talk to these fast log trucks on this highway. Tell them bastards to slow down, or I can."

He was delighted at the present she had gotten for him, but it was overshadowed by Shorty's card. He gave her a quick kiss of thanks. "I'm going to give him a holler." He grabbed the phone on the kitchen wall and stretched it into the front room. He still held the white box with the scanner inside. He placed it on the desk as he waited for Shorty's voice to come on the line.

"Hello."

"Hey, Shorty! How the hell are ya?" They talked for almost two hours until Geraldine told him it was suppertime.

The next day, he quickly ran his milk route so he could meet up with him at his store. When he saw him, he smiled and chuckled. Shorty was still small, barely reaching Charles's shoulders. He could see that the whole top of his head was almost bald.

"Damn! What happened to your hair?" he joked.

Shorty waved his hand at him as if to say "leave me alone," and said, "As usual, you've always had to mess with me. But this time I have to add, you're mighty gray yourself."

The men laughed at one another, then chatted about their lives. Shorty offered Charles a deal to buy him out and take over the discount store. His response was: "Hell, yes! I've been working that milk route for about thirty-two years now. It's about time I do something else." He walked delightedly around the store, taking in all the possibilities of profit.

As Charles dreamed of this memory, he began to feel his right shoulder shake. Then he heard Prunella's sweet, soft voice.

***

"Daddy? Do you want to eat?"

He opened his eyes to see his beautiful daughter standing there with a nice plate of food. He slowly turned to his side. She sat the plate on the nightstand, then helped him sit up.

"I'll be right back," she said and ran to the kitchen. She returned with a chair and a plate of food for herself and said, "I thought we could eat together." He loved the idea of them having a meal together. He was smiling as he poked at the beautiful food, and began to giggle.

She took great joy in seeing her father laughing and smiling. "What are you giggling about?

Charles looked up at her. "I was just thinking about your mama. Do you remember once I bought that store from my friend, Shorty? She loved it, didn't she?" He laughed a little harder, then added, "Yep, up till I messed up."

"Oh, Daddy! I know what you're talking about. I thought she was gonna kill you!"

"Yes, me too!"

They both laughed and began to share their thoughts and feelings about their beloved Geraldine.

Chapter 21

Getting Even

The milk truck sat in the yard collecting spiderwebs and dust. It was deserted because Charles had taken a big step by buying a discount grocery store, located fifteen minutes away from where he lived. Geraldine and Prunella were very happy that he had bought it, for pallets upon pallets of assorted foods would come in the side bay of the large red-brick building, and once those pallets came in, they would open them up. Geraldine anticipated it like Christmas. Prunella loved the fact that she actually got to make money. He kept her apprised of all the business dealings. He taught her how to work hard, and he loved having her around. She was the best help he had ever had, and she caught on very quickly. He could leave to tend to things in town, and she would hold down the fort.

Geraldine found that the store took up a lot of his time, leaving her to maintain everything at home. Loving the silence around the house, she kept it in order: mowing the grass, playing in her flower beds, and keeping the laundry fresh and making sure Charles's clothes were snazzy and perfectly laced with starch, just the way he liked it.

One day when Charles was in a rush to get to the store, he ran out and cranked his truck, then flew back in the house. Geraldine was standing at the door, holding what he had come back in for. "You was about to forget it," she said as she handed him his cell phone and gave him a kiss goodbye.

Minutes after he had left for work, she felt the need to take down the dusty, out-of-date living room curtains and make a new set out of the fabric he had bought for her. She took them in the front room that served as an office for him and a sewing room for her. She began to work with the new material. Wrestling with it, she started to get frustrated as it kept slipping off her sewing table. In disgust, she threw it on the floor and flung herself back into her chair and quickly sat back up, propping her elbows onto the table with her fingers folded around her face. She sat there for a few moments stroking her pinky finger around her bottom lip and then muttered, "Freaking fabric!"

Geraldine picked up her pack of Winston cigarettes and lit one as she looked around the room in frustration. It was cluttered with stuff from Charles's milk deliveries; he had kept every invoice since the day he started. She said out loud, "And he thinks I don't know how to throw away anything...hmm." Her eyes stopped on the white box with the scanner in it, thinking, *Why didn't he hook this up? Maybe he just hasn't had time. Oh well, I'll see if I can do it for him.*

Geraldine pulled the scanner from the box and dropped the instructions on the floor. As she picked them up, she yelled, "Prunella, come here and help your mama."

She came into the room to find her mother fumbling around with the scanner and asked, "What are you doing, Mama?"

"I thought it'd be a nice surprise to hook this thang up for your daddy, seeing as how he's always so busy," she said, handing her the instructions. "Here. See if they make any sense to you."

Prunella read over them and immediately understood how to make the scanner work. She plugged it up, turned knobs, and set the dial. Instantly, they heard a man's voice.

Geraldine stopped what she was doing. "Turn that up!"

The male voice said, "Hey there, darling. Yep, I just left the house. I pulled over to call you. I'll be there in just a few minutes or so."

A cross look weighed heavily on Geraldine's face. She knew that voice, and she stiffened her posture like she always did when she was extremely pissed. The voice of the male that waved through the scanner told her exactly who it was. She immediately jumped up and grabbed her purse and keys, saying to a stunned Prunella, "Get in the car, girl!"

She flung her purse over her shoulder and slammed the house door as she walked out. Stomping to her 1991 Ford Crown Victoria LX that Charles had bought for her, she threw her purse in the seat.

"Hey! Watch where you're throwing that thang. You hit me with it!"

"I'm sorry." She cranked the car and backed out so fast that the tires squealed on the carport floor and spun down the driveway, angrily casting dust into the air.

Prunella wasn't quite sure why her mother was so upset. "Mama, what's going on?"

She slammed her hand on the steering wheel a few times and lit another cigarette, saying loudly, "Your daddy is slipping out on me, and I'm about to bust his ass!" With that, she put the gas pedal to the floor.

Prunella knew to keep her mouth shut because the shit was about to hit the fan. Her daddy was in deep crap. Meanwhile, the words from the scanner fueled Geraldine, ringing in her ears and making her drive faster. She yelled out again, "I'm gonna kill him, that bastard! I'm gonna kill him!" Those were the only words she spoke clearly. Prunella struggled to understand the rest of her rambling, angry rant. The 302 V8 engine propelled the silver car down the highway like a large, screaming bullet. Hot tires burnt the road as she quickly swerved in and out of lanes, cutting corners and running stop signs. She continued flying through town undetected by the police. When they got closer to the store, she could see her mother's knuckles turn white as she gripped the steering wheel harder.

She prayed silently, "Oh, Lord! Please don't let Daddy be there with someone." Her silent prayer was in vain. When they pulled into the parking lot, there he stood talking to a younger petite, dark-haired female in front of the store. He didn't spot them because he was so engrossed with the woman.

Geraldine parked a few cars away, with the engine running, and lit another cigarette, then sat back to watch him with this woman. She could tell from his posture that he was flirting with her. Too many questions ran in her mind: *What is he doing? Why is he with this woman? Just who is this little biddy?*

Although she didn't approve of what he was doing, Prunella wished she could warn her father that her mother was watching him.

Geraldine bit her bottom lip, chewing it as she grunted and mumbled, "Just what the hell does he think he is doing?"

Prunella sat there wondering what she should do for a bit and then unbuckled her seat belt, reached for the door handle, and started to open it as she said, "I'll go talk to him."

Geraldine grabbed her arm. "No, you stay here with me."

She quickly released the door handle. "All right. So what then?"

Sticking another cigarette in between her lips, she looked up to see Charles reach up and touch the woman's cheek. At that very instant, anger raged in her foot, causing it to stomp the gas pedal. The powerful torque of the engine rocked the car. As she revved up the large engine, she yelled, "Buckle up!" Prunella could see that she was about to take off, so she scrambled for her seatbelt and latched it fast. Geraldine let the cigarette hang from her lips as she gripped the steering wheel, pretending to strangle him. She jerked the car into drive and stomped the gas pedal, while letting out a loud grunt past her clenched teeth and tightly lipped, hanging cigarette. "Oh, hell no!"

When he looked up to see what all the commotion was about, he recognized the car and pushed the young woman to the side, yelling, "Run!" He quickly jumped into his truck, and the woman ran to her car, which was parked four cars away, and sped off. As he heard Geraldine's tires spin out toward him, he braced himself, for he just knew she was about to slam into his nice candy-apple-red Ford F-250, but she slammed on the brakes just as she got close to the side of the truck.

Charles rolled down his window and yelled, "Are you crazy, woman?"

She stuck her head out and nodded. "You know it!" She then backed up quickly, putting a little distance between them. Then she just sat there looking at him, and he looked at her. He could see the look in her eyes and tried to crank the truck fast, but he had to wait for the diesel glow light to go out before it would crank. Before he could get it cranked, she was squealing her tires, heading straight for his truck. Just as it cranked, her car slammed into the side of his truck. Sweat beads formed on his forehead as he stomped on the gas, making screeching and scraping sounds as he tried to get away from Geraldine's heavy luxury car. His truck was pinned against the curb by her car.

Prunella yelled at her mother to stop, but she didn't seem to hear her. As his truck became loose, she gave chase right behind him. They screeched out of the parking lot and flew down the road. He stopped at a red light. As he sat there wondering what to do, she slammed into the back of his truck. In fear, he ran the red light. This didn't stop her, for she was still going after him. Crossing through the intersection, they both barely missed a few cars. About a mile down the road, her car bellowed smoke from the front end, which did nothing to deter her. She continued to chase him through town, cursing him with every breath. Within a matter of seconds, two police cars joined the chase. As their lights and sirens flickered and screamed behind her, she did not submit to their warning to stop. Finally the car started losing power, and she had to pull over.

Prunella was crying her eyes out, for she feared for both of her parents. She was just sure that her mother was going to kill her father. Grateful that the car had stopped, she lashed out at her mother: "You've lost your mind!"

Right then the two officers ran up to the car with their weapons drawn, yelling for Geraldine to get out with her hands in the air. She complied with their demands and was soon handcuffed and sitting in the back of one of the patrol cars. Prunella continued to sit in the smoking car until one of the police officers told her to get out. She instantly started explaining the situation of her mother catching her father with another woman. The officers were upset with her for her actions, but had trouble keeping straight faces as the complete story unfolded. One of the men snickered as he asked, "Where is your father now?"

With a frantic look of deep concern, Prunella replied, "At home, I'm sure."

"Well, we are going to have to have you come down to the station with your mother and call your father."

Her mind began to fill with fear for her mother because her father was the only one that could get her mother out of jail, and he was the one being hunted. Once at the police station, Geraldine was placed into a cell. The officers explained to Prunella that they would have to arrest her father, too. They didn't want to, but told her, "Well, our switchboard lit up like a Christmas tree." Just as the officer finished, in walked her father, escorted by another police officer.

He tried to run to Prunella, but the officer pulled back on his arm, so he just said, "Are you okay, baby girl?"

"I'm fine, Daddy. What about you?"

He gave her a half-hearted grin and said, "Okay, I guess."

Charles was charged with leaving the scene of an accident, and Geraldine was charged with malicious mischief. Once they were let go, they rode quietly back to the house in the beat-up truck.

***

They sat in the bedroom laughing at the incident as they gave thanks that nothing major had happened to any of them physically. He burst out, "I wish I had known those things picked up cell phone conversations! You know, your mother never did my clothes again after that day. Shoot! I had to take all of them to the cleaners from them on just to get the starch like I like it."

"Yep, Daddy. She told me she wasn't gonna touch another pair of your drawers."

Both were laughing until Charles stopped and said, "I'm so sorry. I shouldn't have been slipping out on your mama. She was an amazing woman. I was stupid, and I loved your mother very deeply. It hurt when she moved out. You know I wouldn't give her a divorce. I don't believe in that at all." He scratched around on his plate and yawned before saying, "I think I'm getting sleepy again. This nice bit of food has just about put me out."

She could see the sleepiness relaxing his face and body. She took his half-eaten plate of food and stacked it on top of hers. Prunella leaned down and kissed his clammy forehead, saying, "I love you, Daddy. You get some sleep. I'll be in the living room napping. Holler if you need me," and she left him to his vivid thoughts and memories.

Chapter 22

Burying It All

Charles and Geraldine separated that year, in 1995. The oil well had slowly dried up and left them wondering what to do with the land. They both talked it over and came to an agreement to sell it and let her have the money. The account that the oil money had accumulated in was split right down the middle. Both parents agreed to leave sixteen-year-old Prunella right where she was—with her father. Geraldine bought a small two-bedroom farmhouse on three acres not too far from Charles and Prunella. Knowing that they were not going to divorce and that her new house was small, she left a lot of her things with him. He saw and talked to her every day until Christine intervened.

Geraldine had gotten so depressed that she would hide in her room to get away from her daughter's complaints about having to see him when he visited. She had somewhat forgiven him for his infidelity, but Christine would never give him the satisfaction. She would complain over him being a tight-wad and how he would go on one of his cleaning sprees to get rid of collected stuff around the house, and she would fuss over how much time he spent in front of the mirror with his hair. But Prunella loved him and always would. He tossed and turned many nights in his bed, thinking about fighting to keep his marriage together, but to no avail.

Young Prunella was of dating age now and met a young fella named Barlow Brown. She thought he was adorable in his designer clothes and rich cologne. He had long, wavy black hair and kept it clean and combed. She loved his large doe-brown eyes and abundance of facial hair, and in time had fallen madly in love with him. He was from the same town as Geraldine. His father was a car salesman; his mother stayed home with five children. She tried her best to keep all of them straight, and it worked on four of them. They moved on to be quite successful in life, but poor Barlow needed extra care. He was always hurting himself somehow and running back to his mother for comfort. This gave him a lot of excuses for not doing chores.

Charles could see right through him instantly and didn't like him. He played it cool, though, and kept him under close watch. He reminded him too much of Charleen's Frank. Geraldine didn't think too much of him either, because he reminded her of Berry. She warned Charles when he was complaining about the boy, "Oh, let the girl make her choice. If you try to push him out, that will only draw her in. Just stay out of it."

He just couldn't understand why she gave herself to that slacker. He made Prunella promise that she would never move off with him if she chose to marry him, and he rewarded her agreement by buying them a trailer to put anywhere they wanted on the eighty acres. He didn't want her far away from him, especially since losing Charleen.

Barlow would come see Prunella at the discount grocery store. She had worked her way up and now managed the responsibility of employees and paperwork. Charles knew she had great potential to be a businesswoman, and he proudly watched her develop those skills. As he watched Barlow, he worried that he just might have another Frank on his hands.

One day while Charles was at work, Prunella, with Barlow in tow, approached him regarding Geraldine. "Daddy, we just went by to check on Mama, but Christine won't let me see her. She told me that we were not welcome to just stop by whenever we wanted."

His face became red as he said, "I wish your mama had not talked her into staying here. She should have went with her husband to Alabama. But no! She talked her into it by buying her another freaking house. She thinks she can run her mother's life? Well, we'll just see about that!"

He snatched his keys off the desk and said, "Look after things. I'm going over there." Before he disappeared out the door he turned and said, "Hopefully I won't be calling you from the jailhouse." He then gave her a smile and walked out.

In a matter of thirty minutes, Charles was pulling into Geraldine's driveway, parking inches from the Lincoln. He picked up a plastic bag that contained two plate lunches and stepped onto Geraldine's porch. Christine had two boys now, Donovan and Ricky, and they came running to him as he pulled up.

The oldest, Donovan, asked, "What did you bring us?"

Christine was sitting on her porch at her trailer as she watched her kids run to Charles. He threw her a wave, but she didn't wave back. Turning his attention to the boys, he patted around his pockets until he found a pack of peanut butter crackers and handed them to Donovan, saying, "Here. You two split this." He then walked into the house as the boys quickly sat down and devoured the crackers. As he walked in the door, he saw Geraldine lying comfortably on her rose-printed couch.

"Hey, you beautiful thang!"

She waved him off with a smile and said, "Whatever."

Before she had time to sit up and Charles to sit down, Christine came barreling in the door and slammed it behind her, saying, "Oops...my bad."

Her mother didn't say a word. She thought maybe Christine would go away with him there, but she stomped into the small kitchen adjoined to the living room, where they sat with their plate lunches. She fixed a glass of tea and then proceeded to loudly wash the dishes.

Geraldine yelled, "Christine, please!"

She puffed up like a mad ostrich. "Well, all right! Fine! I won't clean your kitchen. Maybe he will before he leaves!" She stomped out with the glass of tea.

Silence fell on the room until he asked, "So what is she doing here anyway? I thought she had an internship at that hospital in Alabama?"

"Well, she got into it with the head nurse at the hospital, and they took her internship away. She's gonna keep working in healthcare. She's going back to Golden Meadows. Oh, yeah! That ain't all. She met some squirrely fella there. He had hurt his arm somehow and come in the hospital where she was at. She brought him back with her. Shit, he's been shacked up over there with her and the boys. You didn't see him out there?"

"Why hell no! What about Jerry?"

She cleared her throat. "Oh, he knows about him. He said he didn't care, but when he comes to town, that Walter had better get down the road."

"Walter, huh? What does he look like?"

"Oh, shit! He ain't nothing to look at. He ain't but eighteen, scrawny and pimpled. Damn! He's still wet behind the ears." She laughed as she took another bite of her turkey sandwich.

"What's so funny?"

She swallowed her food and chucked. "She told me that she wanted her a young one so she could train him the way she wanted a man."

He choked on his food at that, then said, "What does the fella do for a living?"

"That boy ain't got a job. Hell! He don't even have a driver's license or a car. Christine's been chauffeuring him around in that Lincoln."

After sitting with her for over an hour, he made his way out to the truck. He could hear his cell phone ringing and vibrating on the dash, so he answered it. "Hello?"

"Hey, it's me, Oliver. I know it's been a long time, but I got it done. I'm going to bring it by this evening."

Charles knew exactly what he was talking about and became very excited, and he rushed back to the store and closed up. Prunella and Barlow were going to Barlow's mother's house after work. Charles gave his love to her and headed home. Dusk was quickly approaching as he gathered up a few things around the house, and just as he finished, Oliver pulled up.

"Hey, old man!"

"Hey, young sprout! That was perfect timing. So where's it at?"

Ollie gave him a huge grin as he walked around to the passenger side of his black Ford Ranger and lifted out an old, faded-green army ammunition box. He lifted the lid, and Charles took a step forward, leaning down to better see the contents of the box.

"Oh! I think you have outdone yourself this time. Here I thought the cannon was the best, but this—oh, yes! This will definitely do!" Smiling, he looked up at him. "So, does it work?"

"Of course it works!" he laughed.

"I don't know. You didn't try out that cannon before bringing it to me."

"Well now, that's different," Oliver said. "This does not involve gunpowder. I had one heck of a time getting this put together 'cause it took some time figuring on them pencil sketches of yours. I do believe that was the most tedious thing I've ever done. It works! I promise. I give you my word! Shoot! Better yet check it out yourself."

"I can't do it out here. If anybody was to see it..." he trailed off, looking around.

"Well, take it in the house," Oliver urged.

They both went inside for a few minutes, then returned back outside. Walking around to the back of the house, they sat the box on the concrete picnic table, next to a flower pot of calla lilies and a camera. Charles grabbed a shovel, walked under the mulberry tree, and dug a hole. Oliver sat at the picnic table running his hand along the green box.

"So, you are really gonna bury this?" he asked.

Charles stopped digging and looked at him. "Well, from the looks of things, I've got no choice. I hate to say it, but Geraldine knows how to get in the safe. To be honest with ya, I don't trust that Christine; don't know how to. If not now, she will." After running his hand through his gray hair, he continued, "I wish I could tell Prunella, but all I can do is hint. She's a smart girl, you know." He paused. "Now, Ollie, you tell her about this if I leave this world before you, and we never speak of this to anyone else." They vowed to never speak of that day again.

Unfortunately, misery was soon upon the family, as Oliver was diagnosed with a rare blood disease the following year. Within six months, he had passed away, leaving his wife and two grown sons behind. Charles took it extremely hard when he died. Having lost so many loved ones, he began to wonder what he had done so wrong to have outlived them. In honor of Oliver at his funeral, he and his boys fired the homemade cannon for the last time. He could never bring himself to shoot it again. He placed it next to the carport door, where it sat for many years. He tried to visit Mary and the boys, but it became too hard, expecting his friend to walk out the front door to greet him.

Chapter 23

The Hurricane

Years passed and the winds of rumors blew through the town stirring up gossip and assumptions yet again. There were enough whispers whirling around to catch a chill from it all. This caused Geraldine to smoke like a freight train. She lit one cigarette after another, sometimes using one to light the other. Just when she thought she could accept that Charles had made a mistake and move back in with him, Christine would remind her of his infidelity, asking her, "So, Mama...how did y'all meet again?" This kept the hardened truth on the surface as she ranted and raved at her mother, eroding the edges of her clear thoughts. Several years of her living with cold feelings about him caused her to go into a deep depression. She could feel her body and mind slipping as she struggled with her feelings and an unseen illness.

Geraldine was diagnosed with lung cancer two days after her fifty-ninth birthday. All of those years clutching packs of full, rich Winston tobacco had caught up with her. She never let up though, saying, "Well, I see no reason to stop now." Nine months of living with the turmoil of her illness was the toughest thing she had ever faced. Along with this upset was a storm that was on its way, bound for the small town that the Richards family lived in. August 28, 2005, brought fear to all who lived around the Gulf of Mexico. A category-four hurricane left everyone scrambling for canned food and bottled water. Charles opened his store early that morning for the last sale of his items. The shelves emptied quickly.

He pulled Prunella aside and said, "Call your mama and tell her she is staying with us through this storm and I'll be around to get her soon. She needs to be packed and ready to go when I get there." He slicked his hair back with one hand in frustration as he shoved the other in his pocket, adding, "And Christine needs to get her butt with them boys over to the house, too."

She made the call and said exactly what he had said. Geraldine hung up and informed everybody of the plans. Christine puffed up. "You can go, but me and the kids ain't."

As they fussed about the plans, the phone rang again. This time her daughter answered it, then turned up her nose as she handed it to her mother. It was Charles, and he had been keeping a constant ear on the radio for updates. The storm had been upgraded to a category-five. Geraldine told him that Christine wasn't going, so she wasn't either.

"I don't think so! This is going to be a horrible one. I can't in my right mind leave y'all to the possible destruction that's bound to happen with this storm, so you tell that girl to get them kids and that boyfriend of hers together. This ain't the time to be hardheaded! Now y'all get your stuff together! I'll be there in just a few!"

Once he hung up, Geraldine turned to her irritated daughter. "He's gonna make us all go, so don't be hardheaded, and help me get packed."

Her eyes bulged out with madness as she snatched a plastic bag from the kitchen cabinet and stomped back to her mother's room. She slung her mother's clothes into the bag, saying, "You can go if you want to, but we are not going! All he is gonna do is piss you off, and I'm tired of hearing you bitch about him. So I'm not going!"

Geraldine couldn't quite hear what she was saying, so she slowly made her way down the narrow hallway to her bedroom. As she got to the doorway, she asked, "What did you say, Christine?"

Christine spun around on the balls of her feet as she picked up another article of clothing, angrily slinging it into the bag. "Fine! Do what you want, Mother!" She then walked up to her and handed her the bag. "Here ya go! You're all packed."

Christine stomped down the hallway to leave. At the front door, she grabbed the doorknob and jerked it open just as lightning crashed to the ground, striking the large oak tree next to the house. The powerful electrical volts shot down the tree into the root system, traveling through the rich Mississippi dirt. The roots from the tree were scattered underneath her beloved Lincoln. The surge of electricity arced up through the drops of rain streaming down the side of her car, flaring up into a magical blend of colors. This stunned Christine as she stared at the dazzling array of colors fluttering down the large body of metal. When her muscles unfroze from the sight, she quickly closed the door and placed her back against it, as if to barricade the lightning from coming in.

She hung her head. "Dammit! I don't want to go to his house."

Charles's truck was filled with boxes of canned food and bottles of water. Prunella jumped in the passenger seat as he slid in behind the steering wheel. He said, "I think we should gas up the truck and those two cans in the back. Hopefully we won't need them, but you never know."

Rain droplets mixed with small fragments of debris began to fall hard and heavy, blowing sideways with the wind. They soaked the ground, instantly flooding the ditches and overflowing the streets with fury. Charles quickly pulled into a busy station and parked at the pumps. He handed her a hundred-dollar bill and said, "Here, go in and pay them while I pump it."

She went into the store and awaited her turn in line, glancing out at her father, who was reaching over the side of the truck for the cans. A bright flash of light under the truck caught her eye; a fire had started to grow underneath her father's truck. Fear filled her voice as she yelled, "Oh my God! My father's truck is on fire!" Prunella ran out yelling, "Daddy!"

Charles looked up at her as he sat the cans down on the ground and turned to reach for the pump handle. He was confused as to why she was yelling and mouthed, "What is it?"

She pointed at her father and yelled, "Fire! There is a fire under your truck!"

The young female cashier looked up and saw what she was yelling about. She slammed a button to stop all the gas pumps, grabbed a fire extinguisher, and jumped over the counter. A man in a gray business suit in the line grabbed the fire extinguisher and took charge. He bravely ran over to the truck, dropped down, and rolled partly under the truck to reach the fire. Another man at the pumps grabbed Charles by the arm and tried to pull him away from the burning truck, but he fought him off. The thin man was no match for Charles, but he grabbed him again. The man yelled, "Your truck is on fire!"

Prunella dropped to the ground, for fear had victoriously overpowered the strength of her legs. With the intense commotion and seeing his daughter on her knees, all of Charles's senses went off at once, and his body jumped into action. He gave the man one more aggressive jerk. The man threw up his hands and said, "Forget it. You're on your own, buddy!"

Charles scrambled to his open truck door and dove into the cab. As she watched her father climb into the truck, Prunella let out an ear-piercing scream: "What are you doing?" He grabbed the bank bag full of money from the store and tucked it under his arm, as if it were a football and he was making a play, and sprinted off to her, leaving the truck to its chaos. She jumped to her feet once she saw her father running to her. They wrapped their arms around each other tightly. "You scared me, Daddy!"

The man with the fire extinguisher safely put the fire out, then returned it to the cashier. He walked over to them as they held one another. Prunella could see him coming and, taking no time or thought, she leapt forward to the man, hugging him as if he were her long-lost uncle. She spoke loudly, with excitement, "Oh my God! I thank you so much for your bravery, sir."

Once she released him, the man said to Charles with a smile, "Boy, I think you just like danger."

Charles looked up at the man to reply, but to his surprise, it wasn't a stranger who had saved the day; it was Gordon, aka "the good one." He shook his hand strongly as he gave him a huge hug with the other arm, and he patted him on the back, saying, "Oh dear Lord! It's unbelievable! Old Good One! I ain't seen you in ages, and you saved my hide!"

"Yeah, it's been a while. I moved down to the Gulf Coast over thirty years ago. I'm a preacher down there. I come up here thinking I might be far enough from this storm, but I don't know," he chuckled, pulling a wet card from his coat. "Give me a call sometime. I'd love to catch up, but right now I've got to get on myself."

The loud, piercing sound of a fire truck echoed all around. Four young men jumped from the truck and walked up to Charles. One of the men said, "Was it your truck caught fire?"

"Yep," Charles answered, "I don't know what happened." He then looked over at his truck and took a deep breath as he looked at the dents Geraldine had put in it. "Well, I've been meaning to get another one, so I guess you can say it's time."

Another one of the young firemen added, "Yep, mister, I don't think that one is going anywhere. Let's push it to the side of the building, out of the way."

All of the men started toward his truck, so he gave Prunella the money bag, saying, "Here, you hold on to this as tight as you can. Call Barlow to come pick us up, and tell him to hurry. I've got to get to your mama."

Prunella couldn't stop shaking as she made her call to Barlow. He arrived shortly thereafter to pick them up. Strong gusts of wind blew debris across the pavement as they drove to the house. Once they got there, Charles told them to get the supplies in the house. He then ran around to the back of the house and got in Oliver's truck, which Mary had given to him after his passing. Mary couldn't drive it because it was a standard, and her boys were too large to drive it comfortably, and she knew he would love to have it. Oliver had joked many times that Charles loved a Ford almost as much as money.

Charles then sped over to Geraldine's house. The instant he opened the door, a gust of wind blew through the small house, tossing papers from the coffee table up into the air. Geraldine yelled for him to hurry up and close the door. As she fussed about the papers on the floor, he interrupted her. "Come on! We don't have time to worry over this stuff. Let's get to the house. This storm is no joke. It's not messing around, and neither am I."

Christine emerged from the hallway, walked over to the papers on the floor, and picked them up, tossing them back onto the coffee table. She shot a look over at her mother and waited for her to tell him that she wasn't going.

"Come on. Let's make a move!"

"Oh, relax!"

"Relax? I can't relax! Do you two realize that the damn hurricane has up to 145-miles-per-hour winds?"

"So, we're not going," Christine mumbled.

He looked over at her as she stood there with a smirk on her face. Placing both hands on his hips, he replied, "This is one time I'm not going to argue with you. I don't know what your intentions are, but your mother will be in that truck outside and will be over at the house while this storm is going on. You need to get your kids and boyfriend in gear, and do so now! If you want to come with me and your mama, that's fine. But if you're going to stay here, then the kids need to go with us. So what's your plan?"

Geraldine jumped up from the couch. "There ain't no arguing with this silver-haired, hardheaded man. He is right. We all need to go."

Christine pulled her shoulders back, standing up as tall as she could, and looked him up and down. "Well, I'll go get the kids."

"Wait. Where is my overnight bag? Did you put my medication in there?"

She didn't even turn to look at her mother as she walked out the door. "Yep, it's in there." Then she disappeared out the windy door.

Later that night, they found that her medication wasn't in the bag. Christine had said she put it in there, but in fact, she had left them out on purpose, causing her mother to come home sooner once the storm passed. Her plan worked pretty well, for Charles was out with a chainsaw after the storm cutting their way back to Geraldine's house.

Chapter 24

Prunella's Dream

The night had drawn its darkness over the Richards' home. As Charles slept peacefully in his bed, under the spell of the new medication, clouds of rain began to huddle in the sky. Drops began to pound on the rooftop as Prunella lay snuggled on the living room couch, cuddling a soft brown pillow. She rested her chin on it as her eyes fell closed, casting her into a deep sleep.

**

She could see herself walking to the car as she got off from work at the discount store with her father. Once in her Corolla, Prunella pulled out her cell phone and called her mother. Geraldine had received a call earlier from Christine complaining about Charles.

Prunella said to her, "Oh, Mama! I would have thought by now that she would be over this mess and leave Daddy alone. She keeps insisting we talk about the two of you, and I don't want to hear about it anymore."

"She has been in an ill mood ever since lightning struck that car her daddy gave her, and she found out it was gonna cost more to fix it than it's worth. I ain't getting her another one, Prunella; I'm too sick 'cause of this mess right now, so I told her to just take my car. Hell! I don't drive anymore. It's been a little quieter around here now that she has a way of going."

Strumming her thumb on the steering wheel, Prunella said, "Mama, I'm coming over. We'll take a drive and listen to Melissa Etheridge like we used to. That always made us feel better."

Geraldine sat down on her bed, mindlessly pulling at a thread on her nightgown, as she looked out the window and said, "Don't do that. I would love to, but Christine...well, I just don't want to cause any more problems."

"You should not have to deal with that! You need to move back in with Daddy. I'm right there, and I can take care of you myself. Since Daddy bought me and Barlow that trailer for a wedding gift, we have plenty of room for you to stay with us if you'd rather."

Meanwhile, Christine had snuck into the house as she talked to Prunella on the phone. Geraldine didn't hear her come in, and she didn't make her presence known. Hearing her mother talking to someone, she crept down the hall to eavesdrop.

Geraldine adjusted herself on the bed, then balled up her dry, scaly hand into a fist. Bumping her knee with it, she said, "You know, I can't say it don't piss me off knowing he is going to outlive me. Dammit! I've worked hard on that house, and now some floozy is going to take it over one day. I know his old ass has plenty of money to buy him a young gal, but I was broke when we met. Now I have a good bit in the bank, so maybe I should just shut up."

"Yes, Mama, stop that. He loves you and will always love you. I know he does; I can see it in his eyes when he says your name."

"Well, besides all that, did your daddy tell you that we have decided that she gets everything I've got, and you get everything your daddy's got? That's how we drew it up. You'll be all right, 'cause I know what he has in that safe. Did he tell you that the code is in his wallet? I've had a good mind to go over there and clean it out, but that would be taking away from you. So I've pushed that thought out of my head."

Prunella cranked her car as she added, "Look, you just need to get out and get some fresh air. I'm leaving work now, and I've got to stop at the dollar store. I'm coming to get you, and we are going for a ride. I just got a new Melissa CD, and it's awesome!"

Geraldine tugged at her gown as her mind pondered, hesitating to reply. Answering with a positive tone, she said, "Yes, Prunella, that does sound like a good idea. Let me ask Christine if it's all right." Just as she said that, she felt a presence in the room. She turned and looked toward the door to see Christine in her white nursing scrubs listening to her conversation. This made her feel like she was a patient in a mental hospital and her daughter was the warden.

"So when did you have to start asking for permission?"

Geraldine felt that she couldn't address that question at that moment. "Well, let me get off here. I'll call you in a little bit." She started to hang up the phone, but just before it disconnected, Prunella heard Christine say, "It's time for your meds."

Two hours went by and Prunella never received a call back from her mother, so she decided just to go see her. When she got there, Christine met her on the porch, saying, "What are you doing here? Mama is asleep."

She pressed past her corpulent body. "This is my mother's house, and I am going to see her."

"Well, just take your ass on in, then."

Prunella gave her a cold, hard look as she continued through the doorway. She made her way down the hall to her mother's room.

Geraldine lay quietly in her bed and looked to be extremely drowsy. She sat down on the soft bed next to her mother and stroked her cheek. She looked over at her as if she wanted to say something, but her words weren't forthcoming.

Christine walked in, and Geraldine looked over at her, then back to Prunella. She tried again to speak, but her words would not form to relay her thoughts. This was not normal. She could tell that her mother wasn't acting right. "What's wrong with Mama? I just talked to her two hours ago, and she was fine."

Christine only shrugged her shoulders and smirked.

***

The disturbing visions of this memory haunted Prunella as she lay in a state of suspended consciousness. She was tossing around on the couch so much that the soft pillow escaped her grip. Slipping farther into her dream, the memories continued.

***

Weeks had passed since that day, and Prunella was standing in her mother's house. She looked around at all the filth. Dishes were so scattered across the countertops that they masked the location of the sink. Geraldine's small living room was cluttered with articles of clothing, mostly the kids', and McDonald's paper and cups accompanied the beautiful whatnots on the end table. She thought, *What in the world? Where is Christine, and why is Mama's house such a mess?* Looking around in disgust, she called out for her mother.

Geraldine replied with a gruff "woohoo" from her bedroom doorway.

Walking back to her mother, Prunella threw her hands in the air and asked, "Where is she? Why is your house such a mess? I thought she was supposed to be helping you, not trashing the place!"

Her mother interrupted her rant by covering her ears and saying, "Hold on now. Too many questions all at once. I told her to take the boys somewhere. Dammit, there is enough racket around here; I don't need any more."

Prunella quickly apologized in a lowered voice and stepped to her side to help her to the living room couch. Geraldine adjusted her ratty nightgown as she sat down, saying, "I need some new nightgowns."

"I'll get you some, Mama. I'll bring them over next time."

"I sent Christine out to get some for me, but she told me that she forgot because of all the running around she had to do."

Prunella gasped in shock. "I'll bet she didn't forget to eat! Don't send her to do anything again, Mama. I'll gladly do it for you."

"I don't want to bother you."

"Mama, you are never a bother to me. You are my mother. You know that you and daddy were my first loves? Y'all are my world and always will be." They both smiled. Then she added, "So why is the house such a mess?"

Geraldine grabbed her hand, lowered her head, and batted her eyes. "Let's just visit, okay?"

Prunella apologized again and changed the subject. "Your hair is looking better."

She reached up to stroke her straight, white, thinning hair. "Yes, it's thin, and I do miss my gray-blonde curls."

"Mama, you look really good, though. You really didn't lose too much weight with chemo and those radiation treatments."

"Yep, I've always been a healthy-sized gal. Guess I always will be," she laughed.

Hearing her mother say the word healthy turned Prunella's dream into a nightmare. After that day, it seemed the only time she could have a clear conversation with her mother was on the phone. When she visited, Geraldine would be unresponsive to her. This caused her to grow weary and worried of her mother's silent, strange behavior. So on a Tuesday in September, after several weeks of seeing her in a somewhat catatonic state of mind, Prunella phoned her mother's number. The caller ID would show their number, and it had to be either her or Charles.

"Hello," Christine answered unpleasantly.

Prunella wasted no time in saying, "Let me talk to Mama."

"She is sleeping. She had a fever, so I gave her something for it."

"What did you give her?"

"Tylenol," she answered blankly.

"I thought Mama was having trouble swallowing?"

"Yes, but I gave her something anyway. She is fine now."

"Did you get her some suppositories?"

Christine twirled her new, long, blonde salon curls. "What for?"

Prunella began to sweat with anger. How could she possibly be a nurse and not know that? "Well, what did you give her for the fever?" she snapped.

"I told you—Tylenol."

"Did she swallow it?"

"No, I put it up her butt. That's what you do when someone can't swallow it."

"You know they make suppositories with fever reducer, so don't be putting dry pills in Mama's ass! I'm going to bring some. I'll be on my way after work."

She then hung up on Christine, slamming the phone down. She arrived at Geraldine's house just as the waxing crescent moon was on the rise. Prunella burst in the front door without knocking, causing Christine to jump. She threw the box of suppositories on the coffee table in front of her. "That's what you use!" Turning to walk to her mother's room, she stopped and turned around, adding, "Oh, by the way, I'm staying the night."

Once she stepped into her mother's room, the smell of defecation was overwhelming. She stuck her head out the door and spoke loudly down the hallway, "When was the last time Mama was changed?"

Christine jumped up from the couch and huffed, "She probably needs changing now!"

Prunella stayed in the room with her and helped change their mother's adult diapers. After that, she never left her side. She curled up beside her and prayed as she held her hand. Christine never let her truly have any privacy with her, for she was constantly coming in the room.

She came into the room for the final time and announced, "I'm sleeping with Mama. You can sleep on the couch." It was late and she was getting sleepy, so Prunella didn't put up a fight. She lay down on the living room couch and covered up with a throw blanket. She lay consciously on the small couch that allowed her to view the hallway. Not long after she had closed her eyes, a click from the bathroom light switch being flipped on and then the sound of running water caused her to look down the hallway.

She thought, *It's just Christine washing her hands*, so she nestled back into a light sleep. Minutes later, she felt a light touch on her shoulder and heard soft-spoken words from Christine: "Mama is dying."

Instantly, her eyes opened and she jumped to her feet, almost knocking her heavy sister over the coffee table, and ran to her mother's room. As she touched her mother's hand, it was as if she knew she was there. Geraldine sighed with one last breath.

Prunella reached up to touch her clammy, aged face. "Oh, Mama! Please stay with me! You can't go now!" Tears streamed down her face, dropping onto her mother's pink nightgown. As she leaned over, burying her face into Geraldine's chest, begging her to stay, soaking sobs drenched her mother's gown as she wailed with a broken heart, knowing she had slipped into Heaven's light, but Prunella had a deep hope that she could hear her cries and might come back to her.

Christine stood in an undemonstrative stance at the door, saying, "I'm sorry, Mama. I'm sorry."

***

Hearing Christine's unfeeling apology in her dream caused Prunella to toss around on her father's couch. Her thrashing was so violent that she fell off and hit the hard floor, awakening her instantly. The memory of her sister's words caused her stomach to turn. She jumped to her feet and ran down the hallway to the bathroom to throw up. She grew even sicker when she remembered her saying, "I hope the coroner don't say anything about Mama's diaper being on backward."

Prunella began to heave until there was nothing left. She slipped weakly back against the cold tub and thought out loud, "Oh my God! Why didn't I see it then?"

Chapter 25

A Cold Heart

Prunella sat on the cold bathroom floor listening to the sounds of the rain. She watched its transparent drops roll down the small window pane as the lightning lit up behind it. As she continued to watch them, she thought back to the night she lost her mother.

***

She had been so grief-stricken as she made the call to Charles. Sobbing frantically, all she could say was, "Daddy, Mama is gone... She's gone!" Hearing this prompted him to hang up and rush over to his broken-hearted daughter. Charles rushed in the door of Geraldine's house and instantly darted down the hallway to her bedroom. Once he saw that she was indeed deceased, he stood at her bedside tight-lipped and strong, disbelieving he had lost another wife. Charles had truly thought she would recover. She had seemed fine on the days he saw her. All he could do was shake his head in confusion.

Prunella had seen her father come in, and she let go of her mother's hand and latched onto her stiff father, who only loosened up enough to wrap his arms around her. He uttered with a cracked voice, "I'll make the calls."

Christine walked in about that time and, without saying a word, snatched up Geraldine's black leather purse, pulling it to her large boobs. She walked out the room squeezing it tightly in her arms, as if she were protecting herself from being mugged. The sight of her actions made Charles sick. He pulled Prunella from his arms and said, "I'll be right back. I'm going to make a call."

Prunella sat back down next to her lifeless mother and began to cry again as Charles made his way into the living room where Christine was sitting. Stopping instantly, he stood there in shock. She was unaware he was in the room and was vigorously searching through her mother's purse and wallet. He rolled his eyes at the sight, shook his head, and walked out the front door.

When he returned, he looked at her. "I'm going to need you to meet me tomorrow at the funeral home around noon." As Prunella heard this, she came out of the bedroom and stood by her father. Her body was in the room, but her mind was far away with her mother.

Christine rolled a couple of hundred-dollar bills around her finger and smirked, responding with a disturbing level of delight, "Sure, I'll be there."

He was in disbelief of her uncaring attitude at the loss of her mother. She stood there dry-eyed, and he thought, *I wonder if she will ever cry.*

Prunella continued to stand next to him with her arms folded, not saying a word, mindlessly slouching as she stared at nothing. Charles couldn't stand the sight of Christine at that moment, so he said out loud, "I'm going outside to wait for them to arrive."

Prunella still stood numb, fixated in the direction of the coffee table, until she heard the door shut. She snapped back as the unopened box of suppositories came into focus. Then she followed her father outside and stood next to him once again. He reached into his pocket and pulled out a pack of cigarettes and a lighter. Placing one between his lips, he struck the lighter and stood there in the dark watching the life of the flame as it danced in the light breeze. Charles quickly spit out the unlit cigarette and crushed the pack of cigarettes in a destructive manner and tossed them into Geraldine's rusting chair on the porch. He looked over at Prunella and said, "Child, I've never quit anything in my life, but this time I'm gonna."

The next day they met with Christine, who had brought along Walter. It seemed that he was becoming a permanent fixture in her life. Not too many words were shared between them all at first as they walked around looking at caskets and flowers. Christine would walk up to the cheapest items and say, "This one will do." And Charles would look at it and reply, "It's not good enough for your mama." She would ignore him and move on to the next-cheapest item.

The director came in and asked, "Have you decided on anything?"

"We'll take this one," Christine quickly responded as she ran her hand down a pine box.

Charles gasped at her lack of concern. How could she not want to protect her mama's body from the elements? Not wanting to make a fuss, he calmly said, "You should really think about getting one with a gasket to seal it like a vault." He then turned to the director and said, "This one over here is a good choice for us, sir," as he pointed to a beautiful white steel box with gold hardware. It had a beautiful feature of a single pink rose on the white satin interior. He had noted the continuous seam on the casket, which would ensure that her remains would be protected.

Christine reached over and flipped the small white price tag around and nonchalantly snapped her fingers with a twirl of her hair. "I see no reason to get that one. It costs too much."

Charles turned to her aggressively. "Look! I've been through this a few times, and you can't beat the price for a well-constructed casket. This one is the best. It's not that pricey."

She stared coldly into his eyes. "Yep, we all know you have experience in these matters, now don't we? Hmm...so you can buy this one, too."

"Girl, I'm not here to pay for all of this. I'm just here to help you out. I know your mother put money aside for this day. She told me she discussed it with you."

Christine threw her hands up. "Well, you can just take care of it all since you know every damn thang. I'm not spending $2,000 on something that's going into the ground!"

Charles puffed up and spat out, "Why you self-centered little... That's your mother you're talking about putting in the ground!"

The director stood there for a moment in hopes that this disagreement would cease. After looking at their faces, he could tell these two weren't going to agree. He slowly started backing out the door and gently closed it, leaving them to their unpleasant conversation.

Prunella's world started to spin as she stood listening to these two argue. As they went around and around, her face began to turn white, and her palms were sweating and her mouth went dry. She knew her legs were about to buckle, so she took slow, wobbly steps to the main door and walked out, leaving them to argue. She made her way to the front entrance and sat down on the cool concrete steps.

The next day at the funeral, they didn't even look at one another. It soon became obvious that Christine had nothing nice to say about him to friends and family. She even told a few of them that it was his fault her mother had died so young. He received some uncomfortable, guilt-laden stares from some of those people who believed her. He knew he had made a mistake with that other woman. It had made him miss out on the last few beautiful years with Geraldine. Now he was here listening to Christine make a mockery out of their marriage. It was like a knife being twisted in his chest.

The service was about to begin and everyone was sitting down. The director escorted Christine with her two boys and Walter to the same row where Charles and Prunella were sitting. He stretched out his hand and pointed down the row of chairs, saying, "Please take a seat. This is where the immediate family sits."

Walter sat down in the second chair from Prunella, leaving room for Christine to sit next to her. Christine quickly turned to the director, tossed her head to the side to avoid looking at Charles, and blurted out, "I'm not sitting with him! He is a murderer!"

Walter sat there looking dumbfounded and confused. Prunella was so appalled at her sister's behavior and decided she'd had enough of her mouthy meanness. She darted her eyes up at her and, keeping her voice down, addressed her behavior, "Hey! That's enough. It's not right for you to act like this. You have absolutely no right to call him such a thing." She pointed to the beautiful casket. "Now, you look up there. That's our mother laying up there, and here you are acting like this! I can't believe you would be so spiteful!" She then elegantly crossed her smooth, creamy-white legs as she shifted in her little black dress, slightly leaned into her, and said with a whisper, "You may not believe in karma, but karma believes in you. Don't be surprised if one day you regret acting like this. So, whatever hatred you have for my father,"—giving her a wink—"you might want to check it at the door." She straightened up in the chair and waved her hand. "Now, I don't care where you sit as long as you do it with your mouth closed."

Christine adjusted her purse on her shoulder, rolled her eyes, snapped her fingers at Walter, and then pointed to the next row of chairs. "Get up! Let's move."

After the funeral, Prunella and Charles stayed away from her.

She was set up for life and no longer needed them, now the owner of her mother's house, land, car, and a bank account with over $125,000 in it. Being the sole beneficiary of her mother's estate, she was responsible for completing her affairs.

Prunella and Charles caught wind of her life and were glad they were no longer involved. It had been wonderful not having to speak to her or listen to her dramatic twists on life. All was well, but Charles felt he had not seen the last of her in their small town. They would hear new gossip from town folk and share it with one another. Charles heard one day that Christine had abandoned the small house and trailer, with her Lincoln still in the yard, only to live in a newly built house with Walter and the boys. Prunella heard that she was spending money like crazy—buying new clothes, getting new hairdos, and eating out every night. He knew she would run out of money soon, and he was right.

That same year, he received a phone call from a lawyer asking about Geraldine and the store. Charles was frantic when he found out that she was trying to gain more money from her mother's death. Unsure of his rights, he went to several different lawyers to see if there was a possibility of her getting any more money. To his relief, she had no chance. Geraldine had not wanted to be in on the business, so that meant no luck in Christine's pursuit of it.

Word had also gotten around town that Christine's father had passed away. The Rogers family had banned her from going to his funeral. Both wondered what could have possibly been so bad that she wouldn't be allowed at her father's funeral. But they knew the real Christine, so this wasn't much of a surprise.

Months later, rumors began again that she was now broke. Attempting to get money out of the store, she had put herself in a financial hole. In less than a year, every drop of the $125,000-plus was gone, and she was forced to sell the trailer they had once lived in, just to get by. She lost her new house and was forced to move into Geraldine's small house. Her two boys, Donovan and Ricky, had become too much for her to handle, so they went to live with Jerry.

***

Prunella continued to sit on the cold bathroom floor remembering all of this, saying out loud, "What a cold-hearted witch. She never opened the box of suppositories. What was she giving Mama?" The thunder rumbled, instantly following the lightning that engulfed the window with light. She jumped at the thunderous sound and bright flash of light. Fearing the weather, she went back to the living room couch to calm her nerves.

She tried to think happy thoughts and smiled at her memories of sneaking into her parents' room as a child when storms woke her up. With this thought, she eased down the hall to her father's room. Pushing the door slowly open and tiptoeing to the right side of her father's bed, she gently crawled into the bed next to him. She turned on her side so she could look at her peacefully sleeping father. In the dim light, she took in every line on his face. Her eyes moved to his thick silver hair, for it was all completely out of place. Noticing one small strand that lay just over his eyebrow, she reached up to push it aside, and in that moment, he snorted loudly in his sleep, startling her. Giggling, she did not dare try to move it again. She lay there, calmed by his presence, until falling asleep to the sound of the rain, drifting back to her thoughts of her sister Christine, feeling joy because her life had become much more peaceful without having to deal with her anymore. But life hadn't gotten easier.

**

Chapter 26

Business as Usual

In the 2010, Charles became ill. He hesitated in going to the doctor for fear of what they might say. Turning into a complete workaholic, he threw himself into his business, but overworking finally caught up with him, and he became weak and frail. One day he and Prunella were unloading a large truck at the store. He lifted a box from the truck and turned to put it down but dropped it and yelled loudly.

She rushed to him. "What's wrong?"

Holding his side, he grunted, "I don't know. It feels like I pulled a muscle. Let me sit down a minute." He hunkered over and crept to a stack of wooden pallets. Still holding his side, he looked up at her standing there with a scared look on her face. "Oh, now darn it! Take that look off ya face. I'm all right."

She placed her hands on her hips and snapped, "Oh, really? You're fine? Hmmm. Well, I'm going to take you to the doctor, and then we will let him take this look off of my face, 'cause right now it's stuck there."

"We can't just take off and leave the store!"

"Oh yes we can!" Folding her arms and digging deep down into her diaphragm, she yelled sharply, "SHIRLEY!"

In the wake of her echoing voice came an extremely short, older woman. "What's going on?" she asked in a raspy voice.

Prunella turned to her as she stood in the stockroom doorway. "Tell this man he is going to the doctor and you are going to watch after things."

Shirley looked over at Charles, who was still holding his side. Before she could speak, he said, "Oh! Now there ain't no reason to go to the doctor. Y'all just getting all worked up over a pulled muscle." He then looked up at Prunella. "I know she can handle it, but can she really handle it?"

He underestimated Shirley's hearing, for just as he released those words, she clapped her hands together and started walking slowly toward him. She shook her finger at him. "Now you look here, mister. I've been with you for years now. I know this place like the back of my old, wrinkled hands, so you don't worry about this business! I'll make sure to keep the cogs greased, and I'll have you know, you're not a medically licensed physician to make that call about your health." She lowered her finger and lightly patted his shoulder. "You know, at our age, we need to keep a check on our health."

Shaking his head as he lowered it, he agreed reluctantly. "All right, I'll go."

Prunella took him to a nearby hospital, where they found he had broken a rib lifting the light box. His worst fears were realized when they told him he had bone cancer. After meeting with doctors about his health, Charles decided not to take chemo treatments or radiation. He had taken Geraldine to her appointments, and he just couldn't bear the thought of going through that.

He sat Prunella down one day after work to go over some paperwork and said, "I know you want me to take those treatments, but I've decided to let this cancer run its course." She started to cry, for she knew he was too headstrong to change his mind, so she just hung her head. Reaching over, he stroked her soft, Pantene-scented hair and added, "Baby girl, I may be seventy years old, but I have the determination of a twenty-year-old. I have the mindset to tackle whatever obstacle comes my way. Shoot! I've dealt with the loss of my father at a young age; then right after that, I lost Prunella Jackson and the accident with Sharon. Oh, man! Charleen, then Mama, and now I've lost your mother." He lifted her chin to look her in the eyes, then added, "I'm not afraid to die. I think it's been my turn for a while now."

"You may not be afraid, but I am," she said, latching on to him and burying her face in his arms as she sobbed heavily.

He had mulled over her taking over the business. They had discussed it before, but she had told him she didn't want to do it without him. In hopes she would change her mind, he wanted to talk to her about it that day in the office, but he knew it was not a good time and waited a couple of weeks before trying again.

One late afternoon, he walked over to her and Barlow's double-wide trailer. As he made his way across the yard into theirs, he noticed the mess that had piled up in the backyard. It had been gaining his attention for weeks now, but it had gotten much worse. The grass was shaggy around old piles of hoarded junk, and car parts littered the yard. There were two aluminum boats, which seemed to have been used for target practice, that looked like their only use would be as a strainer for fish. He walked over to a bunch of milk jugs that were filled with some sort of liquid. As he picked one up to inspect it, something else caught his eye. He put the jug down and stepped over to the object glaring in the dusky light. Charles fumed as he saw it was one of his tools he'd been searching for. How disrespectful! He tightened his lips, stiffened his arms, and stomped to the front door, where he knocked sternly. He was greeted by a loving smile from Prunella.

"Hey, Daddy!"

He didn't smile back, but grumbled as he walked past her into the house. Turning to her as she closed the door, Charles shook the object at her. "You see this? Do you know what this is?"

"Yes. It's a crescent wrench."

"Very good. Now do you know where I found this?" She shook her head as she sat down on the couch. He stomped his foot. "I'm serious, girly. Do you know where I found this?"

From his tone of voice and posture, she knew that her father was upset. "Okay, so where did you find that?"

His face turned beet red as he spouted off, "I am not letting Barlow borrow any more of my tools. I just found this in your yard. It looks like it has been sitting in the rain for a while now." He pointed to the wrench as he said, "Just look: the dang thang is rusting!"

She sat straight up and, with stiff posture, replied, "Well, I didn't put it out there, so why are you yelling at me about it?"

Charles placed the wrench in his back pocket, then pointed his finger at her and said, "Now you can tell that husband of yours that he ain't borrowing any more of my tools. Just don't touch anything that belongs to me anymore!" He turned to walk out and reached for the knob but turned back and waved his arm. "Clean up this yard! It looks trashy back there!"

Prunella spouted out loud without thinking, "I can't get Barlow to do nothing, Daddy. I tried to get him to clean it last week, so maybe you should tell him yourself!"

He was so upset that he seemed to spin in a circle dance. He suddenly stopped and blurted out, "I don't have to tell him nothing! You dragged him in here. I tried to tell you he wasn't the one for you, but just like Charleen, you didn't listen. You didn't believe me when I said he wasn't good enough for you!" He tossed his arms in the air and added, "Here I was, wondering if I should sell the business or keep it for you, but if you can't get that redneck to do something as simple as cleaning the yard..." He stopped talking and kept his thought to himself.

In his silence, she stood up, placed both hands on her hips, and said, "I don't want to run it without you anyway!"

He looked into her big blue eyes. "Well, that settles it." Then he turned and walked outside. She was so heartbroken by having disappointed her father that she began to cry. Charles didn't know how right he truly was. Not long after marrying Barlow, she had realized he was no good. While they were dating, he had cared about how he looked and smelled before ever walking out the door. He had worn nice jeans with a fresh shirt and smelled wonderful. After landing Prunella and seeing that she would take care of everything, he had let himself go. He was a slob and completely uncaring about everything, mostly hygiene. His looks began to fade quickly, with his teeth rotting and breaking off or just falling out completely.

Prunella suspected infidelity because he would disappear for days, only to return to sleep off whatever fun he'd had. He didn't try to sleep with her anymore, which affected her self-esteem. Then he would lie, saying he was going to his mother's, but when she would call him, the phone would just ring. This made her fear that something had happened to him, for she knew how he drove. She would call his friends and family, but they all would reply in the same manner: "Haven't seen him." However, after that crescent wrench incident, her tears dried up and she let him have it.

When Barlow walked in, she told him he needed to clean up the yard immediately. Giving her a laugh, he retreated to the couch, where he picked up the remote, turned on the TV, and turned up the volume to drown her out. She stomped back to their bedroom and flopped on the bed. While lying there, dry-eyed, she thought, *What am I doing with this loser?*

She jumped up, grabbed a bag from the closet, and started packing. He glanced up at her as she stood in front of the TV with her packed bag. Choosing to ignore her, he looked around her at the TV. She grew angry as she stood there waiting on him to say something. Prunella raised her leg and kicked backward at the thirty-two-inch TV that Barlow couldn't seem to take his eyes off of. It hit the wall and crashed to the floor. She never stopped looking at her shocked, open-mouthed husband. "I'm leaving you and this trailer. You can do what you want with the place. I'm going to Daddy's. I know as long as you are here, it will just be a place where cockroaches hold hands."

She stomped out the door and across the yard to her father's house. Charles didn't know that she moved in with him to save her sanity. He thought she was there to help him with his illness. Like Charleen, who hadn't even been able to utter the word *divorce*, he had no idea their marriage had sunk between the cracks and she was no longer going to try and pull it out.

***

Prunella lay there in her dream state of the past. Charles woke up and rolled over, facing away from her, and started mumbling lightly, as if he were talking to someone. Reaching over to his nightstand, he tried to open the drawer. She didn't hear him bumping it around until he yelled out, "Oliver!" She abruptly woke up to see her father almost falling off the bed as he reached for the drawer. She sat up and jumped to her knees, grabbing him just in time. She yelled, "Stop, Daddy! Stop! You're going to fall!"

He turned to her and, without looking at her, said, "Oliver, where is that photo?"

"Daddy, it's me, Prunella. He isn't here."

He then looked up at her as if he was losing his mind. "Go get the photo, Oliver." He then gave her a light push.

She didn't know what to think, so she ran out of the room, whispering, "Damn. Is he losing his mind?" She instantly returned with the photo of the lilies. As she handed it to him, he said, "Thank you, Prunella."

What in the world? He just called me Oliver, and now he knows who I am? she thought.

He pointed to the partially opened drawer in the nightstand and said, "Reach in there and get that Bible and give it to me." She handed it to him, and he began to flip through the crisp pages. He stopped suddenly and looked up at her as he placed the photo in between the pages, next to something else. Then he closed the book and extended it to her. "You keep that photo in here. Prunella Jackson told me this was a safe place for keeping things." He paused, then added with a chuckle, "Well, that and dirt."

She opened it up and read the paper, then placed it back with the photo. Shaking her head with understanding, she said, "I see. I'll leave these in here."

"It will make sense to you one day. If not, well..."

Prunella started to notice a difference in his complexion. He became pale, and his body was dripping with sweat. "I think I'm going to call the doctor for you."

He quickly grabbed her arm. "No, don't. Please just don't."

***

Chapter 27

Dan Visits

Present day

A cold cup of coffee sat undisturbed in front of a zoned-out Prunella as she sat in her father's office thinking of all the things that had happened. She massaged her temples with her chilly fingertips, trying to remember the whereabouts of that Bible. The curious thought took her down the hall to the door to her father's room. She stood there holding the knob, contemplating opening it. After summoning up all her courage and swallowing the hurt, she pushed the door open.

Frozen in place at the smell of sickness and stale cigarette smoke, she was stunned at how disorderly it was. The room looked deplorable. The bed had been dismantled and now stood propped against the wall. The nightstands were shoved from their usual places, and some of the drawers looked as if they been riffled through. One was tossed upside down, with its contents scattered around on the floor. She stepped into the room bravely and glanced at the wide-open closet doors. She could see everything in it was in disarray as well. Looking away from the strewn contents of the closet, her eyes went to the safe where he'd kept his valuables. The heavy door was cracked open slightly. Her heart sank as she pushed it closed, for she knew it had been emptied of its contents. The sight of his room sickened her so much that she forgot what she had gone in there for. Quickly turning to leave the room, she saw it. The Bible! Happily, Prunella grabbed it and walked back to the office. Entering the drab room, she thought, *This room needs some light.*

Frustrated with the dark, cold feeling of the house, she sat the Bible down on the desk and walked over the large window. The drapes were a dusty, rich brown with small worn holes in them, allowing light to pierce through in an uneven pattern. Knowing they needed to be replaced, she grabbed one of the curtains and snatched it down. Light flooded the room and exposed the dusty clutter as shiny clips rained to the floor. A happy feeling came over her, so she snatched the other one from its sturdy rod. Now she stood there enjoying the sight of the sunlight as it illuminated her face.

Closing her eyes and basking in the warmth of the sun, Prunella opened them to see a nice silver truck pulling into her driveway. She quickly found a plain black long-sleeve shirt, two sizes too big, and pulled it over her head, then scrambled to the carport door. She wondered who it could be until she saw the handsome, tall, slender man slide from the truck and walk toward her. She took a couple of steps out to greet him, and they met in the empty carport. "Hey there, Mr. Dan. What brings you to this side of the pine trees?"

Dan chuckled as he soaked up her sweet smile. "Well, sweetheart, I came to check on ya. I ain't see ya since yer daddy passed. Ain't seen ya in town either, unless I just missed ya." He placed his hand on her shoulders and gave them a gentle squeeze as he looked deep into her with his compassionate eyes, adding, "So how are you really?"

She stood stiff and silent for a moment, looking down at the cold concrete floor. Then, without answering, she turned and took a couple of steps toward the door. Reaching out to open it, she turned to him and said, "Won't you come in?"

Dan nodded and followed her inside. Once in the door, he looked around at all of Charles's things. A feeling of sadness rushed in at the memories of his friend. Nothing looked as it should. The mess seemed to him as if someone had started packing things but knew nothing of organizing. He turned to her and said, "What happened in here?" Feeling he might be overstepping his bounds, he quickly added, "If you don't mind me getting into your business."

Prunella let out a deep laugh. "What business? The business of feeling defeated and destroyed?"

He gasped at her demeanor. "Oh my. Is it that bad?" Feeling true concern for her, he sat down at the kitchen table and patted the tabletop, saying, "Come sit down, sweetheart, and talk to me."

She sighed and went over to the table and plopped down in a chair. Dan relaxed, draping one arm along the back of his chair and sitting sideways. He took a long look at her. She was a beautiful woman who had once carried a brighter smile. Taking note of her oily skin and messed-up hair and the dark circles hugging her eyes, he asked, "Are you getting enough sleep?"

She slowly looked up at him. "Can I be honest with you, Mr. Dan?"

He replied with a fatherly "Sure sweetie. Please do."

She drew in a breath, then exhaled quickly. "No, I have not been doing good at all. My mind is full of wonder, hate, hurt, anger, and loneliness. I'm so frustrated that sleep has not been a friend of mine." She picked at her dirty fingernails. "I've got people wanting Charleen's Corvette—that's been driving me crazy. The taxes are due, and I'm out of money. I've had to sell off Daddy's milk truck, Pawpaw's truck, and my car just to cover the bills these past few months." She paused to look him in the eyes. "And, well, honestly, I've also used the money to buy sleeping pills from a couple of squirrely folks around here. I had a problem there for a minute, but I've gotten myself over that. I screwed up; I know it." Pointing to herself, she continued, "No one has to tell me 'cause me beats me up enough." She slid her upper body onto the table, stretching her arms out straight. "I really screwed up. I let Christine's boyfriend clean my house." Sitting up and waving her arm around the room, she added, "Well, you see how that went!"

Dan didn't know what to say. He just sat there for a moment with his mouth slightly agape and shook his head. She turned back to him, balled up her fist, and bumped it on the table as she said, "All of Daddy's guns are gone. I can't find any of his papers to the bank accounts. Shoot, I'm gonna need a lawyer to straighten all of that out. You know he had a stack of bonds, and they're gone, too. All of that stuff was in the safe." She clapped her hands and burst into nervous laughter. "But oh well, yay for me!"

She stood up and started pacing the floor. Every time he would start to say something, she would interrupt by waving her hand at him. "Oh, no! That's not all. I just had to toss Barlow's butt out. That's a long story. I've got a feeling he has those guns, but I can't prove it." She flopped back into her chair. "And oh my goodness, let me tell you what that dummy told me when he was messed up on something one day. Do you remember when he accidentally shot himself in the foot cleaning his gun?"

Nodding his head, he said, "Yes, I sure do. I felt sorry for that fella. I know that had to hurt."

She slapped the table. "Good! I hope it did. That idiot confessed to me that he did it on purpose just to keep from having to work at that good job Daddy found for him. Can you believe that? And he fought hard to get him that job, too!"

Before he could reply, she slapped both of her hands down on the table, causing him to jump. He reached over to her hands, placing both of his large hands over hers, and said softly, "Let it out."

She looked away with tear-filled eyes and shyly slid her hair back over her shoulder, then looked at him. "I hate Barlow. I can't believe I ever married him. I found out that he was doing that meth—dope! Can you believe that? That idiot came by here before daylight to steal the mop bucket that we used at the store, said Daddy give it to him. He must think I'm stupid. Ha, like Daddy would have give him that." She sat back in her chair, sliding her hands to the edge of the table, adding, "I had divorce papers drawn up. All he needs to do is sign them, but he won't. He throws it in my face that my Daddy didn't believe in divorce, but..."

Dan leaned into her. "If you don't love him, then there is nothing to hang on to. I believe in marriage too, but a loving one. So if it ain't got love, then there ain't nothing to save. You do what you need to do. Your daddy did what was right for him, so you do the same."

"Charleen never divorced Frank, and I know she wasn't happy. Well, maybe at one time, but if she knew what I knew, well..." She paused, not wanting to tell him of the true Frank.

In her silence, he said, "You know Frank was killed about two weeks ago."

A shocked Prunella looked at him with glee. "No, I didn't know. Please tell me more. What happened?" She leaned in toward him so she wouldn't miss a word.

He adjusted himself in his chair and cleared his throat. "Well, yeah. They say he was down at that beer joint on Highway 15. He was with another man in the parking lot, smoking some of that wacky stuff, and somebody in a red beat-up truck pulled up and told him to bark like a dog, and when he wouldn't do it, the person in the truck pulled out a gun and clipped him dead, shot Frank right between the eyes. It was something about him messing around with a man's young daughter." He sat back in his chair. "Ol' boy seemed like a good fella. I don't know why it would have come to that. I don't know. The whole dang thang sounds fishy to me."

She shot him a look. "Serves him right!"

At her look, Dan thought, *Was Frank a bad man?*

Shooting him another look as if she could read his thoughts, she told him that Frank was no angel. "He got what he deserved. I do believe he messed with that man's daughter. As a matter of fact, I know he was a pervert!"

Sitting straight up in his chair, he said in shock, "Oh! You mean he was one of them kind of fellas?"

Prunella retrieved her cigarettes from the bar and lit one. "Yep, he was one of them kind." She sat down at the table, shoving the picture of the lilies further to the side with the ashtray. "Do you want me to tell it, or should I just keep it to myself?"

He leaned in. "Oh, indeed! Do tell." As she began giving the details—times and names—his mouth dropped open. The knowledge she was unleashing into his ears caused him to blurt out, "Oh, Lord! Did Charles know about that?"

"Not until the day before he died," she responded in a huff. "It's a good thing, too, that he didn't know before, because he was gonna kill him the day I told him."

Dan leaned back in his chair in disbelief, pondering all she had said. "Oh my, you never really know people, do you?"

She drew from her cigarette, then let out a cloud of smoke. "The reason you haven't seen me in town is because I've been laid up in here completely out of my tree. With Daddy dying on me and Christine coming back into my life...well, that part was my fault; I mistakenly thought that maybe since it was just me and her left in this world, we could be a family. But...well...yep, I blew a lot of the store money at the casino and going to the doctor for depression. Hell, that doctor caused me to get hooked on them pills."

He leaned in again and asked, "You out of money?"

Covering her face with her hand holding the cigarette, she replied with a sigh, "Yes, I know my sister got into my bank accounts and the things in the safe because she was the only one who would figure out how to get into it. Crafty wench!"

Gasping as he squirmed in his chair, he said, "There is no way you are out of all that. Your daddy has—what about all that other stuff he had? I remember your daddy showing me a solid gold cross he had gotten when his daddy died and the expensive horse statue he got for Charleen. Oh, Lord! Don't tell me she got those?"

The sound of a phone ringing interrupted their conversation. He looked around for the sound, then realized it was his cell phone in his pocket ringing. Excusing himself to answer the call, he walked outside as she fixed a glass of tea.

He returned and they both stood quietly in the kitchen. Dan looked down at the picture frame on the table, then picked it up to see that it was damaged. "What happened to this? Oh, these are nice lilies. Your daddy said something about some lilies he had planted." He placed the frame back onto the table. "Hmm...well, I've got to go load up a couple of hogs to take to the butcher." They walked outside together. Before he climbed into his truck, he turned to her. "Now, if you need anything, you call me. If you don't get me, you can tell my wife, Nancy. She'll take care of it."

Chapter **28**

Charleen's Corvette

As Dan left the driveway, Prunella gave him a final wave. She looked up at the beautiful, clear sky and thought, *Good, it stopped raining. Today would be a good day to check out the Corvette.*

She went back into Charles's office and rummaged around in the big metal desk searching for the keys. As she sifted through the drawers, her hand felt the cold metal of a .38 special Smith & Wesson revolver. Prunella picked it up, surprised that there was still a gun in the house. Guns freaked her out, so she quickly put it back. Pushing back another pile of junk, she saw Tinker Bell. She lifted it up with a smile, knowing this character had watched over what she was searching for. Attached to the ring dangled the keys.

Prunella changed her shoes to prepare for the tall, wet grass that she would have to walk through to get to the car. She went out the back door and around the mulberry tree, taking note of an abundance of different types of lilies under the mulberry tree. *Oh, those would be wonderful if they weren't surrounded by all those ugly weeds grown in between them. Maybe I'll get out here and pull the weeds,* she thought.

The further she walked from the house, the higher the grass became. She carefully weaved her way through, watching her step while walking to the broken-down car parked under the shed. Its beauty was hidden by the years of having sat cold and alone. This was the first time she had been out to look at it in a while. *Stupid, stupid me! I should have fixed the car when I had all that money in my hands. Now it's too late, but I still ain't selling it,* she thought. As she walked out to the molding, dusty car, she continued to curse herself over the mistakes she had made, and her mind turned to the last time she had been out there with Charles looking at it.

274

***

There was a chill in the air that February day. Charles had just returned from the local deli with a plate lunch and sat down at the kitchen table to share it with her. As he was crunching on a fried chicken leg, he watched her pick apart the sweet yeast roll from the dinner. She sat there quietly wondering what he was planning for the day, but he was too engrossed in the fried chicken to speak. She spoke as she tore apart a piece of the bread and stuffed it into her mouth, "So what's your game plan for this lazy Sunday?"

He took another bite of the chicken leg, chewed on it a bit, and wiped his mouth, saying, "Well, I thought maybe we could go out there and take a look at the Corvette. See what it's gonna take to fix her up."

She almost choked on the roll, for this was the last thing she had thought he would say. It was only two days after her nineteenth birthday, and she was in high hopes that this could be a birthday present. Jumping to her feet, she placed the half-eaten roll back into Charles's dinner box. "I'm going to go change my clothes," she said; then she quickly scooted across the living room floor and disappeared down the hallway.

He smiled at her excitement. It took no time for her to return in a plain white long-sleeve shirt tucked down into a pair of flattering blue jeans. She was ready. All she had to do was put on her shoes, and they were at the back door, loosely tied, waiting to be filled. He closed the lid to his dinner box and tossed it into the trash. "Okay, all done. Ready to go?"

She replied by wiggling down into her shoes and snatching the back door open. The intense brightness of the high noon's light reflected into her baby-blue eyes, causing her to squint so severely that she turned back to get her sunshades. In her blind rush to get them, she ran smack dab into her father's chest.

"Whoa! Slow down there, Flash Lightning!"

"Oh, Daddy, I'm so sorry. I can't see a thing."

He laughed at her. "I'll see you out there."

She fumbled around on the kitchen counter until she found her sunshades. He walked out onto the patio, around the large mulberry tree, and past the row of large pines and magnolia trees. Just as the large creosote poles and aluminum roof came into sight, Prunella flew past him. All he could see was long, straight, blonde hair flapping and the bottom of her white Reebok shoes. She was in a mad dash to reach the driver's side of the Corvette before her father did. Her heart pumped with excitement as she approached the sexy car, taking note of its squatting, mean grip on the dirt under the dusty shed. She could envision herself crawling in behind the wheel and cruising down the highway.

Prunella could feel Charleen's spirit flow through her and growing stronger the closer she came to the car. She dreamed of removing the T-top and letting the wind toss her hair. As she reached out to touch the car, it was as if sparks flew from her fingertips as they lightly ran down the sleek body of her sister's beautiful, beloved car. Joy began to fill her as she touched the flat chrome door handle, but disappointment set in instead as she realized the car was locked, and her father was taking his sweet time getting there with the key. She tried to contain herself as she stood next to the Corvette, soaking up every detail of it to occupy her mind. She huffed at the car, then turned her attention to look at Charles's tractor, camper, aluminum boat, and various tools through her dark sunglasses. She dropped her head back, staring at the large wooden beams above her head. Then she spun around and leaned back against the dirty hot-rod, letting out a long sigh. Sliding her sunglasses to the top of her head, she folded her arms in anticipation.

Charles could see her standing there waiting on him, so he intentionally began to walk slower in order to aggravate her. Squinting his eyes to peer to get a good view of her face, he spoke loudly, "What's the matter? It locked?" He turned around and began to walk back toward the house. "Oh, shoot! I forgot the key in the house." He giggled at the look she gave him.

"Just hurry up!"

He spun back around to her, waving his hand. "I'm just kidding, girly. I got it in my pocket."

She gave him a twisted smile. This caused him to pick up the pace. He dug around in his sharply creased khakis for the key and tossed them to her; Prunella quickly caught them with her well-manicured hands. Delight spread across her face as she spun around to unlock the wasting-away car. Uncaring of her white shirt, she jumped into the dusty, dry-rotting red seats.

Charles met up with her at the opened driver's side door. As he approached it, he could see her pretending to drive. This reminded him of the first time she drove his truck as a tiny little thing, with her small feet digging into his lap, swaying with the steering wheel.

He smiled at this memory as he swiped his index finger across the dusty tinted-glass T-top, saying, "So, what do you think it'll take to fix it?"

She looked around at the inside damage. It had not been touched since Frank had pawned it to Charles years ago. It still reeked of stale alcohol and cigarettes. The carpet was stained and worn in places, and the once-beautiful crimson-red seats needed to be completely recovered. The leather had cracked and was torn at its seams, exposing the foam cushion underneath. She reached for the automatic gearshift; it wobbled around, loose, and felt sticky. She ran her hands around the steering wheel, which had the same sticky feel, then looked up at her father, afraid to tell him that it would probably be pretty expensive. So she just sat there wide-eyed and shrugged her shoulders. Prunella knew he liked money enough to not spend it ridiculously.

He walked toward the rear and around to the passenger side, saying, "Oh, I don't think it'll take that much to fix her up. It's a little dirty, but a good washing just might do the trick." Once he made it around to the other side, he stopped talking and squatted down at the door panel. "Shoot! I forgot about Frank's mishap. It looks a little worse than I remember. He said he hit a pole." Charles ran his hand around the nice-sized dent and observed black scratches inside the dent. "It looks more like somebody kicked this door!" She didn't hear him, for the music of her favorite singer was playing loudly in her head, while imagining the T-top off and the wind blowing in her hair as she cruised a beautiful coastline.

Not knowing she wasn't listening, he just patted the dent. "I don't think it was a pole after all." Then he stopped speaking, for he thought she was listening to him and didn't want her to hear what he really felt about the dent at that moment. He continued to crouch down at the door observing the damage and calculating the possible cost to fix it. He looked at the flat, wide, balding tires and began to talk to Prunella, who still wasn't listening to him. "Well, we'll have to put new tires on here. These are too old and dry-rotted. I'll bet they won't even hold air." He paused, then clapped his hands together and said, "Well, I give him ample time to come get square with me on this car, so it's mine now. You know, I think I'm going to paint it a candy-apple red."

She was still in her own little world, but snapped out of it when he said the word paint. Giving him a look through the dirty passenger window, she exhaled loudly. "Excuse me!" Then she jumped out of the car in order to hear him correctly. She closed the door and asked him to repeat himself.

Charles stood up and propped his forearms on the top of the car. In return, she did the same, and they now stood face to face. He said, "I think it would look good painted candy-apple red. What do you think?"

Her smile disappeared and frustration crackled in her voice as she quickly snapped, "No! It has to stay the same as Charleen had it. We can't change it. Besides, what color would you make the interior? You can't have red on red. That would look crazy!"

He pushed himself back, leaned down, and looked through the light-green moss-covered glass. Pulling a handkerchief from his pocket, he wiped the glass for a better view of the inside. "Well, I think it would look good black. Yep! A beautiful blazing-red paint job and black interior." Still wiping the glass with the handkerchief, he continued, "Black interior and trim it in chrome. We'll put some nice clean chrome trim and rims on it. Oh, I can see it, can't you?"

She took two steps backward and slid her hands in her back pockets, then took a deep breath. "Are you going to let me have this car one day?"

He quickly spouted, "Hell, no! Do you have any idea how powerful this car is? You can forget it, girly. This car is too dangerous for you." He waved his hand at her and slowly stepped around the side to the front of the car. Making eye contact with her, he proceeded to lecture her, stopping every other small step to remind her of how careless she was.

She snatched her hands from her back pockets and crossed her arms. "We can't paint over Charleen's memory!"

It was as if she had slapped him with those words. He stopped dead in his tracks at the tone of her voice. His face turned red as he said, "Now look here. It's not like that at all. She had this paint job done at a shop by one of her friends, someone I don't even know. Besides, it would be a pain to find a match to this color!" He quickly turned the tables back on how careless she was. Then he began to quickly walk without looking down. All of a sudden, in mid-sentence, he disappeared in front of the car, out of her view. Charles had clumsily tripped over a bright-green milk crate sitting there.

She was frozen in place. "Are you all right?"

After a moment, he slowly peeped over the large hood. All she could see were the top of his head and his bright blue eyes. He watched the look on her face turn from concern to a big smile. "Now Prunella, don't you say a word."

She gave him a wink with a smile as she slid her sunglasses down onto her face. "Me, careless? Ha! Well, ain't that the pot calling the kettle black. I'm gonna have this car one day."

***

Chapter 29

Putting Her Foot Down

Prunella got to the car with a big smile from the memory of that day. Two wasps were flying around it just as she reached for the door. Her immediate response was to swat at them and run from the car. Eventually, she overcame her fear and walked back, cursing them and carefully watching them fly around. As they disappeared high above the car to a nest in the ceiling, she climbed into the Corvette.

She sat there wishing that the radio would work, wiping the rearview mirror grime with her fingers. Looking at her reflection, she gave herself a half-hearted smile, but then quickly dropped it, looking away and wishing she hadn't looked. Memories of Charleen picking her up from school pained her heart. Charleen had always parked directly in front of the school so all the onlookers could see Prunella climb into the fast, beautiful car with her. Her heart saddened at the thought. *Oh, how nice it would be to have those days as a family again without Christine or Frank.* She then thought back to the last time she'd spoken to Frank. Her mind reflected back to the day of her father's funeral

***

Charles never woke up from his deep slumber on that rainy morning in February. A peaceful smile remained on his face as his body was covered after his soul had escaped to heaven. Prunella stood by tearfully, knowing her father was gone. Friends and family filled the church pews for the memorial of his life, and she greeted people at the door. As her back was turned talking to an older couple, a tall, handsome older man tapped her on her slightly exposed shoulder, and a deep voice said, "Oh, my! You look so much like your sister, it's almost haunting. Beautiful! Absolutely beautiful! Do you remember me?"

Prunella patted his long arm and said, "Well, of course I do, Mr. Mark." She managed to maintain her smile, but she'd seen Frank standing just past Mark in the doorway, watching her interact with Mark and his wife. A disgusting smirk appeared on his face as he rubbed his hand over his mouth as if he were trying to hold in his thoughts. Age had not been a good friend to him. Those attractive looks Frank had possessed had long been lost. He was now frumpy, as he wore a dingy white button-up shirt and pants that looked as if he'd pulled them from the bottom of the waste basket. And now that long, dark mane of hair was gone, leaving only a few sprigs of gray hair.

After their conversation came to a close, she hugged the couple and thanked them for coming. Mark walked right past Frank, completely ignoring him. After he passed, Frank unfolded his arms and wobbled over to Prunella, who rolled her eyes at his approach.

As he got closer, Frank spouted off, "What's he doing here? Your daddy would be bent out of shape if he knew Mark was here."

She could smell the strong odor of alcohol coming from him and asked, "Have you been drinking?"

"No, Prunella. You know I wouldn't come here like that!"

"Calm down. You're too loud."

"So why is he here?" he asked too loudly again.

Frustrated, she pulled him away from the doorway so people couldn't hear him. She reached out, pulling him by his shirt sleeve. "I suggest you get a grip on yourself, or you're going to have to leave." Now standing a good distance away from the door, she gave him an evil look and added, "Now, you listen to me. My father and Mark may have had their disagreements, but they are nothing compared to yours!"

"What's that supposed to mean?" he huffed.

She glanced around to see if anyone might be listening. Unable to contain her thoughts and feelings about him any longer, Prunella leaned in close to him and whispered, "My father wanted to kill you, and I'll bet if I tell Mark what I know..." She paused, lifted her hand to his face, and tapped him hard right between his eyes with her French-tipped fingernail, adding, "I'll bet you'd receive a bullet right there!" She relaxed her arm and continued, "So honestly, I think after today you need to toddle along and never look back. You spout off at the mouth about Mark being here, but you're the one who truly has no business here!"

"Now you hold on there just a minute. I've got plenty of business being here. As a matter of fact, you and me have the matter of a Corvette to clear up before you ever get to stop looking at this pretty face."

She tossed her head back and laughed at his arrogance, then replied, "Oh, please! You old, dried-up turd! You are the most disgusting man I've ever known!"

He reached out, placing both of his short, stubby hands on her shoulders, and began to slowly rub them. "If that redneck husband don't give it to you like you need it, you just call me. I'll tickle your fancy anytime."

Shoving his hands off of her shoulders, she walked away from him. Frank reached out to pull her back, but she had moved too quickly for his reach, so in a loud tone he said, "I'm coming to get that car. You can just get my title ready!"

Once he spoke those loud, threatening words, she stopped dead in her tracks. It was if he had slapped her in the back with his words. Their eyes met as she slowly turned and walked back to him. Growling with anger, her words were like sparks flying in a steel mill: "Did you pay him back?" Prunella was now standing face to face and nose to nose with foul-smelling Frank, unmindful of his stench. "Did you pay him back the money he loaned you? Well, you know what? Whatever financial dealings you had with my father are now mine, which means you are going to have to pay me in order to get it back. And truthfully, your money isn't good enough to get it back, so I'm keeping my sister's car!" With a hard, fiery stare, she added, "My father wanted to kill you. I know how you treated my sister. All those drunk fits she had to put up with."

He reached out and touched her hand, but she jerked back, saying, "Don't you ever touch me again or anybody else for that matter! I don't know if Charleen knew what a sick, twisted pervert you are, but I do!"

Reaching out and touching her hand again, he pleaded, "But you are family to me. I loved your daddy, and Charleen was the love of my life."

Her stomach turned at his words; the word *family* coming from his mouth had forced this conversation beyond disgust. She snatched her hand from his sad grip. Waiting for a couple of people to walk by, she discreetly said, "Leave right now! Don't stay for the service.

You will never be a part of my life. You may have a lot of people fooled, but I know what you did to Janet." He tried to look away, but she followed his head movement, making sure to maintain eye contact with him. "Oh? You didn't think I knew about that? Well, I suggest you leave now and never come back around." She turned to leave him standing there, but turned back around to face him and said, "If you come out to the house harassing me about the Corvette, remember: Daddy has a lot of land." Tossing her hair and giving him a wink, she added, "Like looking for a needle in a haystack." Then she smiled and walked away.

***

Prunella sat there stewing over thoughts of Frank until the two wasps returned, grabbing her attention. As they slammed into the dirty windshield, it seemed as if these two beautiful creatures were in some sort of disagreement, rather like a pair of sisters arguing over clothes. This reminded her of her own sibling rivalry.

Life had been so peaceful until Charles had passed away. The day after the funeral, Christine had re-emerged into her life. Now unprotected, without her father's presence, she felt like a sitting duck on eighty acres. She thought back to the day Christine had fluttered back into the doorway only to darken it.

***

It had only been one day since Charles had left the world. Late that afternoon, there was a knock at her door. A drowsy Prunella rose from the cool leather couch and stumbled her way to the door. Her head was swimming and her vision was fuzzy from the medication she had taken. This caused her to move much slower than normal, and just as she reached for the door, it popped open. Shocked at the sudden entry, she snapped, "What the hell? I was going to open it!"

A much-thinner, beautiful Christine pushed past an unkempt Prunella. "Oh, don't I look good? It looks like I could give you and Charleen a run for your money. I'll have all the boys after me," she said, as she sashayed about.

Prunella rolled her eyes, thinking, *Oh my God. She is still intimidated by Charleen, who's been dead for eighteen years. Whatever!*

Walter trailed in behind Christine as if he were her shadow. As she stopped twirling, she quickly said, "Well, I know you're jealous," looking her up and down. "Damn! What happened to you? It's 3:00 in the afternoon, and you look like crap. What are you doing? Letting yourself go? Never thought I'd see this!" She grabbed her cigarettes from the counter, lit one, and replied with only a cloud of smoke as she walked over to the couch and sat down. Christine was frustrated at her silence and snapped, "Well, aren't you going to ask me how I lost all that weight?" But she didn't allow time for Prunella to answer. "I had a gastric-bypass operation last year. It sucked for the first few months, but don't I look gorgeous?" Seeing that Prunella didn't even look up at her or appear to have any interest, Christine began sifting through the unopened mail on the counter.

She was still not looking at her but replied, "Well, you look really good."

"I need you to buy me a car."

Prunella thought, *Oh great! Daddy hasn't been gone long, and here she is looking for money!* She crossed her feet and placed them on the coffee table and said, "Well, you meet me halfway, and I'll consider it."

She flared up but smiled at her once she looked over at her. "I don't have half."

"Where's that car your daddy give ya?"

"It's still at the house. Why?"

"Well, take it to the scrapyard. That would be something."

"I'm keeping the only thing my daddy ever give me. So, no!" Dropping the sour-sweet smile, she said, "Oh, come on! You got more money than I did."

"Oh, my God! Really?" she gasped.

Christine could tell this conversation wasn't going her way, so she changed the subject. "Have you seen my kids?" she asked, slapping Walter on the top of his head, adding, "Go get my wallet from the car."

Walter grabbed his head and looked at Prunella, embarrassed. Without saying a word, he scurried out to the car. While he was gone, Christine saw an unopened envelope on the counter that struck her interest. While her sister wasn't looking, she slid the envelope in her back pocket. Walter opened the door just in time to see her do this. She gave him a look that told him to hush up or she'd smack him. He didn't say a word and handed her the pink wallet.

290

They both walked into the living room. He sat on the loveseat, and she plopped next to Prunella as she relaxed on the couch, jarring her from her comfort. Christine flipped out a plastic photo binder, which was connected to the wallet, and pointed at a photo. Prunella gasped at the sight of this child, for he had been six the last time she had seen him, but he was now nineteen and looked a lot like Frank. She cleared her thoughts as she recovered from her shock and said, "Oh my! He sure has grown! Where is he now?"

"Oh, he hates Mississippi, so he went to live with his daddy for the summer and decided to stay." She stuck another photo in her face. "Look. This is my baby, Ricky. Ain't he just precious? He is my pride and joy."

Prunella looked at the pictures of both boys, but she just couldn't stop wondering if Frank was the father of Donovan. Not thinking, Prunella blurted out, "Did you hear about Barlow having a wreck? Yeah, I had to buy him a new truck. The one he had was on its last leg."

Christine complained at her confession, "Oh! I see. You'll buy that lowlife a ride, but you can't buy one for your only sister?"

She had a way of pulling on her heartstrings so hard until they popped one by one. Prunella thought that maybe if she gave in, Christine would back off and let her live in peace. From that day forward, the visits from Christine were with false intentions. There was always something to do with Prunella's fortune.

Chapter 30

Tractor Troubles

Prunella climbed out of the Corvette, closed the door, and leaned against it. She looked at two large holes dug out in the ground close to the Corvette, and she kicked the dirt. "What was he thinking?" It brought to mind another crazy part of her life.

Christine and Barlow were constantly driving her crazy with phone calls about one another. She would complain that she'd seen him coming out from behind the house with a load of stuff. Then he would call and say that he'd seen her messing around Stella's trailer. Prunella couldn't keep her eyes on them all the time. She didn't trust either of them, but they were all the family she had to hold on to. Dealing with them pushed her further into a depression. She would take a few of her pills and escape to the bells, whistles, flashing lights, and spinning reels of the Gulf Coast casinos. The sounds and lights mixed well with her medication and seemed to help her shake off the depression. She'd been so often that she was quickly granted a VIP card, but unbeknownst to her, Prunella's inheritance was slowly RIP.

***

Walter approached Prunella one day and asked if he could buy Oliver's old truck. She was hesitant about selling the truck because she wanted to save it for someone in need. Unfortunately, it was he who was in need. Walter didn't have any money; Prunella knew that. Christine was surely no help either, so she thought, *I could use some help with this big yard*. Walter seemed to be a good fit for it, so they traded to meet their own needs.

After a couple of times of him using the equipment, the riding lawn mower and Weed eater stopped working. They convinced her that neither of them were working right to begin with, and within a short time, the grass was soon beyond a lawn mower's ability. She knew of only one thing: the tractor. Prunella called him and asked if he knew how to operate a tractor. A confident Walter assured her that he could. "I'm going to be leaving for the coast in a few minutes," she told him. "I'll leave the tractor key under the carport behind the cannon."

Not long after she was coast-bound, he and Christine decided to take on the yard. He was excited to operate the tractor, for the farm where he had once worked had plenty of them, but the farm boys wouldn't let him operate any of them. He was like Rudolph the Red-nosed Reindeer: they would laugh and call him names. But if you had seen Walter work, well, you would know at least Rudolph had that red nose.

He jumped out of the little truck almost before it came to a complete stop. He looked all around but didn't see the cannon. Christine rushed madly across the yard. She couldn't wait to venture into Stella's trailer, thinking no more of him as she anticipated "antique heaven," and her money-grubbing hands were anxious to inventory all that lay in her reach.

Walter yelled, "Hey, where is the cannon?"

An aggravated Christine stopped, turned around, and yelled back, "Damn! Are you blind? It's next to the door!" She then turned back and set out to rummage through Stella's trailer, mumbling about how stupid he was.

In the meantime, Walter was searching for the cannon, but it was not to be found. He walked toward where it should have been and found the key on the bare floor by itself. Not caring that the cannon was gone, he picked up the key and ran to the tractor with a huge smile was on his face. His heart fluttered with anticipation. It was like redneck heaven to him. With a touch of swagger, he stood there between the tractor and the Corvette, only giving the car a glance but staring lovingly at the tractor as if it were a hot girl he was about to approach for her phone number. Walter walked big and tall to the big blue Ford tractor and climbed aboard, placing the key into the ignition and turning it. Nothing. He tried again...still nothing! Cursing, he suddenly remembered. "Oh, yeah!" And he cranked the tractor and tried to back it up. Finally, after a few adjustments, the tractor quickly backed up. Once it cleared the over-sized shed, he threw the gear into forward. The speed was set from the last time the tractor had been used, and it was too high for him. He made a few very speedy circles in the small, open field trying to figure it all out, but as he was looking down at the levers and gages, a panicked Walter didn't realize that he'd made his way back to the shed. He maneuvered the speeding tractor past a row of magnolia and pine trees, barely missing them. His mind raced, trying to figure out how to stop it, as he steered it back to the small, open field. He circled in the field, frantically praying and cursing at the same time, trying to figure out how to stop it. Before he knew it, the tractor came back around toward the shed. It was too close to the trees, and he quickly swerved to miss them. Having overcompensated for the trees, the tractor was now heading straight for the shed housing the Corvette.

BAM! The tractor's front end slammed into the large creosote pole just next to the car. It lodged itself in place as the bulky tires began to dig deep down into the ground. It was bulldozing the deeply planted pole of the shed. He couldn't think straight. All he thought of was to jump from the tractor and get Christine for help. Leaving it running as it ripped and tore through the soil, he ran across the yard to the trailer where she was plundering. He flew in to see his now-thinner love digging in silverware.

While he was telling her of the catastrophe, Barlow pulled up at the house. He drove around the back of the house to the shed, but as he got closer, he could see the running, unattended tractor. He jumped from his truck and climbed onto the tractor and turned it off. In the silence, he sat there wondering what was going on. Just as he was climbing off the tractor, Walter came running toward him. "Man, am I glad you dropped by! I didn't know what I was going to do!" Once Barlow knew that Walter was the culprit, he took no time in confronting him about his abandonment of the running tractor. They began to argue until, suddenly, the sound of someone being decked in the face echoed across the yard. Christine screamed at the sight of Barlow throwing a punch at her smaller man. Feeling that it wasn't a fair fight, she continued to yell and scream at him as she ran to them, "Stop! Stop, Barlow!"

Meanwhile, Prunella had stopped at a store just a town away. As she was about to go in, she realized she'd left her wallet with her ID in it at home, so she turned around to get it. Christine called Prunella as the two men pushed one another around, but Prunella couldn't hear the ringing of the phone over her tunes and her singing harmoniously and loudly along with the music. Christine kept calling, but unbeknownst to them all, Prunella was only minutes away. Within seconds of pulling into her driveway, she caught a glimpse of her husband's truck at the shed and a wad of bodies scrambling around on the ground. She was already frustrated to be back at the house, and to top it off, the people she wanted to run from were all there. So in an instant of madness, she quickly tore across the open front yard to the shed, pulled up quickly, slamming on the brakes, and stopped inches from the sight of Barlow sitting on top of Walter. He had his arms pinned to the ground, and Christine was cursing for him to let him up.

Prunella jumped from her car. "What is going on here? Barlow, stop that! Let him up!" He looked up at her through his sweaty, long black hair, sat back, and huffed as he let the fella's arms free, releasing him and standing up. Walter rolled away to safety, then stood up next to Christine. She helped him up and fussed at Barlow all the while, sending him voodoo cursing looks.

Prunella looked over at the tractor and the mess that had been made. Her face became cross as she slowly turned back to the trio and asked, "What the hell happened here?" All three started to talk at once, but she held up one hand, commanding them to stop. She then pointed her finger at Barlow. "Okay, now you tell me. Why are you beating on him?"

He brushed the grass and dirt from his clothes, pushed back his tangled hair, and exhaled as he pointed his finger. "That dumb-ass boy rammed the tractor into the dang pole. Then Mr. Stupid left it running, while in gear!" He stomped over to the tractor, which was just one foot from the Corvette, then added as he pointed, "Look! See! His stupid ass liked to have hit the Corvette!"

She folded her arms in disgust, for she didn't know what to think as she stewed over the fact that the car had almost been pulverized by the tractor. Her face grew red, and a blazing fire began to burn deep inside her. Tilting her head back, exposing her face to the dusk sky, she let out a loud, blood-curdling scream, jolting them all into silence. She looked back at them and thought to herself, *I can't stand to look at them any longer.* Hanging her head down, she said, "Leave. Please just leave. Every one of you, just leave me alone. I can't deal with this right now."

As she turned around to walk to her car, Christine tried to plead with her, but her words were never heard. Prunella kept walking to the car, got in, slammed the door, cranked the car, and then turned the music up to escape the chaos in her world at that moment.

She drove back through the yard and pulled underneath the carport. Just as she opened the car door, an out-of-breath Walter popped up in her view, startling her. In her mind, she screamed, *Oh my! Not now! Please go away!*

"I'm really sorry about that. I...I..." he said.

She held up her hand to say stop, then turned it over and exposed an open palm. "Just give me the key to the tractor." About that time, Barlow's truck ripped through the yard, racing down the driveway to the highway and leaving a cloud of dust.

As they watched him speed away, Walter asked, "Hey, what happened to your cannon?"

She quickly spun around looking to where it should be. "Where is my cannon? Where is it?"

Walter shrugged his shoulders. "I don't know. It wasn't here when I got here."

Her mad thoughts rang out loud, "Can this day get any worse?"

He reached out to her, but just as he touched her shoulder, Christine turned the corner. "What the hell is going on here? You're under here flirting with my sister!" She pulled at his short brown hair.

"Don't do that! That hurts!"

Prunella sighed loudly. "Oh yes, this day can get worse. It just did." Anger was still in her, so she turned to Christine and snapped, "Where is my cannon?"

Giving her a smile, she replied, "What are you talking about? I don't have it. Maybe if you asked your husband, you might find out." She looked down at her fingernails and picked at them, then added smugly, "But I doubt it."

"What did he do with it? If you know something, you need to tell me."

Still looking at her fingernails, she replied, "Hummm," then with a light laugh, "You know Barlow. He probably took it to the scrapyard. I've been told he has been going there a lot lately. I'd start there if I was you."

Prunella could have spit fire at that moment at the thought that someone would steal her fondest memory. Oliver had made two cannons. He had given one to Charles and kept one for himself. At every family gathering, Charles and Oliver would fire them, but once her uncle died, they were never shot again. It had been sitting under the carport in that same spot for over a year, and now it was gone. She could feel that her tears were on the verge of falling, and she didn't want them to see her cry, so she stomped her foot and pointed to the road, yelling, "Leave! Now!"

Christine grumbled as she spun around, snatching Walter's arm in the process. Once they left, Prunella called Barlow, while pacing the carport floor in frustration. After several tries, he finally answered the phone. "What do you want?"

"Did you get my daddy's cannon?"

"I don't know what you're talking about. What cannon?"

"Don't play dumb. You know damn good and well what cannon I'm talking about!" she seethed.

"I don't know what you're talking about. Don't bother me with it. I don't know nothing."

"Yes, you do, Barlow! The one Daddy and Uncle Oliver shot all the time!"

"Whatever, Prunella!"

The phone disconnected, and she thought to herself, *See if I ever help you again.*

Chapter 31

Nasty Barlow

Months later, on a cold October night, Barlow totaled his truck. His life was spared, suffering only a broken leg and arm and a nice-sized goose egg on his forehead. Prunella knew no matter what story he tried to tell her that it was more than likely he who had caused the wreck. They were still married, but they lived apart. She felt obligated to take care of him, so she moved him into the house with her and gave him the spare bedroom, although she didn't want him there, for he'd never kept a job and was a lazy slob. She took care of everything. so he was very happy to be living with her again.

She passed on the same stipulation that she had given Christine and Walter: "Stay out of Daddy's room." Six months went by of her dealing with a pitiful Barlow. Finally he was up and running again with only a slight limp. She felt it was time for him to go, but she didn't know how to tell him. It was killing her inside to be living in his hell again; his old habits hadn't changed. She had thrown her hands up before with him, and now she was doing it again. It was almost impossible to keep the house orderly. He would leave empty cans around and continue to use the ashtrays even if the butts were overflowing onto the tables. Every dish he used was left dirty to decorate the living room. He also left nasty spit bottles lying around, some with a lid and some without, so there were disgusting spills from the opened ones. The floors were scuffed from his dirty boots. Plain and simple, he was ruining the house. He didn't care about keeping anything clean, including his body.

He had no problem going hunting and fishing and then coming in unwashed to lounge on the couch. Charles's once-nice brick home was now becoming condemned with Barlow's help. He had to go! His actions finally gave her the strength to put him out. Around 2:00 a.m. one night, she awoke thirsty. As she opened her bedroom door, a small light down the hallway caught her eye. The soft glow was coming from underneath Charles's bedroom door. Her heart fluttered because no one was supposed to be in there. A sense of wariness turned to straight fear as she crept down the hallway to her father's door. The door was slightly cracked. Fear hung in her throat as she stood there wondering what was on the other side of the door. After collecting her thoughts for a moment, she slowly pushed it open. No one was in the room, and everything was still the way Charles had left it, except a few things had been moved around on his dresser and nightstand.

She could see that the bathroom light was on through the slightly cracked door. Hearing someone stirring around in there, her heart beat faster with every sound. In fear, she stood outside the bathroom door wondering, "Should I look in there or just go get Barlow?"

Her small frame stood frozen in place with muscles that seemed of no use. She couldn't even lift her arm to push open the door. *Come on!* she thought. *You're a tough chick. You know this house like the back of your hand, and you'll be out that front door before whoever this is can even see you. They will never catch me.* Her face dropped as the door opened and light from the bathroom lit up the shadow she stood in. Now standing face to face with a bloody Barlow, she screamed, causing him to jump with a burly cry.

Throwing a punch into his chest, Prunella unloaded on him. "What the hell are you doing in here?" Looking him up and down, she noted the blood all over his clothes. She poked her head into the bathroom past him and saw all she needed to see. "Barlow Benjamin Brown! Get the hell out of my house now, and take that half-skinned deer out of my father's shower!"

"I can't see out there to clean it. Besides, I told my buddy I'd have this done for him by morning."

She was so angry that she lunged at him, thrusting both of her fists into his chest, screaming, "You nasty, disrespectful piece of crap! Get out of my life! I hate you!" The words I and hate rolled off her tongue so easily that she backed up from him and looked at him with tear-filled eyes. "Please leave! I can't take this anymore. I want a divorce!"

Shocked at her words, he yelled back, "No! I ain't gonna give you one. Besides, what would your daddy think if he heard you say that?"

He reached out to touch her, but she recoiled from him. "Don't touch me. Oh my God! Look at your hands. Yuck!"

Barlow left that night with the deer in hand. An exhausted Prunella popped a few pills, then went back to bed to lie down. As she lay there thinking, she knew he had left a big mess in her father's bathroom and it'd be up to her to clean it up. It looked like a crime scene. She sank further into a depressed state and finally drifted off to sleep.

The next morning, she refused to get out of bed, knowing the mess left behind in the bathroom. She mulled around the thought of giving Walter another chance to help her. Surely he couldn't tear anything up with just a wet sponge. She felt she needed to pay him for this nasty job, but she didn't know how much. Lying there until her bladder couldn't wait any longer, she got up and made the call to Walter. He was excited to take the job and make a little money.

His eagerness brought him and Christine to the house within minutes. They arrived to a fresh, beautiful Prunella, all ready to go enjoy the perks of her VIP card at the casino while she left him cleaning. She gave him a hundred-dollar bill and said, "I'm going to give you this now. I'll give you another when I get back. All I need you to do is gather up the trash and clean out the back shower where he had that deer. If you run across anything that looks like it may be important, don't throw it away. Just put it up here on the kitchen bar. I may not be back until late tonight, so just lock the door when you leave." She pulled Christine aside, just out of his hearing, and repeated the instructions to her, pleading with her to keep a close eye on him. Christine assured her that everything would be fine and that she wouldn't leave him unattended.

Once Prunella left the house to escape to the coast, there was one thing Christine had been dying to do since losing all her weight: go through Prunella's closet. She left Walter to the nastiness of the bathroom and began digging around in the closet. She spotted a wooden box on the top shelf and opened it, thinking at first it was junk until she found an old driver's license that belonged to Prunella. She let out a big laugh as she slipped the old ID into her bra. Then she found a beautiful light-blue dress and put it on. It fit her perfectly. So happy that she was finally small enough to wear her size, she danced in front of the large floor mirror, blowing kisses at herself. She thought about going in and surprising Walter, but as she entered Charles's bedroom, she remembered finding all those wonderful things in the closet as a little girl.

Christine flung the closet doors wide open. The closet was almost as it had been all those years ago except for a few cardboard boxes stacked in the bottom. She pulled some from the closet to make

307

room for her investigation, unafraid of being caught this time. She took her time looking around.

After a little while, unable to find what she was looking for, Christine turned to the boxes and sifted through old papers, photos, and sweet letters from Geraldine to Charles. This was frustrating. She sat down on the floor, intensely looking through them all, thinking, Where is it? It's got to be here. Tossing items to the side and making a huge mess, she suddenly stopped searching. Her hand had run across the beautiful black velvet box that had contained the gold cross, and she remembered how it had fallen to the floor when she was snooping as a child. It had been nothing to her then, but now she wanted to get her hands on it. The beautiful ribbon was gone, but she didn't care. The feel of the box in her hands gave her the happiest feeling as she flipped back the top in high hopes of seeing that beautiful solid-gold cross. She was anxious to see if there was a stamp indicating its weight and purity.

The joy dropped from her face as she found the box empty. She threw the box across the room toward the bathroom door where Walter was scrubbing the shower. Her fit of anger drew him from the bathroom, and he looked around until he saw her sitting on the floor. "What the hell? What was that racket?" He walked toward her and saw his beautiful woman in that dress. He leaned down to her and said, "Hey! Let's do it right here."

She pushed him, causing him to fall backward into the boxes. She flung her head around, looking away from him. "Serves you right. Now go on and get back to your job!"

As Walter struggled to get up, he saw her searching through Charles's belongings. "What are you doing?"

"Don't worry about it. Just keep doing what you're doing. Now go away!"

He quickly left her and went back into the bathroom. Another of her memories from years ago was of the metal box. She lay back on the floor to look under the bed, saying, "Damn it! It's got to be here somewhere." Then she saw it but couldn't quite reach it, so she stood up and tossed the bed aside like it was nothing. When she picked the metal box up, to her surprise, it wasn't locked. She held her breath as she lifted the lid expectantly only to be disappointed. More pictures and letters! She threw the box to the floor in anger and huffed at it. Then she saw something that made a sneaky smile stretch across her face. On the floor was Charles's worn-out brown leather wallet. She ran into the bathroom to Walter. "I'll be right back. I've got to go to the house for just a few minutes." She gave him a kiss on his sweaty cheek and left him to the filthy bathroom.

Later that night when she turned into her driveway, Prunella didn't see Walter's truck. She thought how wonderful it was going to be to walk into a clean, quiet house, but as her headlights lit up the carport, the porch light came on and out he walked. She felt a sinking feeling in her gut as she stepped out of her car, while maintaining eye contact with him. "Where is Christine?"

He shrugged his shoulders. "I don't know. It's been all day, She took my truck, and I've tried to call her but no answer."

Not another word was said, because she was upset with Christine and didn't want to take it out on him, so she tightened her lips and walked in, dropping her purse in shock at the sight of the house. The only thing that was clean was the kitchen counter bar, where she put all of the mail. She didn't say a word as she started toward the hallway.

Walter spoke out, "Barlow stopped by. He took some guns out of here. He said they were his."

She stopped, frozen in place, as she slowly turned back to him, shooting him a mean look. "There isn't anything in this house that belongs to him!" Sprinting down the hallway to her father's room, Prunella thought, *The only place Barlow could have gotten those guns was from the large safe in that room.* She flung open the door to the bedroom and instantly fell to her knees as she looked at the destroyed room and saw the safe door, wide open.

Chapter **32**

Behind the Photo

Prunella stood outside the Corvette continuing to think about the day she had left Walter down the road in the dark. Then, with great pleasure, she had called Christine and told her she could pick him up from the side of the road and had stressed to her, "And y'all stay away from my house! I am done with you two!" While standing there thinking of her past trouble with her so-called family, she had scrubbed a hole in the dirt with her foot. It was getting late, and she had stood there in thought long enough.

She lovingly gave the Corvette one more touch with her eyes and walked back to the house, taking a shortcut through the beautiful patch of lilies growing underneath the mulberry tree. Bending down to pick a couple, she heard the loud sound of a truck rapidly approaching. She left the lilies unpicked and walked around the front of the house to see who it might be. To her shock, it was Walter. As the truck slid to a stop and the dust settled, he stepped out with his hand in the air as if to surrender. She couldn't believe the gall of him. She thought she had made herself clear when she told him to get lost, so she crossed her arms and snapped, "Just what do you want?"

Walter pulled up his sagging blue jeans and walked toward her. "I know I'm the last person you wanted to see today, but I was wondering if you had heard about Christine?"

Prunella expelled a woof of air. "Gosh! Yep, I sure have. Jerry called me early this morning to tell me the news, and to be honest with you, I can't seem to care."

He stood there with his mouth open in shock, and his eyes teared up. "I tried to go see her, but Jerry told me that if I came back over there, he was gonna beat me up." He slid to his knees, crying heavily. "What am I gonna do? I love her."

Prunella had always thought that he had a few loose screws, but she now realized he didn't have any screws at all. She began to feel sorry for him and just couldn't understand how he couldn't have seen this day coming. She leaned down to him, placed her hand on his shoulder, and said, "Jerry isn't ever going to divorce her. Even if he did file, she won't sign it. It's time you run and go find you a nice girl your own age and settle down and have some kids."

He looked at her and gave her a half smile. They stood up together, seeming to leave some of his despair on the ground. He hung his head and said, "I've got to tell you something."

Standing there quietly for a moment, she started to fear that he was about to ask her on a date. Every time he would try to speak, she would say, "Shush, you don't have to say anything."

As she fought off his words, he became frustrated and snapped, "Would you just stop and listen to me?"

She shushed herself, for she was shocked that he seemed to have found his manliness. So she stepped back and crossed her arms. "Okay. Spill it."

He drew in a deep breath, then exhaled with an exhausted expression. "I should have stopped her." His thoughts were scrambled as he tried to figure out how to tell her that Christine had stolen all of her money from the bank accounts and hid it under the back seat of the car her father had given her. He didn't want to say all that he was thinking, but it fell out. "She stole your money and hid it in that old Lincoln, She has always been on the hunt for something."

She grabbed him by both of his shoulders. "What all did she get?"

He began to backtrack. "I...I don't know. Did I say she stole something? I've never seen anything," he stammered.

In that moment, she felt scared, angry, and sad. These emotions were swimming throughout her body, causing a nauseated feeling. She gave him a half-hearted smile, saying, "I don't think I can take any more information today, so if you don't mind, I need to be alone. I'm going to lie down."

He nodded with understanding and gave his apologies for upsetting her. Then he left her in her anguish. She went into the house and shut the door and threw her frail body across the kitchen bar, unmindful of the mail falling to the floor. Her tears had evaporated on that last bit of information, and she was exhausted from the domino effect of bad news. As she lay stretched out across the countertop, anger came to the surface. Prunella was known for holding back her feelings and maintaining a strong outer appearance, but her nerves had been strung out and twisted so much that she snapped. She stood up straight and looked over at her purse and vigorously searched until finding a bottle of pills. Pouring the little blue oval pills into her hand, she popped them into her dry mouth. Before dissolving her insanity, she spit them from her mouth across the kitchen, showering them everywhere. She slammed her hands down onto the countertop, clenched her fingers, gripping what they touched, and slung everything off the counter. She had never felt so much anger, and at that moment, she was not afraid to let it all out. She yelled, "That's right! Let's just mess it up! Who cares, right? Nobody cares about my house or my life! All they care about is money, and it's gone now!"

Walking around the house looking for anything to throw, she picked up one of the kitchen chairs and threw it, kicked the big yellow mop bucket, and slung the lamp. Then she spotted the picture of her sister Christine. She picked it up and looked at it and said, "I wish I had listened to Grandma Stella. I should've watched my back. I can't believe I ever helped you...and your man!" She then smashed it to the floor.

Still unsatisfied and wanting to break something else, she looked around and saw the gold picture frame sitting on the kitchen table and thought how satisfying it would be to shatter the already-broken glass. She snatched it from the table, lifted it over her head, and slammed it to the floor. Prunella jumped back and let out a high-pitched squeal, for she loved the sweet sound of that shatter. She began looking for anything that would give her ears that same satisfaction. Her eyes found a boxful of cheap figurines and trinkets, and she began throwing them on the floor, using her sister's picture for a target. Crash after crash, she continued to throw them. Before realizing it, she had broken the entire box, and to her surprise, she was still angry. It just wasn't enough. She pushed up her sleeves, clenched her fist, and slung her arms about like a sloppy boxer fighting a fly. This movement caused her to become unsteady, and she fell to the cold, hard floor covered in the shattered mess.

Rivers of tears broke as if a dam had burst. Streams of sadness rolled down her face, flooding onto the floor. She cried out to the heavens, pleading loudly, "God help me! I can't take this anymore. I just can't! Why didn't I just swallow that handful of pills and end all of this? There's no one left to care about me!" She was in so much pain and aware she had fallen in all the glass. Her hair tangled over her face, giving cover to her cries as she lay there, stretching out her arm, unaware of raking it in the shards of glass. She was unable to feel the glass tear through her flesh as her sorrows pulled her down. Prunella was teetering on life's edge.

Pulling back her messy hair and gazing across the floor, her vision was blurred. She lay there regaining her composure, and every peaceful breath seemed to make everything clearer. The sparkling shards of different-colored glass came into focus as she slowly pushed herself up. Realizing she was lying in all that beautiful broken glass, she carefully got up and went out the back door to shake the fragments from her long blonde hair and clothes. Then she went back into the house and truly saw the mess she had made. She had a gut-wrenching thought: *This is no better than something Christine would do. I need to clean this up.*

A disappointed Prunella took a shower to rid her body of the small fragments of glass, and put on a pair of gray jogging pants and a white t-shirt with pink house shoes. She slung her wet hair back, not giving the blow dryer a thought, so she could quickly return to the destruction and clean it up. With every sweep and scoop of broken glass going into the trash, she felt relief. Sweeping around the busted gold frame, she leaned down to pick up the loose photo from the broken mess, gave it a flick with her fingers, and tossed it on the kitchen table without a thought; then she continued to sweep.

Satisfied that she had cleaned the house enough, she sat down at the kitchen table and slid the photo of the lilies closer to her. A sad smile appeared on her face as she remembered looking at it after Charles had first hung it on the wall. He would say to her, "You'd never have guessed I'd take such a pretty picture! Hmm...they say a picture is worth a thousand words." Then he would laugh loudly, adding, "Yep...thousands!"

Her mind pondered the thought as she looked at the picture of the lilies, trying to remember what year the photo was taken. Turning it over to look for a date, she saw only those strange markings. As she sat there wondering what they meant, she suddenly remembered the Bible. Prunella jumped from her chair in excitement as she scrambled to Charles's office and grabbed it from the desk. She went back to the kitchen table and flipped it open. She removed the photo and the deed to the eighty acres that was hidden in it. *Hmm...at least she didn't get this deed. Smart thing to put this in a Bible, 'cause Christine would have caught fire if she'd tried to crack these pages,* she thought.

Prunella tucked the deed back into the Bible, took it to her bedroom, and hid it under the mattress. Returning to the kitchen table, she picked up the two photos and held them side by side. She couldn't see any difference in the colorful photos, but they had different writing on their backs. She read them out loud, "Mulberry" and "NO OOM." Then she thought, *Well, damn! Did Daddy misspell this word? What is "NO OOM"?* She flopped back in her chair and let out a long sigh, tossing the pictures onto the table. *What was he thinking? It's just flowers, so why was he so adamant about that picture?* After that thought, it was as if Charles had whispered the secret in her ear. She sat back up and spun the photo around. "What if...naw...no way!" She laughed out loud, turning one picture sideways to reveal "300 OZ." 300 OZ Mulberry.

She sat there shocked for a short time; then she jumped to her feet and flung open the back door. Looking at the beautiful, twisted mulberry tree growing a few feet from the edge of the concrete patio and shaking her head, she closed the door in disbelief. Then she returned to look at the pictures again. "Naw...no way! Surely not! Lilies, there was something about the lilies, but what was it? Dang it!"

Sitting there in wonder, thinking back to what Charles had tried to tell her, she remembered what Prunella Jackson had said: "Lilies are like Mother Nature's narrator for our feelings." What did that mean? Suddenly she remembered everything he had told her about the tiger lily. The evening light was almost gone as she wondered, "Should I really go out there with a shovel and dig up those beautiful flowers? What if there isn't anything there and I make a mess of things?" Laughing, she said, "Well...how much worse can it really be? Ha! It would just fit in real nice with the rest of the place now."

She grabbed the rusty shovel that leaned against the fireplace, then slowly headed out to the mulberry tree, ducking down under the low-hanging limbs. She looked over all the assortment of lilies. There were pink, yellow, and red ones, which had grown together over the years, but the tiger lilies were not there. She knew she had seen them out here, but where were they now?

Chapter **33**

The Discovery

Prunella stood under the dark mulberry tree looking for the tigers lilies that she knew existed. As she wondered where they could be, it suddenly dawned on her. It was April and she had only seen them in the summertime. The dusk light was her only source of illumination, so she thought about waiting until morning to see better. As she walked back to the house and pondered what her father had told her about Prunella Jackson's lilies, her curiosity and anticipation took over, and she went into his office and found a big green flashlight. She flipped its switch and said with a loud laugh, "Wait! Naw, I can't wait!"

She returned to the mulberry tree and pointed the flashlight at the ground in search of the tiger lilies. Remembering vaguely where they grew, she started digging. The ground was soft due to the rain, making it easy for her to penetrate the dirt. As she dug around under the mulberry tree, the sweet scent of her blood lured the pesky mosquitoes to her. They nipped at her, causing her to curse and slap at them, distracting from the dig. Roots would give her a false feeling that she had found something, causing her to become frustrated. As time passed and she found nothing after digging up three spots, while enduring the zinging mosquitoes in her ear, she grew tired. She grumbled, "Unbelievable! I've dug up all these places that I thought those tiger lilies would be. So where are they?"

She sat down on the ground. "What am I doing? I'm just dreaming. There's nothing here." When she picked up the flashlight and saw what a mess she had made of the lilies, she started to cry. Sitting there running the light over them, back and forth, she dropped it. Pushing her long blonde hair back with her dirty hands, she started to hyperventilate. She leaned forward into the dirt and released a loud, wailing cry. "I can't breathe here anymore! I'm suffocating here!"

Then she heard her father's voice whisper in her ear, "Wrong lilies, girl."

Prunella jumped to her feet in hopes of catching a glimpse of him, but all she saw was darkness. "Daddy?"

Charles's light, chuckling voice vibrated in her soul, and she heard him say, "My lilies. A picture is worth a thousand words."

She grabbed the flashlight and pointed it at the golden calla lilies growing scattered about. She slung the shovel at the dirt randomly, sinking it into the midst of them all. Several minutes went by, and she kept digging until her shovel hit something that felt different from roots. Falling to the ground, she ripped at the object, slinging dirt over her head, until a rectangular metal box was uncovered. She pulled at the object, but found it wouldn't come out easy, so she dug deep down its side to loosen the earth around it. Finally it was loose, but it was too heavy to lift. She stood up, bent at the knees, and let out a loud grunt as she lifted it from the dark hole. Her small arms were no match for the metal box, and the weight of it forced her to set it down quickly. Wasting no time, she flipped up the latch of the box to look inside.

A soft brown cloth was stuffed inside, covering the contents. Her heart thumped in her chest as she pulled back the cloth to expose what was underneath. Quickly grabbing the flashlight and shining it into the container, she let out a gasp and quickly covered it up, slamming it shut. She looked around to make sure she was completely alone; then she jumped to her feet, bent down, lifted it out with a loud grunt, and marched with a struggle to the back door. Once at the door, she set the box down and exclaimed, opening the door, "Dang! This thing is heavy!"

Prunella slid the box inside the door, then closed it, and with one more grunt lifted the box onto the kitchen table. Then she ran to all the doors and windows to make sure they were covered and locked before returning to the kitchen table. Her heart raced with anticipation as she looked down at the dirty metal container. Curiosity was getting the best of her, and she quickly flipped open the top of the box. She reached up to the retractable kitchen light and pulled it closer to the table. Prunella stood there frozen in place, staring at the box. She was anxious to get a good look at what was underneath the brown cloth.

Pulling back a kitchen chair, Prunella half sat in it on one leg as she pulled the box closer. Reaching down and pulling the cloth back, she gazed at the shiny object. She could see her reflection looking back at her; this caused her to lose her breath and slide down into the chair. After regaining her breath and her heart rate returning to a normal beat, she stood up again and pulled the wrapped object from the metal box and placed it on the kitchen table. Her hands shook as they uncovered it.

There, sitting in front of her, was a gold box. It was approximately eight inches long, five inches wide, and four inches high. She wondered how it opened, as it looked like it should. The intense beauty of the box stunned her, and its shine made her fingerprints easily visible. She quickly buffed her fingerprints off with the soft cloth, but this did not deter one curious finger from exploring a seam around its top. As she pushed the top of the box, the top plate moved. She continued to push until it came off. Exposed to her were the contents of the box. Inside were what seemed to be several small squares. In the center of these squares was a two-by-two opening containing different jewels and stones. She looked at the top plate that had come off and flipped it over. There stamped in beautiful print was "OL," circled largely. Under it was stamped "12 OZ 999.9 FINE GOLD."

Her mouth fell open at the sight. *Oh my God! This is real gold! she thought. What is "OL"?* Prunella screamed in her head at the magic of this gold box as she slowly took it apart, placing the top plate aside and removing the stones inside the small opening. She could see that the inside walls of the small square were removable, so she pulled them out. Stamped on their sides were the words "OL 2 OZ 999.9 FINE GOLD." Her eyes grew larger, and she seemingly couldn't breathe as she continued to examine this magnificent work of art. She wondered why she had never seen this beauty. She removed the small squares to find that they were as deep as the box and stamped precisely on their slender sides was "OL 1 OZ 999.9 FINE GOLD." She noted that there were 224 small squares. After removing all of the squares, she saw a piece of paper. She unfolded the paper to see that it was a certificate of authenticity, reading, "300 Ounce Golden Puzzle Box Collection, an original design by Charles Richards II, created by Oliver Longmon."

Prunella put the box back together and sat there looking at it in amazement. Then it hit her. Why was the box so heavy? So she looked into the metal box again, and there at the bottom was another dark cloth. Thinking there might be another fancy box, she removed the other cloth. A heavy brick of lightly pitted gold was underneath. In disbelief, she turned the heavy bar over to see if it had markings. Sure enough, stamped on the back was "300 OZ. P.J.C." The C hung from the J as if it were dangling from it. She laughed hysterically at the sight of all this gold and couldn't believe that Charles and Oliver had put this marvelous box together. This was the best news she had ever had. Laughing as she looked over this fortune in front of her, she said, "I'll bet this is what Christine was looking for. I'll bet

Daddy knew she would come looking for that stuff, so he melted it down to make this and hid it. What a clever man." Picking up a couple of stones from the center of the box, she recognized them: black opals, benitoite, red beryls, jadeites, rubies, sapphires, and a couple of diamonds. "Oh my! These things range in price from $2,000 to $20,000 per carat, and I've got a small handful!" She placed the jewels back into the small hole in the box and slid the lid back on and covered it. Her mind was going a mile a minute, for she didn't know where to hide this. And with the luck she'd been having, it would need to be well hidden. She thought about putting it back in the hole, but knew she couldn't just hide it; it needed to be shared with someone first, so she made a phone call.

Forty-five minutes later, a freshly dressed Prunella stood anxiously at the locked door awaiting Gregory Longmon's arrival. Finally, two bright headlights pulled into the driveway. She went out and met him as he got out of his truck, wrapping her small arms around his hefty body. This hug felt like home to them both because they had grown up together. He embraced her, asking, "Is everything all right?"

She pushed back, wiped her tears, and sniffed. "I've got to show you something. I know you won't believe it, but I've got to have you look at it and tell me if this is really happening or I'm dreaming."

Confused by her statement and by the way she had leapt into his arms, he knew something wasn't right. "You can't tell anybody. I mean anybody!" With her strange behavior, he began to fear what was about to be shown to him, because she was acting like it was a dead body. He began to resist as she pushed him through the opened door. She looked up at a frightened Greg and gave him a chuckle as if she'd read his mind. Giving him another tug, she said,

"Come on now. There ain't nothing in here that's going to hurt you."
Directing him over to the kitchen table, she sat him down where
the brown cloth lay covering the treasure. He looked up with scared
eyes as she laughed, "Oh, Greg! Just lift the cloth!"

Carefully, he eased his hand over the cloth and slowly pulled it
back. Sitting in front of him was the gold puzzle box that their
fathers had made. Prunella didn't show him the other bar. Both sat
mesmerized; then they began to talk about the sheer genius of the
box. She told him how she'd found it by following Charles's clues,
and they laughed. Their fathers had made something out of the
gold, hidden the jewels inside it, and buried it. They sat there for
several hours just talking. Finally, she opened the puzzle box and
took out five stones and handed them to him. "Take these and fix
Charleen's Corvette for me. You keep the rest for yourself."

He blinked repetitively as he looked down at the expensive stones
in his hand. He replied with a stutter, "I...I'm...I'll come get it
tomorrow, and it will be done in no time."

Both gave each other a smile as she said with a touch of flare, "Life
is about to change!"

One month later, the house looked great. Prunella had newfound
strength. She had cleaned the house entirely, and the yard was
trimmed beautifully. She had been spending a lot of time and
money on the house fixing it up. Grabbing a "FOR SALE" sign, she
headed out to the front yard with it. As Prunella drove the sign into
the ground, the sound of a sweet roar caused her to look up. It was
the Corvette rolling down the highway toward her. Greg pulled up
in her 1981 candy-apple-red Corvette, painted just the way Charles
would have wanted it. Approaching it, she could smell the beauty.

She laughed at Greg as she watched him squeeze out of the seat. "How in the world did you get in there?"

Greg gave her a wink and a laugh as he tossed her the keys, replying, "Very carefully."

The loud sound of a truck coming down the highway stole their attention from the car. It was Barlow pulling into the driveway.

Chapter **34**

.38 Special

Mad emotion stirred in Prunella as she stood there holding the keys to her newly rebuilt Corvette. Barlow was the last person she wanted to see. He flew into the driveway and jumped from his truck, spitting a wad of tobacco out of his mouth onto the ground. "Just what the hell do you think you're doing putting a for sale sign up in the yard?" he spouted. "You ain't selling this place!"

He would have been better off just slapping her rather than to stand there and tell her what she was and was not going to do. She snapped inside but kept calm, giving him a smile. About that time, Greg's ride pulled into the driveway to pick him up. She thanked him as she kept an eye on Barlow, who was just about to touch the shiny Corvette with his nasty hands. "I'll call you later." Just as he reached out to touch the car, she snapped around with a grunt, clenching her teeth. "Don't touch my car!" Then she turned back to Greg with a smile. Still looking at Greg, Prunella pointed to the house. "Barlow, let's go in the house. I want to show you something."

Greg gave her a look of shock as he mouthed, "What are you doing?"

"Oh, don't worry," she whispered. "It's not what you think." Giving him a final wave, she walked toward the house with Barlow behind her, just like she wanted.

He kept asking her, "How is that your car? Where did you get it? Is that the Corvette from the shed?"

She ignored his words, but once they were in the house, Prunella went into the office and sat down behind the desk. "Go get you one of those kitchen chairs and bring it in here and sit down. We need to talk about things."

Disregarding what she said, he turned around looking for something to sit on. Spotting a low chair covered with stuff, he rudely threw it all in the floor as he asked, "What in the hell is going on? How did you get that car fixed? You can't sell the house!"

She rolled her eyes at his lack of respect. Not wanting to repeat herself, she just got up and got the chair from the kitchen. Once she brought it in and placed it next to the desk, she pointed at it and said, "Now get your ass up and sit here."

He sat down in the chair, still rambling on about how she couldn't sell the place. Sitting back down, Prunella drew in a deep breath. "Hey, you know what? I've had enough of this crap with you. You have stolen everything that my father had outside. I know it was you that took the cannon my uncle made, plus all my daddy's guns, and to top it off, you come by early this morning and tried to steal my mop bucket. You are a piece of work, you know that?" He tried to speak, but Prunella shouted, "Shut up! Just shut up, and you listen to me!" Opening one of the drawers in the metal desk, she pulled out some stapled papers. She threw them over to him, then rolled a black ink pen toward him. "I need you to put your signature on that paper there 'cause I'm done with all of this." She adjusted in her chair, then continued, "I'll be damned if I'll keep dealing with you. When I look at you, I see Frank and, honey, that's not good!

After looking at the papers, he tossed them onto the desk. "I ain't signing them."

She slammed back in the swiveling chair and let out a loud growl as she flung her hands in the air. "Damn it, Barlow! I had a feeling you were going to tell me that. I think I know what you are trying to hang on to, but you know what? I don't love you. As a matter of

fact, I can't stand you, and my days of taking care of you are over!"
She didn't even wait for his response; she just fearlessly reached
down into the drawer and pulled out the .38 special. She picked
up a couple of loose bullets and placed them into the cylinder.
"Unbelievable! You missed one! But then again, I thank you for
leaving it. Hmm...well, it's like this: you don't have a choice anymore
whether or not we stay married." The cylinder slapped closed, and
now she was pointing the gun at him, looking hard. "So I'll tell you
like I told Frank. My daddy has a lot of land. It would be like looking
for a needle in a haystack. So I suggest you put some ink on those
papers, or you can sign them in red. I'll give you that one choice."

Barlow looked into Prunella's beautiful blue eyes, and for once he
didn't see that frail little girl he could push around. It was as if he
were looking at his death certificate, so he lowered the pen to the
paper and signed.

After he signed the papers, she said, "Now show yourself out, and
don't touch the Corvette when you walk by it or..." She patted the
gun and gave him a smile, enjoying the powerful feeling of the
scary gun in her hand. Then she tucked it into her waistband.

 His dust had not even settled before she heard another vehicle pull
into the driveway. It was a panicked Walter. He jumped from the
little black truck, drenched in sweat and dirty like he had rolled
down a hill. He ran to the door where she stood. "Oh, please help!
Jerry won't let me talk to Christine, and he's about to haul off her
Lincoln, and all that money is still under the back seat!" Walter took
a big swallow, then added, "That's where she hid all that money
she stole from you. It'll kill her to see it get dragged off. Could you
please come help me stop him?" She gave him a laugh but kept her

thoughts to herself. He kept looking over his shoulder at the red Corvette sitting in the driveway, then asked, "So who's here?"

Giving him a small giggle, she replied, "Nobody is here. She's mine." Before he could form a question, she added, "What can I say? Miracles happen."

Ignoring her riddle, he asked again, "Will you help me?"

The feelings she had with Barlow came rushing back, and the cold steel of the gun barrel in her waistband made her smile. "Sure, I'll help you. I'll meet you over there."

As Walter thanked her, she muttered her under breath, "I wouldn't thank me just yet." On her way over to Christine, the thought kept repeating in her head, *All the money Christine stole from me was hidden in the car this whole time.*

Once Prunella drove up to the house, she could see Christine sitting in a wheelchair on the porch. Jerry was hooking up the Lincoln to a tow truck. She parked the Corvette at the end of the driveway on the other side of the rusty fence; then she walked up to Christine. She gave her a big smile as she said, "How you like that fine-looking Corvette?"

Jerry gave her a wave from the Lincoln as he shouted out, "You came to see my old, hateful biddy. Well, you might get a word in edgewise with that one now!"

Christine tried to reply to Jerry's comment, but all she could get out was, "Dah...dah...dah." Her left arm was drawn up close to her body and shook.

Jerry looked out at the fence and saw Walter standing there and yelled out at him, "I done told you to get on down the road. You ain't got no business here anymore. This is my wife!" He turned back to the car and proceeded to hook it up.

Christine kept watching his every move as she continued to try to speak, "Dah...dah...dah."

Prunella looked down at her half-sister sitting in the wheelchair, speechless for a change, and said, "Oh, ain't that a bitch! Look at that! He is fixing to take off with all that money. Oh, what a shame!"

Christine turned her head to look up at her. She could hear and understand every word Prunella was saying; she just couldn't reply. This was a bittersweet moment for Prunella as she moved around to get a good look at her cold-hearted sister's face. She bent down in front of her, now face to face with her. "Oh, your little man slipped up and told me where you put all of my money. He is so dumb that he didn't even realize he had told me. I can't believe I trusted you enough to let you back in my life." Leaning close to her, almost nose to nose, she whispered, "You never opened that box of suppositories, and you were afraid the coroner might say something about Mama's diaper being on backward. That's why you kept apologizing to Mama that night she died...because you killed her." She paused, looking over to make sure Jerry was still far enough away to not hear her, then added with a laugh, "All that stuff you were looking for? Well, I found it! And damn, is it nice! Hmm...Donovan sure don't look like his daddy." She put her hands on her hips. "Now I know why you didn't like Charleen. She had yo' baby daddy!" She turned to walk away but stopped and looked over at Jerry and then back at Christine. Prunella blew her a kiss goodbye as she said, "Have a nice life. I sure hope he don't love you like you loved Mama."

Walking to her car and opening the door, she yelled back up to the house where her sad wheelchair-bound sister sat, "You know what a Lincoln will never be? A Corvette!" She cranked the car, and a Melissa Etheridge song came on, bringing a huge smile to her face. Turning it up because it was a song Charles liked, a tear fell from her eye as she reached into her back pocket and pulled out a picture of him, Geraldine, and Charleen together. She placed it by the gearshift and pulled off her father's dog tags and hung them on the rearview mirror.

One year later, Prunella sold the house and traveled around the world. Greg Longmon walked out to the mailbox one day to find a bright-pink envelope. The note read, "Dear Greg, I finally decided to settle down. I bought a place here in Oceanside, California. I met a really nice man who has horses. He seems very promising, but I don't want to rush it. I do look forward to you and your family visiting me sometime. I love you all and miss you deeply. I took this photo of my olive tree and the purple lilies in my backyard. I hope you like it. Give everyone my love, and I'll talk to you soon. Love, Prunella. P.S. Keep up with the picture. It's worth a thousand words...ha ha—THOUSANDS."

He smiled as a single tear rolled down his cheek. He knew she could finally breathe.